To Bradley,
Enjoy!

THE ERICKSEN CONNECTION

A Mark Ericksen Thriller Book 1

BARRY L. BECKER

Barry L. Becker
11/3/2021

Dedicated To
the brave American men and women in uniform
who risk their lives to protect our country and our freedom.

Chapter One

On April 18, 2002, at Zero Dark Twenty, an MK-47 Chinook Helo lifted off from Bagram Air Base, Afghanistan, into a moonless night with a roar, escorted by two Apache gunships, headed to the village of Zarghun Mekh, twenty miles from Khost, Afghanistan. Mark Ericksen, a Navy SEAL lieutenant, and second-in-command leaned forward on the webbed bench. He took a deep breath and reflected on his wife Karen's last words to him as he gritted his teeth.

I'm proud of you for protecting our country, but I want you back home in one piece. I love you.

He glanced at several of his men, and his squadron commander, Major Jeb Templeton, nodded and gave them the thumbs-up sign. Eighteen men of Bravo Team, part of the elite tier-one operators from the Joint Special Operations Command, JSOC, were on a High-Value-Targets-Mission. The men wore their battle dress uniforms, and all had beards and long hair to blend into the Afghan culture. The team's painted camo green and brown earth-tone faces highlighted the whites of their eyes. Several minutes into the flight, many men closed their eyes to rest, and silence prevailed except the helo's noise. The rotor blades thumped in cadence to a "Whop-whop-whop" beat, and the gears made a whining sound like a high-speed chainsaw.

Ericksen had been on thirty-two missions since arriving in Afghanistan at the end of 2001. He thought about their most recent mission briefing. Eleven days before, the Agency, as the military referred to the CIA, received actionable intel on the targeted leaders' meeting set for April 18 at 0900 hours. The Predator drone had conducted recon and surveillance in the village over the past six days. He transferred intel back to the Agency at Bagram Air Base's Tactical Operations Center, the TOC. Two days ago, the Predator drone's live-feed video camera had picked up the Taliban's second-in-command, along with a senior military commander.

Late on April 16 Bravo Team sent a small advanced team to conduct recon and surveillance. The next morning, Delta's Fico Delgado, using a camera with a telephoto zoom lens, collected photos of Saad Al-Fulani, a key Saudi Al-Qaeda leader, leaving a compound. Al-Fulani reported directly to Osama Bin Laden, his presence confirmed to the CIA/JSOC Command the meeting's significance.

Ericksen reflected on the horrific terror attacks just seven months earlier, on 9/11: the planes that hit the World Trade Center buildings, the Pentagon, and the fourth hijacked plane, United Air Lines flight #93 on course to Washington DC. Had it not been for those brave Americans who rushed the terrorists and fought to take control of the plane, the White House or the Capitol building would have been destroyed. Sadly, the aircraft crashed in a field in Pennsylvania, killing all on board. On that day, over 3,000 people died on American soil.

With a few minutes to go before insertion, the pilot voiced a warning: "Ten minutes out." Ericksen and the men adjusted their helmets and night-vision devices with their gloves. Ericksen was all about duty, honor, and country, and expecting less than one hundred percent from his team was an intolerable thought. He trusted his men and knew should he get injured or killed in action, they would never leave him behind. Failure wasn't in his vocabulary.

The helo approached the Infrared Landing Zone (LZ), which glowed on a plateau two kilometers from the village where the high-value-targets were reported to be staying. The air turbulence shook the helo as it hovered forty feet above the landing zone, kicking up dust, sand, and rocks. The men fast-roped to the ground on the plateau perched above the village, which stood over 3,000 feet in elevation.

The team quickly assembled one hundred yards away at the staging area. The winds howled out of the east at fifteen miles an hour, the temperature held at fifty-eight degrees fahrenheit, while the rain pelted the ground into a mud-soaked path. Their eyes began adapting to the low-level light with the phosphorus screen's intensified images to best direct their line of sight in green. The team met Bashir Sadozai, an Afghan intelligence officer who was embedded on several JSOC missions. They also met four operators from Bravo Team: Vinnie Goldman, the SEAL Team-Six two-way radio/satellite comms operator; Delta Force Sergeant Delgado; a CIA paramilitary operative; and an Air Force combat controller.

The infrared technology illuminated the houses at which two nights ago their Pashtun informant had installed guidance beacons. They could be seen only by certain types of night vision goggles and by the Predator drones' thermal-imaging cameras. The two targeted mud and brick homes were located at the far end of the village, adjoined by three other houses and surrounded by a brick wall enclosure. Should the mission fail, the Predator operators stood ready to fire Hellfire missiles into those designated targeted homes.

By 0145 hours, they had traveled one kilometer and had another kilometer to go to reach the assault vantage point. The team momentarily stopped, took out their water packs, and drank some water. The vantage point sat perched on a bluff overlooking the targeted homes. Most of the operators carried Heckler and Koch submachine guns with suppressors, each affixed with a green laser and a white strobe light, three magazines apiece, many flashbangs velcroed to their vest, body armor, a secure two-way radio, lip mic, and headset. Some carried rocket launchers with high explosives, a couple of sniper rifles, machine guns, and explosives to breach doors.

At 0155, Goldman received a call on his encrypted satphone from the TOC. Ericksen stood twenty feet in front of the team when he and the team heard Goldman's voice through their two-way radio headsets, "Abort mission! We've been compromised!"

"Shit!" Major Templeton said to the men through his mic. "Back to the landing zone."

One minute later, a barrage of bullets rained down on them like a hailstorm bombarding a field of spring corn. Finding themselves targets in the kill zone, the men scrambled for cover. A bullet pierced Templeton's shoulder, knocking him to the muddy ground. Seconds later, a rocket-propelled grenade exploded fifteen feet away from him, spraying shrapnel into his legs. His mangled leg below the knee bled heavily. Ericksen turned to Sadozai, ten feet behind him, and waved his hand in a follow-me gesture, "Bashir!" They rushed to Templeton's aid, pulled him behind the nearest boulder, and applied a tourniquet to stop the bleeding.

Loud crackling and pops from AK-47s and grenades spit out rocks, dust, and debris tumbling down the mountainside. A minute later, a SEAL and a Delta were killed in a hail of bullets. A Delta operator went down, shot with a bullet to his thigh. A SEAL combat medic charged to his aid and began patching him up when a bullet sliced through the medic's neck, killing him. The Air Force combat controller and another operator ran into the kill zone to fetch the Delta who had gone down, and as they carried him toward another boulder, bullets struck and killed both men. The acrid smell of explosives permeated the air. AK-47 rounds and rocket-propelled grenades continued to blast away at the team as they fired up the slope.

Goldman received a call on the satphone and gave it to Ericksen, who was now in command. "Oscar-Foxtrot-Zulu-Gold Eagle, Condor is down. Do you copy?" said Ericksen.

"Roger that. The QRF [quick reaction force] is on its way. Do you copy?" Pathfinder asked.

"Roger and out," Ericksen said.

Ten minutes later, Pathfinder called. "The video link from the Predator spotted twenty-five armed insurgents (terrorists) moving fast up the ridge. We've called in a couple of C-130 gunships and the Medevac from Jalalabad.

"Thanks, Pathfinder, Roger and out." He had good cover behind a large boulder as the bullets continued to rain down. He readied up his lip-mic and passed the word to his team.

A few minutes later, the fighting stopped. Fear and uncertainty penetrated his mind for a moment, as one would expect of any brave SEAL Team-Six or Delta operator, but he was battle-hardened and mentally tough like many of his fellow brothers. Their focus zeroed in on their mission: capture or kill the insurgents. If it came down to a survival firefight: kill the enemy before the enemy kills you. The men carried their dead and wounded back up to the LZ. He realized the extraction would be dangerous, and the chance of the helo being blown to bits magnified his concerns for his men's safety.

Twenty minutes later, the fighting erupted again. The team ran for cover. Twenty terrorists raced down from the foothills shooting at the team. The terrorists who remained on top of the ridge fired at the pinned-down team from concealed positions.

Ericksen yelled, "Fire!" They immediately blasted them with their submachine guns on full auto. Three terrorists ran towards him from thirty yards away. With his heart racing and his adrenaline pumping, he shot and killed one man, then turned to his right and shot the second man dead. The third man ran at him, stopped, and aimed to shoot, yelling, "Allahu Akbar," when Ericksen cut him down with a three-round burst and watched the man's brains and blood fly out of his skull. He swiftly turned to his left and saw Delgado firing at several terrorists. When one aimed to shoot Delgado from ten yards away, Ericksen shot him dead. Delgado glanced at the dead man as he hit the ground. He turned and nodded his head in a thank-you gesture to Ericksen as their eyes met.

The Predator shot a Hellfire missile at a group of terrorists on the ridge. The team heard the sound of the boom and felt the explosion as the ground shook around them. Rocks, dirt, and body parts tumbled down, barely missing them. Glancing to his left, Ericksen spotted a charred head and a leg rolling past him. He turned to Goldman, adjusted his helmet, and brushed the sweat off his beard with his right glove. His heart kept pounding faster.

"Vinnie, call again and get the ETA on the Medevac and the gunships."

At that moment, Vinnie got hit by two rounds in the neck and thigh. Ericksen heard a groan, turned, and saw Petty Officer First Class Vincent "Vinnie" Goldman down on the wet shale and muddy rocks. He ran to Goldman, pulled him a few feet behind the large boulder, and leaned over him. He glanced for a second at his blood-soaked camo uniform,

"Extraction is minutes away, bro. You're going to make it."

"Mark, please listen, tell my wife and son I love them."

A minute later, he coughed up more blood and died, holding Ericksen's hand. His eyes stared up at nothingness. Goldman, a SEAL Team-Six operator, had been on several missions with him in Kandahar Province, and they were good friends. Both he and Goldman were former teammates on SEAL Team-Eight before being selected for SEAL Team-Six. Ericksen's tears rolled down his muddy, sweat-filled face.

Ten minutes later, the firefight went silent. Master Sergeant Lech Pulaski, the lead non-commissioned officer, raced over to his position. "Mark just got a call from TOC; they said a Pashtun village elder they detained claimed Sadozai is a Talib (a member of the Taliban)."

"What!" said Ericksen with a puzzled look? Can't be."

"They said Bashir Sadozai."

He had established a bond with Sadozai, who was recently assigned to Bravo Team. In several firefights, he fought side-by-side with the team, killing many terrorists. He had intelligence, dedication and performed courageously. The men trusted him.

Ericksen shook his head in disbelief. "I don't believe it. Get me, Colonel Dawkins."

"Oscar-Foxtrot-Zulu-Raven...Do, you copy?" said Pulaski.

"Roger that. Sadozai is a fucking Talib spy. Put Gold Eagle on."

"Gold Eagle, we have confirmation Sadozai is a Talib who provided intel to the Taliban about our missions," said Dawkins. "Do you copy?"

"Roger that, Iron Fist." Iron Fist was Colonel Dawkins' code name.

"Sir, let me take him back for interrogation. It wouldn't be the first time a tribal village informant flat-out lied!"

"Gold Eagle, goddammit! Now terminate Sadozai, and that's a fucking order. Do you copy?"

He knew killing an unarmed person violated the Rules of Engagement. He wished Dawkins' boss at JSOC, a Rear Admiral, was available, but the Pentagon had called him back for a briefing. Ericksen didn't respond.

"Gold Eagle, I've given you a fucking order, so you best not give me any shit! Do you copy?"

He handed the satphone back to Pulaski. He shook his head and didn't say a word. He needed time to think. "What the fuck!"

The ambush could be attributed to any number of possibilities: It could have been the local tribal village informant who set us up; maybe the first team had been spotted or heard during infiltration. Based on Bravo Team's briefing, Pakistan's Inter-Intelligence Services (ISI) provided the intel. Did they double-cross us? Perhaps Bashir Sadozai was a spy. The colonel said he had hard evidence. But why wouldn't he let me take Sadozai back for interrogation and give him a chance to disprove the allegations against him? Disobeying his orders in the heat of battle would have grave consequences for me, even though my instincts might later prove me right.

Time was running out. He had to make a decision.

Chapter Two

The TOC at Bagram Air Base was situated in a large, heavily fortified tent, surrounded by barrier blast walls. It housed a sophisticated array of technologies, hi-def monitors, command modules, and computer workstations manned by over forty JSOC technology specialists. They managed the critical satellite links to the command headquarters at Centcom, JSOC, USSOCOM, Pentagon, NSA, and the CIA.

The Agency's Special Activities Division, the CIA's paramilitary clandestine section, shared the TOC and ran Predator Drone Operations in Afghanistan out of the UAV Ground Control Station, a thirty-foot, triple-axle trailer situated eighty feet from the TOC. Their primary mission focused on guiding the predator drones through a line-of-sight data link for take-offs and landings by pilots and sensor operators, who used joysticks as controllers, similar to those used in operating video games.

Once the drone reached cruising altitude, the Agency passed on the controls electronically to pilots and sensor operators, located thousands of miles away at Indian Springs Air Field, near Nellis Air Force Base in Nevada. Those operators based in the United States watched on large hi-def-flat-screen monitors live-video feed from the Predator Drone cameras via satellite communications.

They operated the controls in the same manner as their Agency operators at Bagram Air Base. The decision to fire the Hellfire missiles resided with the President, the National Security Council, the CIA director, and the recommendation of the Agency's station chief in Afghanistan.

Colonel Shane Dawkins stood two-inches over six-feet, his muscular physique filling his camo fatigues as a cyborg warrior rolled off of the assembly line. At forty-two years of age, the Delta-trained officer wore a military crew-cut and served as the Deputy Task Force Commander of JSOC. He struck fear in his men. No subordinate ever crossed him if he wanted to keep his rank. He took another puff of his cigar and walked back to a bank of workstations.

He stood next to Clyde, the Agency commander and chief-of-station, and Dex, the Agency's operations chief. They watched the action on the hi-def flat-screen television monitors displaying the Predator's cameras' view via the military satellite relay communications passed back to the TOC by one of their satellite uplink vehicles parked outside.

"Our Medevac and C-130s should be there momentarily," said Dawkins.

"Let's hope so. We've lost too many men already," Clyde said. Dex glanced at Dawkins' right hand, gripping his satphone. He turned back to Clyde. "I better get back to the team." He supervised technical experts from the Ground Control Station, including pilots, sensor operators, satellite communications engineers, and staff. Dawkins took a draw on his cigar, watched the smoke rings leave his mouth, and then abruptly left the TOC. He was standing thirty yards from the entrance and made a call.

"Oscar-Foxtrot-Zulu-Raven," said Pulaski.

"Raven, I have Agency decoded intercepts. Get me Gold Eagle."

"Roger that." Pulaski moved closer and handed Ericksen the satphone.

"The colonel just received Agency intercepts...Sadozai's a spy."

"Gold Eagle, the Agency handed me decoded intercepts with proof. Now terminate that fucking bastard. Do you copy?"

Ericksen shook his head, put his satphone down, and closed his eyes for a second. He tensed his jaw, clenched his teeth, and opened his eyes. "Roger that, sir." He glanced at his desert camo uniform and hands drenched with Templeton and Goldman's blood.

"Mark, kill that fucking traitor for Vinnie and our brothers."

"Where the hell is he?"

"He and Delgado carried the major up to the LZ."

He grabbed Pulaski's arm and handed the satphone back to him.

"Get Vinnie to the LZ, and let's get the fuck out of here."

"Right on!"

Ericksen heard the approaching Chinook MH-47 Medevac and AC-130 gunships by their increased noise levels as they sped closer. Three operators took defensive positions behind the boulders, fifteen feet apart, while the team carried the dead and wounded to the LZ.

A few minutes later, he spotted Sadozai, dressed in the traditional Afghan shalwar kameez and vest along with a wool beret. He bolted toward him. He grabbed the thirty-five-year-old Afghan, slammed him against a boulder, and hit him with a right to the jaw, sending him crashing to the ground. Ericksen kicked his AK-47 away. Sweat ran down his face.

"You fucking Talib, you set us up."

Sadozai got on his knees, his face bloodied, tears and sweat rolling down his face. He looked up at Ericksen and pleaded, "I'm not a Talib. I hate the Taliban!" He removed a photo from his vest pocket and pointed to it.

Ericksen took out his Sig P226 and aimed it at him. "You're lying."

"Please, sir, I have a wife and two daughters. I'm telling you the truth. I beg you." Two shots pierced his face as he hit the ground. His lifeless, bloody body lay a few feet away from the photo. Blood poured out of his left eye socket and from the bullet hole in his forehead.

Delgado and Ericksen made eye contact. He motioned for him to come toward him. Delgado's eyes widened, almost surprised by the killing. He shook his head briefly.

"Fico, check his clothing for any intel."

Delgado nodded, still in disbelief, and sighed, "Why did you kill him?"

His right hand trembled a bit as he put his gun back into the holster.

"The Agency provided the colonel with proof Bashir was a Talib."

Delgado shrugged his shoulders and shook his head. He had been on several missions with Ericksen, and like most soldiers in combat, especially JSOC operators, he knew killing terrorists and collateral damage came with the territory. Ericksen bent down and picked up a photo of Sadozai's daughters and wife and noticed to his surprise Bashir's wife lacked a burqa. Her unveiled face and casual clothing surprised him. He placed it in his pocket next to his wife's photo.

The screeching, metallic sound of the Medevac and the gunships approached the LZ. The piercing noise could be heard even with their headsets on.

The AC-130 gunships escorted the helo to the LZ. The pilots blasted the terrorists' positions with 105mm and 40mm cannon rounds as the men ran down the mountain toward the village. Explosions lit up the dark sky, sending dirt and rocks downhill. If there were any terrorists still alive, they weren't a threat to the Bravo Team now. Some of the debris hit the men. Sweat and mud-covered their faces as they moved up along the trail to the LZ.

The Predator Drone launched its last Hellfire missile and, within seconds, hit one of the targeted houses, exploding into a giant orange fireball, spewing mud and brick in all directions. Seconds later, the next home burst into flames like a thunderbolt from Thor's hammer, killing several people inside. The sound could be heard for miles.

The Medevac pilot landed on the LZ. The cargo door opened, and the men loaded up the wounded and the dead. The remaining operators rushed on board, and they lifted off. The risk to the Medevac would have been greater if it tried to hover above the LZ while the men hoisted up the dead and wounded, besides attempting to climb up to the helo. Time was critical. The gunships escorted them back to Bagram.

Once they arrived at the airbase, Ericksen went back to his tent. This fucking hellhole! A stream of thoughts flowed through his mind about the men on Operation Daring Eagles. He felt a deep sadness for his brothers who had died in the ambush, cut down like ducks in a shooting gallery. He had known many of them since arriving in Afghanistan.

They did everything as a team: ate, drank, trained, fought, slept side-by-side, and killed insurgents. In quieter moments, they shared family and life stories. His brothers, which numbered six, would no longer return home and be with their loved ones again. Death delivers permanence. He would always remember the battles and the men who didn't return.

Ericksen tried processing and questioning what occurred.

Why would Bashir insist he was telling the truth? And why would Sadozai have a photo of his wife during an operation showing her without a burqa? Had Major Templeton been able to command the team, would he have followed the kill orders? Colonel Dawkins said he had solid proof from the Agency intercepts.

The teams' lives and missions depended on the character of their commanders and the trust the team had in them. Those threads built the fabric of moral leadership. Without that trust, their honor, duty, and country would lose its moral integrity.

Chapter Three

On April 19, Ericksen entered the TOC wearing his desert camo fatigues, looking for the comms sergeant. He wanted answers, like those the Agency and JSOC sought from the debriefing session Bravo Team endured, shortly after they returned to the base. Ericksen rushed toward Pathfinder, the master sergeant who operated the communications console station. He glanced down on the sergeant's desk and raised his eyebrows, startled by the front-page headline of the Operation Daring Eagles collateral damage report.

"Eleven Afghan family members killed by a Predator drone in a village night raid near Khost."

"Is the tribal village elder still being detained?" asked Ericksen as his eyes focused on the sergeant. "The one who claimed Sadozai was a Talib."

"Sir, we don't have any village elders locked up here," Pathfinder replied, shrugging and staring up at him. Sir, with all due respect, I don't know anything about Sadozai being a Talib."

"Is Colonel Dawkins available?"

"No, sir. He left for lunch a few minutes ago."

"Thanks, sergeant." Ericksen turned and left the TOC.

He jogged to the Agency's headquarters office; a tent situated one-hundred-fifty-feet from the TOC. The Agency maintained two offices. One at Bagram Air Base to control Predator drone operations, direct high-value-target-ops with JSOC, and another known as Kabul station, located in the Ariana Hotel in Kabul, near the Afghan government offices, American Embassy, foreign embassies, and ISAF headquarters.

He approached two armed soldiers guarding the office.

"I have an appointment with Clyde." The guard waved him forward. No one knew the last name of the Agency men at Bagram and understood their first names were an alias. The guard took out a phone and called, "Dex here," said the voice.

"Sir, Lieutenant Ericksen has an appointment with Clyde. What should I tell him?"

"Send him in."

Dex opened the tent flap, greeted Ericksen, and escorted him into his office. The room had the latest high-tech predator drone scientific equipment, signal intelligence devices, three hi-def flat-screen monitors on a large table, several computers, and cipher locks on file cabinets. Dex appeared to be in his late thirties, with short brown hair, medium build, and a nameless military desert camo uniform.

"Clyde stepped out and should be back in a few minutes. Please be seated."

Dex moved toward his desk, stood, turned, and faced him. "I just want a confirmation," Ericksen said, as he stared with his deep-set blue eyes at Dex. "Did you or Clyde provide intercepts to Colonel Dawkins during Operation Daring Eagles that confirmed Bashir Sadozai conspired with members of the Taliban?"

Dex's jaw dropped, and he shook his head, "Hell no! We never had anything on Sadozai."

At that moment, Clyde rushed into Dex's office. He was tall, bald, lean, and muscular. His posture and military bearing were reminiscent of a man who had spent several years in a combat command. After serving fourteen years as a US Marine intelligence officer, Clyde resigned his commission as a major and joined the CIA's para-military group.

"What's up, lieutenant?"

Ericksen's face flushed red. "Dex just gave me my answer, sir. Dawkins is a lying, fucking bastard! He first claimed a village elder fingered Sadozai as being a Talib. Then he claimed your Agency gave him intercepts with proof." He shook his head. "The colonel ordered me to kill him."

The forty-two-year-old Clyde motioned with his right hand, "Lt. Ericksen, please follow me to my office." He turned to Dex; his lips tightened with a scowl on his face.

"You too."

He thought Clyde seemed unhappy that Dex got involved. His office appeared larger and also loaded with high-tech equipment, computers, monitors, and maps. He and Dex sat down on two chairs facing the Agency station chief. Clyde shook his head, "Colonel Dawkins told me insurgents killed Sadozai during the ambush." He lifted up a water bottle, took a sip, and placed it back down on his desk.

"Did your satellite communications record the conversation between the colonel and me?"

Clyde's face tensed up, surprised by the question. He looked at Dex and then at Ericksen, "Sorry, we don't."

Dex interrupted, "That's right."

"Shit." Ericksen shook his head and made a fist. "That leaves me with only one witness."

"Sorry, I wish we could help you," said Dex as he shook his head and cupped his chin.

Ericksen gritted his teeth and glanced back at Clyde. "I'm going to confront him."

Clyde shook his head, looked directly at him, and slammed his hands on the table, "Be careful with Dawkins. I had a couple of run-ins with him when he served as the military attaché in Riyadh several years ago. Listen up, the Admiral recommended you for the Silver Star two months ago and got you registered at the Naval Postgraduate School. If you keep your mouth shut, you'll probably get promoted to a lieutenant commander once you complete your master's program."

Ericksen sighed. "Sir, I killed an innocent team member." He looked down for a moment and then raised his head. "Tell me how the hell I'm going to live with that memory the rest of my life!"

"You're in a dangerous environment, and all kinds of shit can occur. Do you get my drift?"

Ericksen shook his long, sandy-colored head and appeared puzzled by Clyde's comment.

"Don't forget your squadron rotates back to the States in two weeks. Stay alert and be smart," Clyde said.

"Do you believe Sadozai had anything to do with this ambush or any in the past?" Clyde turned to Dex and then back to Ericksen.

"I doubt it. Three days after receiving the intel, we sent Sadozai, Delgado, and one of our officers to Khost to meet the informant at a safe house. We had Sadozai under our control. The next day Sadozai impersonated a livestock broker, and along with a vetted Pashtun asset, entered the village to collect the on-the-ground assessment and check out the foothills nearby to determine the best place to serve as our LZ insertion and extraction point besides the video provided by the Predator."

"So tell me, sir, why do you think the colonel ordered me to kill Sadozai?"

"I can't answer your question," he said, shaking his head and shrugging his shoulders.

He began walking out, stopped, turned, and looked at Clyde. "Why did you shoot the missile into the house?"

"I felt the Pakistani ISI probably set up the ambush and hedged their bets. They probably threatened Walid to work with them and the Taliban; otherwise, they would have killed him. It's also possible they hatched a plan where he portrayed himself as the village informant. Our relationship with Pakistan isn't good, but there are times when they've provided us with good intel. When your team got ambushed, I had a gut feeling there was a twenty percent chance the bad guys were in the house. I recommended to Langley to kill them. Those terrorists killed lots of good men, and if they are in that house, they will die. No doubt, when we fuck up, it turns these tribes against us."

"Sir, thanks for your time." He turned and left the tent.

Clyde glanced at Dex, raised his eyebrows, shook his head and he placed both hands on his desk. "We have to keep our stories straight. I would advise if you heard any of their conversations to erase it from your mind. The White House, DoD (Department of Defense), and the intelligence community would wash this story before it ever reached the media, even if Dawkins is a sadistic commander. We can't win this fight."

"Trust me, I didn't hear a damn word," said Dex.

"Good."

Dex suspected no more than twenty people at the highest levels of the DoD, CIA, and the White House heard Ericksen and the colonel's NSA-enhanced satellite encrypted communications beside himself. Dex wasn't his real name, either. He had graduated from the Air Force Academy with a degree in electrical engineering and received his commission as a 2nd lieutenant. After spending several years as a US Air Force captain in Special Operations, he was recruited by the Agency's Directorate of Operations into their Special Activities Division.

Dex had a streak of integrity and honor in him, with no respect for anyone who acted unethically, was dishonest, or lacked character. After he intercepted and listened to Dawkins's encrypted satphone communications with Ericksen, he felt sad that he couldn't help him. He wasn't about to risk his career and place himself in harm's way, but no one could erase the truth he knew: Dawkins broke the military trust, lied, disobeyed the DoD's Rules of Engagement, and ordered Ericksen to kill Sadozai.

Chapter Four

Ericksen jogged three hundred yards to the mess hall, entered, looked around, and spotted Dawkins seated at a table on the officers' side in the far corner along with a major and Master Sergeant Pulaski. They appeared to be halfway through lunch, eating their turkey breast, mashed potatoes, and cranberry sauce. He approached the colonel's table. "Can I talk with you outside, sir?"

"What's this about, lieutenant?" said Dawkins, as he looked up from his chair.

"This matter is extremely confidential, sir."

Dawkins chuckled, "You can talk in front of my staff."

Ericksen took a few steps closer and stared into his eyes. He had a face that resembled a heavyweight boxer, with a strong jaw, scar tissue over his right eye, and a broken nose.

"I discovered your claims were all lies. What happened?" Ericksen said, his face tense and flushed red. "You ordered me to kill an innocent man."

Dawkins' jaw dropped open, and stared at him. "Is that what Clyde told you?"

Ericksen shook his head. "No, Dex did."

Dawkins suddenly stood up, his face filled with anger. He dropped his fork on the table. "All right, let's step outside and discuss this in private."

They stepped outside, and the other two men followed, leaving their meals on their plates. Dawkins wore US desert camo fatigues and the bird-colonel insignia. They walked 100 yards and stopped in front of the colonel's tent. He waved Ericksen and Pulaski inside his sleeping quarters while the major stayed outside. Dawkins put his hands on his hips and raised his voice,

"You're a damn good officer, but I'll bust your ass if you ever attempt to imply that I lied to you."

"Colonel, what the hell do you call this?" Ericksen said, his anger written all over his face.

"What's one fucking Afghan to you in this medieval country? Shit happens!" Ericksen's piercing eyes stared at him. He had nothing but contempt for him because he had destroyed the trust and honor bestowed on him by the US military.

"I'm going to request a meeting with the Admiral as soon as he gets back. We'll find out who's telling the truth."

"Listen up, don't be stupid. You have two weeks to go before you leave this hellhole. Think again, if you pull that shit, Pulaski will testify under oath that you killed Sadozai in cold blood."

Ericksen turned and moved inches from Pulaski's face. "Tell the colonel exactly what you told me he said about Agency intercepts," Pulaski smirked.

"Sir, I don't know shit about any Agency intercepts, but I saw you kill Sadozai with my own two eyes, and he wasn't armed."

Ericksen stared at him with a shocked expression and disgust. He yelled, "You're a fucking liar!"

Dawkins put his hands up, palms facing Ericksen. "Don't forget if there's a court-martial, they could also order Delgado to testify under oath and ask what he witnessed. I would think twice about your plans. A murder conviction could send you to Leavenworth for a long time."

Ericksen's face was red again with anger, and shouted, "Colonel, did you just go fucking nuts?"

Dawkins tensed up. He yelled loudly at the major outside the tent, "Get this fucking asshole out of here!"

"Yes, sir," said the major.

He turned and left the colonel's tent on his own. He had an intense hatred for the man and recognized he couldn't do a damn thing about it. He loved serving his country, and now his career as a Navy SEAL was in jeopardy. The colonel had him by the balls. As he walked back to his tent, he felt speechless. What could he do now?

———

THE NEXT MORNING Ericksen spotted the six-foot-four, 225-pound Pulaski leaving the mess hall. He walked up to him. "You're not fit to wear that uniform." At six-foot-one and 185 pounds, he was just a pound over his collegiate wrestling weight. "We'll find out, won't we?" Pulaski responded, his face flushed red with anger. Pulaski enjoyed beating the shit out of warriors who either challenged him or verbally disagreed with him. He hadn't lost a fight in over two years. Both men were experts in close quarters combat. Soldiers leaving the mess hall gathered to watch.

Pulaski threw the first punch at his head and missed, and in less than a tenth of a second, Ericksen delivered a swift, powerful kick, buckling Pulaski's knee. Pulaski momentarily lost his balance when Ericksen's right-hand punch landed flush on his temple, knocking him to the ground. The former All-American college wrestler took Pulaski down with a burst of speed, pummeled him with vicious shots to his head and face, smashing his nose, cutting his right eye, and splitting his lip open. Ericksen continued pounding his bloody face and then finally stopped. He stood up and looked down at Pulaski. "Go to hell, you lying bastard!" Pulaski groaned in pain as Ericksen turned and walked toward the mess hall.

———

SEVERAL HOURS LATER, he entered the field hospital searching for Templeton. An Army doctor and a nurse approached him. "What can we do for you, lieutenant?"

"I heard Major Templeton is scheduled to be on the afternoon flight to Ramstein Airbase, and I would like to see him." Both of them looked at the lieutenant and thought the major could use some cheering up.

"His left leg below the knee was amputated yesterday. He's still groggy. Five minutes, okay?" the doctor said. He nodded, followed her into a partitioned section of the tent, and looked at Templeton's bandaged shoulder.

"Hi, Jeb."

Templeton pointed to his leg under the sheets. "Mark, they amputated my leg below my knee. There goes my fucking military career." He knew any words he expressed would not change his friend's mental condition, but he made up his mind to try.

"Jeb, I'm proud to have served under your command."

The West Point grad nodded. "Thanks for pulling my ass to safety."

"Bashir and I were only doing our duty." He didn't want to mention anything regarding Sadozai. "Let's hope for a speedy recovery."

"I'll be at Landstuhl for a week, and then I'll be off to Walter Reed for rehab."

"Let's stay in touch," said Ericksen.

He went back to his tent and reached into his footlocker. He retrieved the photo of Sadozai's wife and children, stared at the picture, and shook his head. He thought it was morally wrong to kill another human being in cold blood, even under orders. He closed his eyes. The image of Sadozai appeared in his mind, "I'm not a Talib. Please, I beg you." The memory of killing an innocent man sent chills down his spine. He placed his face in his hands and whispered, "God, please forgive me."

He retrieved a large picture of his wife from his footlocker. Why her and not me? Reflecting again on the last words she spoke to him a week before she was killed in June 2001: I'm proud of you for protecting our country, but I want you back home in one piece. I love you. She was four months' pregnant, and the ultrasound indicated they were going to have a girl. He promised her that when he reached his tenth Navy anniversary in December 2002, he would resign his naval commission and find a job in civilian life. They both agreed being away on long deployments wasn't good for marriage. That memory was freshly etched in his mind like it had happened yesterday.

After her death, the glue that held him together emotionally, physically, and spiritually was a renewed dedication to SEAL Team-Six. In August of 2001, he made up his mind to make a lifetime career commitment to the Navy.

He couldn't get Dawkins out of his mind. He knew if he demanded a military hearing, Pulaski would serve as a prosecution witness against him in a court-martial. Dawkins might also bring in Delgado as a witness to testify. The likely outcome would be a first-degree murder conviction and a lengthy prison sentence at Fort Leavenworth. Besides the ruling, the dishonorable discharge would devastate him and his family. Right then and there, Ericksen made a decision on the only course of action available to him.

Chapter Five

On May 9, 2002, Ericksen arrived at his condo in Virginia Beach. He shaved off his beard and mustache and drove his Silverado pickup truck down Virginia Beach Blvd for his Ship Ahoy Hair Salon appointment. The hairstylist led him to chair number one. The middle-aged woman said with a strong Southern accent, "Wow! You sure need a haircut, honey. What would you like?"

He looked in the mirror. "I need a trim, Ma'am."

"Okay, honey," she said with rosy cheeks and a big smile.

She stared into his blue eyes and turned to another hairstylist. Her mouth opened wide to silently lip the words wow, as her head did a little movement side to side to suggest this handsome guy is hot.

The other hairstylist lady silently agreed with her by motioning her head up and down and thinking damn right.

"I'll bet you don't have trouble getting a date with the ladies.

"I lost my beautiful wife last year. She was killed in an automobile accident."

"Very sorry…Would you like shampoo too?"

"Yes, Ma'am."

THE NEXT DAY he left the US Naval Special Warfare Development Group's building at Dam Creek, Virginia, dressed in his white summer service uniform, his military separation papers in hand. He had officially resigned his commission from the US Navy. When he entered his master bedroom, he glanced at the top of his dresser at their framed wedding photograph stood. They were married in May 2000, at a church in Charlottesville, Virginia. His wife had brown shoulder-length hair and sparkling brown eyes. He wore his full Navy white dress uniform, Navy SEAL Trident breast insignia over his service badges, and the Naval Parachutist insignia below.

For a few seconds, he rubbed his eyes and lowered his head. She had been a certified maternity nurse at a Virginia Beach Hospital. She loved her job. They both were looking forward to the arrival of their baby girl when tragedy struck and robbed their future. On June 24, 2001, her car got hit head-on by a drunken driver on Richmond's road to Virginia Beach. She died instantly.

He whispered to the photograph, "My God, I loved you very much." He didn't have time to bereave during his deployment time, and each time he entered the condo, he felt a deep sadness and loneliness.

The next two weeks were spent fixing up his two-bedroom-two-bath condominium and selecting a realtor to sell the unit. He and his wife had purchased the oceanfront condominium on Atlantic Avenue in November 2000, for close to $400,000. His clothing, furniture, and personal effects had remained in the condo. He gave her clothing away to a charity, except two dress outfits and a pair of her high-heel shoes.

The handsome ex-Seal wore a designer blue sports shirt, khaki tan slacks, and shiny, Sperry Top-Sider loafers. He could easily pass for a yachtsman. He sat down by the computer and printed out a letter thanking the Admiral for his efforts in getting him accepted at The Naval Postgraduate School, and explained his decision to enter civilian life. He couldn't risk telling him the truth as long as Dawkins and Pulaski were willing to seek a hearing and, ultimately, a court-martial against him. He dropped off the letter at the post office an hour later.

———

A FEW DAYS LATER, he got into his pickup truck and headed to Charlottesville to the Monticello Memorial Garden Cemetery. He glanced at all the graves in her section and finally approached her gravesite. Looking down at the inscription on her headstone, he read: Karen Graham Ericksen, December 10, 1974–June 24, 2001. His in-laws lived in Charlottesville and maintained the gravesite regularly. Ericksen held a bouquet of red roses, knelt down on the grass, placed the flowers on the right side of the headstone, and closed his eyes.

He thought about Karen, remembering one summertime when they went backpacking in the North Cascades of Washington State. They had laughed and enjoyed each other's company on that memorable vacation, smelled the food they cooked over a campfire stove, drank fine wine, and held hands while they hiked along paths in the forest and mountains. Those memories captured love, serenity, being part of nature, and sharing the natural beauty of the old-growth trees, plants, and flowers that created a glowing calm within their hearts.

Tears rolled down his cheeks as he continued thinking about her kindness, her sense of humor, and holding her in his arms. He removed a picture of her from his wallet and glanced at her kind and beautiful face. In one moment, Karen was full of life, and in a split second, she left his world forever. Now he confronted life without her. The numb feeling and emptiness compounded his other problems.

He remembered a profound anonymous quote etched on a tombstone in Ireland that appealed to him:

Death leaves a heartache no one can heal. Love leaves a memory no one can steal.

He stared down at the headstone, closed his eyes for a few seconds, then turned and walked away.

He contacted a moving company to pick up the furniture and personal belongings and place them in storage until he decided where his next move would be in the DC area. While in Virginia Beach, he didn't want to meet any of his old SEAL buddies. His nightmares and flashbacks had begun taking a toll on him, and his only thoughts centered on going home to visit his family. He jumped into his Chevy

Silverado and left town. He figured it would take several days before he finally reached his parents' home in Washington State.

He gripped the steering wheel tighter. "Heading toward home at last." Dating was the furthest thing from his mind. It was like being submerged in ice, frozen without feelings.

He didn't have any desire to discuss his PTSD or his nightmares. He hoped for the day to come when he could manage them, but now all that mattered was the love and warmth of being with family.

———

SIX DAYS LATER, at 7 pm, he pulled up the driveway to his parents' Tudor-style home on SE 61st street in an upper-middle-class neighborhood on Mercer Island, Washington. Ericksen and his sister Mia had immigrated to the United States from Denmark in 1981 with their parents. His father accepted a position with a Danish shipping company in Seattle. In the privacy of their home, the family spoke Danish.

His mother enjoyed being a homemaker. Over the years, she took him to Boy Scout meetings, judo, soccer, football, and swimming practice and took his sister Mia to soccer, piano, and ballet lessons. Both he and Mia were well-behaved children.

He made the varsity football, wrestling, and swim teams at Mercer Island High School and graduated in the top one percent of his class. He received All-State honors in football and wrestling. When he received a full scholarship for wrestling at Oregon State University, he and his family celebrated at the Space Needle Restaurant in Seattle.

When he walked up to the door carrying his luggage, his parents' eight-year-old German shepherd dog Bjorn started barking. When his father opened the door, Bjorn jumped upon him, and he immediately dropped his luggage and gave the dog a hug. He walked into the living room and embraced his parents. Over the next several minutes, they shared a teary-eyed reunion and updated each other on the latest news.

On the mantel above the fireplace in the living room were several family pictures, including him catching a football in the end zone against their biggest rival, Bellevue High School, and one of him with Karen on their wedding day.

"We only hope one day you'll find the right woman again and start a family," his mother said in Danish, as she smiled and looked right into her son's eyes.

"Maybe one day, Mor," said Ericksen. By the time he left for college, he had begun answering them in English, with only one exception, he still called his Mom by the Danish word Mor, and his Dad, Far.

He heard several knocks on the door and advanced towards it, and opened it. He smiled and overjoyed at the sight of his sister Mia, her husband, and their two boys, seven and nine. They entered the house and immediately hugged each other. Mia looked at her younger brother. "I hope you're going to stay awhile," said Mia in English.

"I'm planning to stay a few weeks and then head back to DC to search for a job."

She looked directly into his eyes and said, "We missed you all those years, and more than ever, we need you back home." She gently placed her right hand on his shoulder as tears began flowing from her eyes, "Why not submit your resume to one of those tech companies like Microsoft or Amazon?"

"Mia, I'm not interested in being a computer programmer or software engineer." He knew his parents, sister, and her family was precious to him, but he recognized his JSOC and SEAL Team-Six background would generate more career opportunities as a defense contractor. His father walked toward him and spoke in Danish as he escorted him into the dining room, "You're home now, and that's what counts."

Ericksen now had a critical mission facing the challenges that would await him: dealing with his post-traumatic stress disorder (PTSD), losing his wife from the previous year, regaining his mental toughness, and his self-confidence in his pursuit of landing a good position in the defense establishment.

Chapter Six

Dawkins hunkered down on the couch in his hotel room in Geneva, Switzerland, on June 5, 2002, reading a novel entitled *Absolute Power* by David Baldacci. He heard four knocks on the door and walked up to the peephole. He viewed a slim, tall man wearing a business suit with light brown hair in his thirties.

"The code."

"Andromeda," the man said.

He turned the knob and opened the door. The man carried a small suitcase with a combination lock on it and handed it to Dawkins.

"Timberwolf gave it to me yesterday at Ramstein Air Force Base. He told me it's a present from Shogun." The man removed a large envelope from his portfolio. "This is for you too."

"Thanks, Randy," he said, as he shook the hand of a former British SAS officer who had served as a junior military attaché for Great Britain in Riyadh, Saudi Arabia, from 1998 to 2000. He had resigned his commission in 2000 and worked as a freelancer. Randy didn't know the contents of the briefcase or the letter in the envelope. He just followed orders, and like some of his duties, he didn't have a need to know. Dawkins had flown to Nassau, the Bahamas, to set up a private numbered account for his company, The Conestoga Fund. This procedure provided him with another security shield in protecting his identity at the Swiss bank he intended to use in opening up a private numbered account.

The room overlooked Lake Leman and offered a panoramic view of the majestic mountains. The clear blue skies with daytime highs in the upper seventies created a perfect day for the average tourist strolling along the lake's promenade. However, Dawkins focused more on the contents of the small suitcase. Shogun was the code name for the leader of their group. His secure cellphone rang, and he picked it up. "Iron Fist."

"Shogun," the booming voice said. "The combination number is 0502. Two months ago, I deposited four million dollars into Banque Matthias Reiter. From this point on, you'll be our sole contact for depositing funds in our Swiss and Liechtenstein banks. I've made an appointment for you to meet Jurgen Reiter at 1400 hours today. Swiss respect punctuality, so don't be late."

"Yes, sir."

The Banque Matthias Reiter SA was located on the Rue du Rhône in Geneva's business section. The building had five floors of office space, and global financial investors considered the Bank one of the leading small private banks in Switzerland. Founded in 1907 by Jurgen's great-grandfather Matthias Reiter, the bank had started in Geneva and added branches in Lugano, Lucerne, Zurich, and Bern. By 1990, the bank established offices in Vaduz, Sao Paolo, Frankfurt, London, Paris, Tokyo, Singapore, Grand Caymans, and Dubai. Their total assets reported in 2000 exceeded thirty billion dollars, and they had over 1,000 employees.

Dawkins faced Jurgen Reiter, an athletic-looking man in his mid-forties, who served as executive vice-president of wealth management at the bank. Two older brothers held the top positions, CEO, and COO, respectively.

The conference room conveyed exquisite paintings: pictures of racing cars, seascapes, abstract art, Zermatt and Jungfrau Mountains, and a portrait of the founding father of the bank. Reiter sat at the head of the table with Dawkins to his left. Behind Reiter hung a beautiful stained-glass painting on the wall. It was about ten-feet-in-height by seven-feet-wide and featured a scene of Bellagio, Italy.

Dawkins opened up his suitcase, counted one-million-two-hundred-thousand-dollars in $10,000 packets of shrink-wrapped one hundred dollar bills. After a few minutes of counting the money, Reiter issued him a form to sign and gave him a card with only the private number of the account on it.

"Please read this carefully, Mr. Dawkins, because this form explains our bank operations and instructions on how to make deposits, wire-transfers-of-funds, and withdrawals, either in person, by phone, or online. Please excuse me; I'll be back in a few minutes."

Three minutes later, Reiter re-entered the conference room and sat down. Dawkins looked at the card and read the numbers BMR7073385JR/1.

"Please memorize your company's private bank number. BMR stands for the name of our bank. After the seven numbers, you'll notice my initials JR and 1 represents our headquarters location where you opened your account. I will be your primary contact. If you call me, you're to ask for my employee number and my grandmother's maiden name. My number is 0145, and the name is Keller. I will respond by asking you for your account number, date of birth, passcode, and access code. We will provide a new access code to you every three months. Your new access code will be Jungfrau."

After ten minutes of further discussions regarding private numbered accounts, filling out the bank terms, bank intranet access, personal and corporate information, he signed the agreement and returned to Reiter.

"Excellent. We have your date of birth and your passcode. I find it interesting you would choose Terminator for your passcode," said Reiter, cupping his chin with his hand.

"It has a ring of finality, don't you agree?"

"Yes, a ring of finality," Reiter said with a tight-lipped smile. He pressed a button. Fifteen seconds later, a female administrative assistant entered the conference room, took possession of the cash, and placed it in a large zippered bank bag. "Here's your transaction receipt. Please put the receipt in a safe deposit box with the card. If you like, we can provide a safe deposit box for your convenience."

"Thank you, but I'm covered."

Reiter slid the papers in his portfolio on the table. He stood up. "Please tell your chairman we'll take good care of your company's numbered account. Welcome to Banque Matthias Reiter. We value your business, and we assure you of our commitment to protecting your identity."

"On my next visit, I would like to invite you for dinner and discuss our mutually profitable arrangement," said Dawkins as both men stood and shook hands. Reiter escorted him out of the conference room.

He rode the elevator down to the lobby and left the bank. He entered a coffee shop at Rue du Mont Blanc 26 and ordered a hot latte. A smile appeared on his face as he thought of the upcoming opportunities to profit from the Afghan War.

Chapter Seven

JUNE 2003

E ricksen tossed and turned in his bed. He hit the wall with his closed fist after seeing Sadozai on his knees, begging for his life: "I hate the Taliban. I'm not a Talib; Mark, I have a wife and two children, please don't shoot." He suddenly yelled, "No, Stop!"

Sweat drenched his face, body, t-shirt, and boxer shorts as he awoke from his nightmare. He squinted his eyes, reached for the nightstand, and turned on the light. The radio/alarm clock illuminated the time: 3:45 am. He couldn't sleep anymore. He got up and went into the kitchen to retrieve a bottle of water from the fridge. He shook his head and thought to himself, it wasn't my fault.

It had been a little over a year since he resigned his commission from the US Navy. In September 2002, an executive recruiter in Arlington, Virginia, had an entry-level project management position at Cambridge UAV Systems in Washington, DC. The company designed and manufactured top-security drones for the Department of Defense and the CIA. The work required a college degree with several years of experience in clandestine operations and Special Operations Forces background with a top-secret security clearance.

His impeccable recommendations from the Admiral, the Task Force Commander of JSOC in Afghanistan, Major Templeton, and an anonymous person at the Agency sealed the job. He wondered if that person's alias from the Agency was Dex. After several interviews, senior management hired him with an excellent benefits package, including a base salary of eighty thousand dollars a year.

Ericksen put on his jogging outfit and sneakers and headed out. He resided in a one-bedroom apartment on Becontree Lake Drive in Reston, not more than two hundred fifty yards from Lake Fairfax Park. Ericksen ran at a good clip, a six-minute mile. After running for forty-eight minutes, he returned to his home, took a shower, got dressed, and left at seven.

Once a month, he made the trip to Charlottesville to visit his wife's grave. He jumped into his vehicle and drove to a restaurant on Highway 28 for a full breakfast. He arrived at ten in the morning at the Monticello Memory Garden Cemetery with a red roses bouquet.

The next day he drove his Silverado pickup to Alexandria. He entered a three-story medical office building, walked up to the 3rd floor, made a left turn, and walked to suite 320. The signage on the door read: *Dr. Ann B. Moore, Psychiatrist.*

He entered the large office, approached the medical administrative assistant seated at her desk behind a window partition in the reception area, and handed her an envelope. "Here's the statement and money." His new phony driver's license and social security number displayed the name of Rory Taylor. A retired SEAL buddy had provided him with a forged ID and address to receive invoices and statements.

"Please take a seat," said the assistant. She looked up at him. "We'll call you soon." A minute later, the medical technician opened the door and called "Mr. Taylor."

She escorted him to Dr. Moore's office. The doctor smiled and shook his hand. He walked over to a large leather chair opposite her chair and sat down. Trim and appearing to be in her mid-forties, she had short, layered auburn hair, wore fashionable, large eyeglasses, and displayed a large diamond wedding ring on her finger. She wore a navy blue knit top and matching skirt. Moore sat down and pulled up a chart. "Any more luck with your job search, Rory?"

"No, Doctor."

"Anything new?"

Ericksen had a frown on his face as he motioned with his hands, "The Prozac isn't helping...in fact, I'm having a difficult time sleeping and more anxiety attacks."

She shook her head and glanced at his chart. "My records show I gave you a six-week supply of fifty-milligrams a month ago. Do you still have any left?"

"No, I threw them out," as he shook his head and tightened his lips.

"Okay, we'll continue with the Prolonged Exposure Therapy... though I must admit, your lack of progress puzzles me." She shook her head. "Please start again."

He removed his sports jacket and placed it on his lap. He glanced around the room for a moment, observed the same paintings, the university degrees, and a fancy Board Certified framed professional certificate.

He intentionally lied to her almost about everything: his name, being unemployed, the branch of service, and the rank he held. He repeated his fictional story again. "It was April 27, a week before I was scheduled to go back to the States. Our Ranger platoon's convoy spearheaded forward in broad daylight on Kabul's road to Jalalabad when the Taliban ambushed us. The lead Humvee hit a land mine and exploded. Men screamed, and the smell of explosives filled the air. Suddenly, I lost some of my hearing. Rounds fired from AK-47s rained down on us from high above the mountain. At that moment, I felt a burning sensation – a bullet hit me. It ripped through my upper left arm. The sound of two more explosions reverberated, and the earth shook."

"What went through your mind when you got shot?" she asked.

"I don't remember. Before I lost consciousness, I saw a few RPGs hit one of our trucks. It exploded into a fireball. Five platoon brothers burned to death. I'll never forget the sight, the smell of body parts, and the fumes from the wreckages of our vehicles. It was horrible. The next thing I remembered was waking up at a field hospital and treated for my wounds."

Ericksen had been shot in the upper left arm while on a SEAL Team mission in Somali, a few years earlier.

Dr. Moore stood up, walked over to him, shook her head, and placed her hand on his hand. "I honestly can relate to your pain. Seeing your buddies dying before your own eyes, most horrifically, would cause most of us to continue to have nightmares and depression." She looked straight into his eyes and softly said, "But Rory, we've been together addressing your PTSD for the past five months. We've tried Cognitive Behavioral Therapy first and transitioned to Prolonged Exposure Therapy. You kept a diary of these events, but you haven't made any effort to confront those images of atrocities. I believe you feel a sense of guilt because you survived, and some of your buddies did not." He didn't respond.

She walked back to her desk, stared directly into his eyes, shook her head, shrugged her shoulders, and had a troubled look on her face. "Truthfully, I'm at a loss for words; either my methods have not helped you, or you're hiding something from me. I don't enjoy saying this, but I think you should look for another psychiatrist." Their eyes met, and their heads nodded in agreement.

"Dr. Moore, I'm sorry." He got up and walked out the door. He thought about the toll the missions had on him, but even though they were traumatic in most cases, he knew he could handle it. His motto always focused on duty, honor, and country. He had loved being a SEAL. However, killing Sadozai under his commander's orders proved too hard to grasp. Broken trust seared his heart and mind like a terminal disease that ate at him until there was nothing left in him to go on.

The nightmares and the flashbacks drove him crazy. He just couldn't confide in a psychiatrist and own up to that horrible event. He couldn't tell her he worked on classified projects for a defense contractor. As far as she knew, he didn't have a job. When he started treatment, he always paid in cash and could not produce a health insurance card.

He left the building and drove to his office in Bethesda, Maryland. His determination focused on being successful at Cambridge UAV Systems, and at the same time do his best to hide his PTSD. He had received two raises and one promotion since he joined the company. His supervisor received approval for Ericksen to start an Executive MBA program in September at the University of Virginia.

Chapter Eight

US EMBASSY, BAGHDAD

In June 2004, Dawkins took a seat in the Republican Palace's dining facility, now the headquarters for the US Embassy in Baghdad. He faced an Iraqi interim ministry official. The thin, middle-aged economist with the bushy mustache and oversized eyeglasses glanced around the room, chewing his lunch entrée of lamb stew. After a few seconds, he turned back to him. "Colonel, I'll be in London next week, and I'll do the wire transfer."

Dawkins nodded. He assumed the monies would reach his Liechtenstein numbered bank account soon. Once deposited, he sent the money the next day to his other bank numbered account in Geneva. Dawkins recognized he had to be cautious in any negotiations with any Iraqi ministry officials, for one never knew when a corrupt official would double-cross him and tell the authorities.

"In October, I'll deliver another thirty million in cash to your ministry, and I expect you to continue our ten percent deal. It's a win-win for both of us."

The official lifted the glass of orange juice, took a drink and placed the glass back down on the table. "Colonel, you can always count on me to be a partner to our secret arrangement," he said as he smiled and nodded.

Over the past year, he had added another responsibility besides his JSOC role: he served as head of security to distribute monies for the Iraq Relief and Reconstruction Fund managed by the Coalition Provisional Authority (CPA). The CPA reported to the Secretary of Defense. Dawkins saw this as an opportunity to persuade other senior ministry officials to secretly partner with him. The primary requirement focused on the delivery in cash, in one-hundred-dollar bills, shrink-wrapped, and placed in footlockers and file cabinets. Then Pulaski would load and transport the money on heavily guarded armored trucks in the wee hours of the morning.

On June 28, 2004, the US government dissolved the CPA, and the Iraqi interim government took control. The Project and Contracting Office (PCO), along with the Iraq Reconstruction and Management Office, replaced the CPA and now was under the oversight of the US State Department in Baghdad. He became an active participant with the PCO, a Defense Department branch reported to both DoD and the State Department. At the end of June 2004, he asked two senior US Army contracting officers to meet him and Pulaski in Germany the following month.

On July 17, the contracting officers flew to Ramstein Air Base from the Baghdad Airport on an Air Force cargo plane, arrived at two o'clock in the afternoon, and rented a car. They made a quick stop along the way, picked up a twenty-five-year-old German woman, and continued on their journey to Wolfach, a sleepy, small village in the Black Forest region.

Three hours later, they registered at the front desk of the thirty-room rustic Hotel Steigerwald Eich, situated close to many hiking trails. The colonel and the woman shared one room, and the major had the other room. Dawkins had told the men they would be going to his Zurich bank on Monday to open private numbered accounts. The officers awarded contracts to Iraqi contractors for reconstruction projects and retained a percentage of the award in the form of cash. Once officers received their kickback, they would contact Dawkins and arrange for the monies to be picked up by Pulaski. For these services, he charged the officers twenty-five percent of the funds collected.

His access to a Gulfstream jet was secretly authorized by an intelligence group operated in the shadows. And provided his classified trips to the US Air Force base at Ramstein, Germany, whenever he submitted a request. Most flights from Afghanistan and Iraq flew wounded soldiers or those killed in action regularly to Ramstein AFB. This method offered a veil of secrecy.

Dawkins and Pulaski landed at twelve-noon and were met by one of his Air Force friends who drove a US military truck up to the plane to retrieve luggage and two-foot lockers filled with cash. He drove the vehicle back to a hangar where both men unloaded and transferred everything into a Humvee.

He planned to drive to Switzerland and deposit the monies into his private numbered accounts. Once there, he would transfer a smaller cut to Pulaski's numbered bank account and a larger share into Shogun's account.

Dawkins thought of every detail to make sure no one could trace their every movement. He removed his cellphone from his briefcase and made the call to one of the officers.

"Hello."

"It's Iron Fist. I hope you're enjoying the accommodations."

"We are. It beats the sound of rockets and IEDs," the colonel said.

"Enjoy the cuisine. I'll see you soon."

"Thanks, sir."

On Sunday, July 18, the colonel and the German woman with auburn hair and a curvaceous figure enjoyed a walk along a Black Forest path. The warm weather in the late afternoon reached eighty degrees fahrenheit. He observed them as they walked. The couple slowed their pace down the trail, surrounded by the forest's large trees and a wide variety of plants. They talked occasionally and seemed happy. He wore a Bavarian-type outfit, a hat, a pair of sunglasses, and a beard and mustache to disguise himself. His stealthy moves went unnoticed. As he came within sixty feet of them, he removed his Glock 9mm handgun with a suppressor from his backpack. The couple heard something, turned, and faced the man with the gun.

"Good afternoon," Dawkins said in German, as he took a few more steps and aimed his Glock at the startled colonel, who raised his hands. The bullets penetrated the colonel's forehead, spurting blood down his face and body as he crumpled to the ground. Dawkins looked straight into the woman's eyes.

"Please, don't kill me," she cried out in German as she raised her hands up near her face. '

"I'm sorry," he said in English and fired off two rounds into her head and neck. Blood engulfed her blue dress as she lay dead on the ground, a few feet from the colonel. He looked both ways before he bent over the colonel's body and searched for a wallet with his gloved hands. He pulled the wallet out of the colonel's trousers' rear pocket, removed all the money, and placed the wallet back into the colonel's pocket. He then pulled the bodies off the trail and deeper into the brush.

He moved at a fast pace through another trail till he reached a parking lot three miles from the murder scene. Pulaski opened the passenger door, and he jumped in. After driving for a few minutes, they pulled off the road, and he removed his disguise and changed shirts.

Dawkins thought about the first time he had killed someone. It was his father. He grew up in rural Oklahoma, the only child of an abusive, alcoholic father and a timid, kind mother. The family-owned a two-hundred-acre cattle ranch that generated a decent income. One evening he heard screams coming from his parents' bedroom. He opened the door and was shocked to see his mother being beaten violently by his father. At sixteen, he was already six-feet-tall and had an athlete's build. He screamed at his drunken father. In a fit of anger, he ran straight at him, threw several punches to his head, and pushed him out of the bedroom and against the second-floor railing. He lifted his bloody, dazed father up and threw him down the flight of stairs, breaking his neck. He checked for a pulse and discovered none. He had killed his father.

THE NEXT MORNING, his mother, still in shock, her teary eyes red, watched as her son placed her husband's body in the trunk of his car. He drove to an area near a creek on the property, dug a deep, unmarked grave, and placed large tree stumps over it.

Being from a small town, he had little time other than helping with the family's cattle ranch focused on sports and the weekends, getting drunk at parties and fighting. He enjoyed being a bully by inflicting pain on students whom he didn't like or who appeared to be weak, a trait Dawkins believed he learned from his father.

As an outstanding high school athlete lettering in two sports, wrestling, and football, he received a football scholarship from the University of Oklahoma. After he had received his degree, he entered the US Army's Officer Candidate School (OCS) and received his commission as a second lieutenant upon completing his OCS training.

Dawkins snapped back to the present. He called the major at four o'clock.

"Hello," the major said, after picking up his cellphone on the third ring.

"This is Iron Fist. Let's meet at six instead of seven."

"That's fine, sir."

"I don't know if you're up to it, but I'm going for a three-mile hike into the woods."

Do you want to join me?" asked Dawkins.

"I'll pass, sir."

"No problem...By the way, Pulaski wants to drop off a bottle of your favorite brandy, but I don't have your room number."

"I'm in 311."

"I'll see you downstairs in the lobby at six," he said, as his face formed a smile. Thirty minutes later, he spotted Pulaski walking at a brisk pace to their Humvee in the parking lot. He stopped, and Pulaski jumped into the car.

"Did you leave the room sterile?"

"Of course."

They headed for Geneva with over five million dollars in cash. Life is good. His secure cellphone rang. "Hello."

"It's Shogun. Have you taken care of everything?"

"Yes, sir."

"Timberwolf will meet you after your friend departs from the bank. Let's talk soon."

Chapter Nine

Pulaski opened a private numbered bank account with Dawkins' assistance at Banque Matthias Reiter. After depositing cash into their newly acquired numbered account, he left Geneva in their Humvee and headed to Ramstein for a military hop back to Afghanistan.

Timberwolf observed Dawkins at a store near the bank. He took out his encrypted cellphone and made a call.

"Hello Iron Fist, you copy?" asked Timberwolf.

"Roger that, Timberwolf."

He scanned over the second page of the *International Herald Tribune*. "I'm at Starbucks. I just ordered you a black coffee."

He entered Starbucks a few minutes later, checked out the coffee shop, and spotted his contact reading a newspaper. He walked up to his table and sat down opposite Clyde, the station chief for the Agency, who now directed Predator Drone operations in Iraq. Shogun had selected Clyde's code name, Timberwolf. Agency clandestine case officers, which included SAD officers, used aliases at all times. However, when conducting transactions involving private numbered accounts, the bank had to know one's official name or corporate name to establish an account and provide security.

"Did you transfer the funds into my account?" asked Clyde.

"Yep. Three hundred thousand Swiss francs."

"Thanks."

He continued to serve as the key contact to Reiter over the next two years, conducting most business under Shogun's direction.

"I have an appointment at the Grand Hotel Kempinski in a few minutes. Meet me at 1500 hours in the lobby. The Gulfstream will be ready for takeoff at 1700 hours." He left Starbucks and walked to the hotel on Quai du Mont-Blanc 19.

A few minutes later, he entered the hotel lobby, took out his cellphone, and called.

"Hello," said a man.

"I would like to talk with Senator Campbell."

"Who's calling?"

"Tell him Iron Fist."

A few seconds later, the man said, "We're on the 4th floor. I'll meet you at the elevator."

He approached the bodyguard, who escorted him to the suite, and opened the door. "Raise your hands; this won't take long," as he frisked him. The bodyguard looked at Campbell, reported,

"He's clean, Senator," and left the room. Dawkins entered and greeted Campbell, the US senator from Kansas. Campbell looked much younger than his age. He had a slim build, medium height, with grayish-brown hair. He glanced through his rimless eyeglasses at him. "It's good to see you, Shane." They walked into the living room. "We conducted a bug sweep yesterday."

Dawkins nodded and glanced around, appreciating the luxurious furniture and ambiance of the suite.

"Very classy, sir."

"Would you like a drink while we wait for lunch?"

"Yes, thank you, Senator."

Campbell walked over to the mini-bar, opened it, glanced at the contents, and grabbed two small bottles of Scotch from the side section. He poured the bottles into two clean glasses and gave one to

Dawkins, who sat on the leather couch. They both raised their glasses. "Cheers."

"Jurgen Reiter sends his best regards to you. He's meticulous about details and smart."

"Your observations are correct, but you left out his enormous ego." They both smiled.

"I first met Jurgen in 1990 when I was Ambassador to Switzerland. He had just joined his family's bank, and his father handled my account. When I realized it would put me in good standing with the Swiss banking industry if they knew I had an account in their country like other diplomats, foreign businessmen, and business-women. Naturally, I reported my savings account to the IRS. I didn't want any unnecessary trouble. You can't get rich in these government jobs, but being connected to decision-makers can create profitable opportunities."

"I agree."

"My sources told me you'd been passed over for Brigadier General."

"Yep. Probably the Admiral had a hand in it."

"What are your plans for when you retire?" As the bodyguard opened the door and let the room service waiter bring in the lunch, Campbell asked. The waiter placed the food on the dining room table and left along with the bodyguard.

Both Campbell and Dawkins removed the top of the tray, glanced at the sea bass fillet, potatoes, and asparagus, and began their lunch.

He looked up and stared for a few seconds at Campbell. "I've been offered several business proposals, but I haven't responded."

Campbell leaned forward. "Our mutual friend Chuck Huntington would like you to join his firm. His primary mission is to bid on State Department private security contracting jobs in the Middle East and Central Asia. Naturally, the competition in this field is tough. Blackwater USA, Aegis Defense Services, Titan Corp, and others control the majority of the contracts. They all strive to hire experienced Special Forces Operations personnel. That's why his company needs to have a competitive edge if they intend to be profitable."

"How much investment does he have behind him?"

"He raised significant capital from major investors and is ready to take advantage of the upcoming State Department budgets, starting in October. He needs the best professionals to fill in several executive positions. Would you be interested in joining Stealth Dynamics in the capacity of vice-president of recruitment and training?"

He treasured his friendship with Campbell. Campbell had served as Ambassador to Egypt in 1994–1996 when Dawkins worked out of the US Embassy as a military attaché. Campbell had made his career as a diplomat in the State Department. He retired from the department in 1997 after serving twenty-five-years at State. In 1998, he won the race for US Senator in Kansas.

He took another shot of Scotch. "How much money are we talking about, Senator?"

"$250,000 per year, all expenses, excellent healthcare package, four weeks' vacation, and a two percent commission on all net revenues."

He nodded, "Sounds sweet, sir. Hopefully, you'll be getting a slice of the action." Campbell maintained a few seconds of silence.

"Since the Iraqi government replaced the Coalition Provisional Authority, State has taken an active role in coordinating the reconstruction efforts in Iraq. My role is to use my influence in the awarding of bids to Stealth Dynamics for projects in both Afghanistan and Iraq."

Dawkins nodded his head and looked around the room before turning his head back to face Campbell. "I'll certainly consider your proposal. When do you need an answer?"

"We'll need your answer as soon as you finish lunch. Both Huntington and I want you to take this position starting October first because of your leadership abilities and our trust in you to keep sensitive matters from leaving your lips."

"Where is the company based?"

"McLean, Virginia. However, we want you to set up an office in Geneva to monitor and manage our banking transactions periodically, as well as run our training center near Williamsburg." He thought this opportunity delivered several decisive advantages: lots of cash, a rewarding career, wars against terrorists, and personal enjoyment.

A few minutes later, he placed his fork and knife at the four o'clock position on his plate. He looked at Campbell and smiled.

"Sir, I accept the position."

"Shane, one final thing. From this point on, we'll use code names when calling or emailing each other. My code name is Spotlight."

He concluded his business, went downstairs to the bar, and met Clyde. They walked to the bellhop station, and Dawkins retrieved his luggage from the security room. They left the hotel in Clyde's rental vehicle and drove to the Geneva International Airport. Two hours later, their Gulfstream jet took off bound for Baghdad, Iraq.

Chapter Ten

ANBAR PROVINCE, IRAQ

In August 2005, on the road between Ramadi and Habbaniyah, US Marine Expeditionary Force of seventy Marines headed east in convoy toward Fallujah. The temperature reached 115 degrees fahrenheit. Two Marine helo gunships covered the convoy from the air. Five Al-Qaeda terrorists observed their movements awaiting when the lead Humvee would be within ten feet of the telephone pole alongside the highway. Hidden near the pole, covered by dirt and debris, laid an IED loaded with C-4 explosives, connected by wires to a remote detonator two hundred yards away.

When the lead Humvee reached the target, Abdullah Al-Suhaimy, a tall, muscular Arab man wearing a headband, black shirt, and jeans, activated the detonator and watched the Humvee burst into flames. A few seconds later, the explosion engulfed the second Humvee, killing Captain Ryan Sullivan. Most of the Marines in both vehicles burned to death. A few from the first Humvee managed to escape, though seriously burned. One terrorist fired his AK-47 assault weapon into the trucks, and another fired an RPG at the oil tanker, which burst into flames.

A plume of smoke shot into the sky as another terrorist activated another IED remotely from his cellphone, destroying the comms van instantly, killing three comms operators. Several Marines died, and many suffered severe injuries. The other Marines took positions behind the remaining vehicles and returned fire. Four Marines ran into the desert sand parallel to the highway and fired back at the insurgents.

One Marine fired two rounds and hit another terrorist. He fell and yelled, "Allahu Akbar" before he took his last breath. A Marine sniper fixed his aim at the back of another terrorist, squeezed the trigger, and the shot smashed into his head. Brains, blood, and skull fragments flew onto the desert sand.

A shot hit Abdullah's right arm, but he managed to get to his motorcycle and take off. By using a shortcut, he arrived at a safe house located a mile from Al-Ramadi Hospital. He knocked three times, stopped, and waited five seconds, then lightly tapped twice. A young armed terrorist opened the door. There were four other men inside the living room.

He approached Ziad Kabbani, a short, thin man with a black beard. Abdullah was a rugged-looking Saudi man with jet black hair and beard, a distinctive hook nose, and a scar etched along his right cheek and one above his eyebrow. "Allahu Akbar. Welcome back," Ziad said in Arabic.

He held his right arm as blood seeped from the wound. "Allahu Akbar, my friend." Ziad embraced him and kissed his cheeks.

"Your wound looks serious. We'll get a doctor."

"It's nothing. We must never stop the attacks until the Great Satan leaves our Muslim lands. We need more bombers ready to shed their life for Allah and Al-Qaeda," Abdullah said.

Ziad approached two men in the room and handed each bag loaded with explosives, explosive vests, and devices. "My brothers, tomorrow, you'll become martyrs in Fallujah. Mohammed will open the gates of heaven for you, and seventy-two virgins will welcome you in their arms." Ziad and Abdullah embraced both men. Everyone said,

"Allahu Akbar" as they carried their large duffel bags out of the house. Ziad raised his hand and waved Abdullah to follow.

"Our cook has prepared some lamb kebabs, baba ghanoush, and coffee for you."

"Our work is getting counter-productive. Al-Zarqawi is hurting our cause with the tribes. He's killing innocent Muslim women and children." He shook his head and clenched his teeth.

"Bin Laden's courier left word we need to have a meeting with him and persuade him to change his tactics," said Ziad.

"My Saudi brother, you keep making bombs; let me worry about the Jordanian asshole. If he continues on this path, I'll slit his fucking throat."

————

In September 2004, Ericksen joined Avanti Biosystems, a biometrics company sold to the DoD, as vice-president, military affairs. Over the past year, he had spent much time in the Middle East supervising training in technology use. Ericksen's team of biometrics trainers from Avanti Biosystems and the DoD's Biometrics Task Force spent the next three weeks of August in Baghdad (The Green Zone) and Balad Air Base. Then set off to several US military bases in Afghanistan, training American, Coalition Forces, and contractors to implement their systems.

His company had received a no-bid DoD contract to train them to execute the enrollment of both iris and fingerprints of foreign nationals and known or suspected terrorists' via fingerprint scanners and hand-held iris scanning devices. The templates were sent into a Biometrics Automated Toolset that would capture and collect the data and electronically store them at the FBI's West Virginia biometrics data center and the DoD's Biometrics Fusion Center monitoring and analysis. The critical analysis would occur at the National Counterterrorism Center. If the analysts discovered that an individual was in the country, they would immediately be placed on an international terrorist watch list. If anyone of those individuals appeared anywhere globally, the database would be available to all US government agencies; and other allied countries who would use

Interpol. When law enforcement stopped or arrested a potential terrorist in Europe or North America for a misdemeanor or felony, and their biometrics ID in real-time matched those collected in Afghanistan or Iraq, they would be held indefinitely.

———

HE HAD MIXED emotions about returning to Afghanistan. On the one hand, leaving one-hundred-twenty-degree heat in Iraq to a more tolerable ninety-five-degree temperature was beneficial. Still, his memories of Sadozai would create a challenge for him on his last stop – Kandahar.

In Bagram Air Base's auditorium stood twenty trainers from Avanti Biosystems and the DoD, along with two hundred troopers and contractors. After they had watched a fifteen-minute video on the enrollment and verification process of the dual-biometrics system on the large screen, the lights came on. Ericksen stood at the podium and advised everyone to get in a line behind each trainer's duty station and get hands-on experience with the technology.

Ericksen spent the next day at Kandahar International Airport's joint military base, which consisted of US and NATO armed forces under the International Security Assistance Force (ISAF). After his company and the DoD group had completed training, he walked over to an Afghan Armed Forces building located at the military base for his scheduled meeting with Jannan Sadozai, Bashir Sadozai's older brother.

His efforts to locate the family of Bashir Sadozai had taken a few years before the State Department, and the Afghan government finally got back to him. Correspondence between both men started two months ago. He learned both Bashir and Jannan had spent most of their years in Quetta, Pakistan, during the Taliban occupation, and they were close to some of Hamid Karzai's inner circle. Bashir had trained as a journalist and Jannan as a teacher.

A British SAS major escorted him to the building. The Afghan soldier at the entrance waved them through. After signing in at the front desk, he was accompanied by an Afghan to a room. The staffer introduced him to Jannan Sadozai, a man in his forties with a full dark beard and a knee-length shirt, a sheepskin cap, and baggy trousers. Ericksen reached out with his extended hand to shake Sadozai's hand. After fifteen minutes of conversation, Ericksen stared into Sadozai's eyes.

"Bashir was an excellent Bravo Team operator. His knowledge and Intel were crucial for our operations."

Jannan tightened his jaw and moved around in his chair. "Mr. Ericksen, the Afghan Security Service claimed Bashir had been killed at close range by two bullets from a handgun – probably a 9mm." He coughed nervously, placed his hand to his mouth, and asked, "How is that possible?"

The question surprised him. His mouth dropped a bit. "The Taliban ambushed us. They charged down the mountain from all sides, firing their AK-47s like a herd of goats on a stampede. Some of our brothers died during the exchange. I believe a Talib grabbed one of our Sig-Sauer handguns, then shot and killed Bashir at close range."

Jannan's facial expression froze for a few moments, deep in thought. "Thank you for the explanation. You cleared up some concerns I had."

He wasn't sure if Jannan believed him or not; he couldn't muster the strength to tell him the truth. He removed his wallet and handed over twenty-one-hundred-dollar-bills to Sadozai. "This is the least I can do to offer some assistance to Bashir's widow and her children."

"Mr. Ericksen, though I appreciate your good gesture, we can't take it," he said as he handed the money back to him. "Bashir and I are Pashtuns, and we're proud people. We have endured over thirty years of war in our country. Someday we hope peace and freedom will grace our people's hearts."

He nodded, "I understand."

"Bashir told me you're a strong leader and a man of honor."

He gave him his business card, took out a pen, and wrote his personal telephone number on the back of the card. "If you ever need help, please don't hesitate to contact me."

"It was kind of you to meet me," Sadozai said. He stood, smiled, and reached into his pocket and gave him a photo of two girls. "This is a picture of Bashir's daughters."

He looked at the girls' photos and smiled. "What are their names?"

"Laila and Ranrha."

"They're precious."

"Thank you." He clenched his teeth and tensed his jaw. Ericksen tried to hide his feelings but knew each time he looked at the girls' picture, the image of killing their father would generate a pain he could not stop. He had to find a way to help them. But how?

Chapter Eleven

I n May 2006, Ericksen joined his former JSOC commander, Jeb Templeton, in The JW Marriott Hotel bar on Pennsylvania Avenue in Washington DC. The hostess seated them at a table, and a waitress took their order.

Over the next fifteen minutes, the two former JSOC officers brought each other up-to-date. Templeton had gone through a year and a half of rehabilitation and learned to use a prosthetic leg, and now worked as the deputy director for the DoD's defense biometrics and forensics enterprise out of Arlington, Virginia.

Both men lifted their shot glass of bourbon. "Cheers." Templeton poured down his shot of bourbon in one gulp.

"The CEO of EyeD4 Systems, an Oregon company involved in biometrics and encryption software, contacted me and asked if I could recommend anyone for the position of senior vice-president of marketing. I immediately thought of you."

Ericksen's eyes lit up, and leaned forward. "I've heard about the company. If a good position opened up, I would move back to the Pacific Northwest in a heartbeat. If this startup offers me an excellent compensation plan, I'm all ears."

For the next five minutes, He gave him an overview of the

company. It had been four years since *Operation Daring Eagles*, and he needed to ask Templeton a question that had always been on his mind. He appreciated his efforts in recommending him for his current job at Avanti Biosystems, as well as his first job, but didn't want to talk to him about his PTSD. Did fear of being ridiculed by a former Delta Force Commander have something to do with it, or was it fear of losing his top security clearance and livelihood?

Ericksen had to know. He gritted his teeth. "Jeb, if you weren't shot during *Operation Daring Eagles*, would you have killed Sadozai on Dawkins' orders?"

"Hell, yes! Shit, Rules of Engagement are one thing, but as a career Army Special Ops officer in the thick of battle, I would have been insane to challenge Dawkins' orders."

He leaned closer and asked, "What if you found out later that Dawkins lied about Sadozai being a Talib?"

Templeton's jaw dropped. "What the fuck are you saying?"

"There were no Agency intercepts. It was all a fucking lie."

Templeton tensed up, his eyes staring at him. "Don't tell me you have PTSD?"

"Hell, no!" He replied, rubbing his hand against his chair. Templeton shook his head. "Mark, let it go. We've both seen the horrors of war. No good can come of it."

He thought about Templeton's last words, "No good can come of it." *Templeton was right; I couldn't prove it because I had no witnesses, except Pulaski.*

Chapter Twelve

BANQUE MATTHIAS REITER SA

Upon the death of one of his brothers in May 2008, Jurgen Reiter received a promotion to President and COO of the bank. The fifty-year-old banker wore a blue pinstriped Italian designer suit and Testoni dress shoes, reflecting the meticulous taste of a man who rubbed elbows with the upper-class gentry. His neatly trimmed goatee and mustache looked perfectly in place. His fifth-floor executive office had a view of Lake Leman.

He handed an envelope over to Elizabeth Caldwell, an American businesswoman, who sat in a leather chair facing him. In her early thirties, the attractive blonde, her curvaceous figure elegantly clothed in a Marc Jacobs purple suit and white silk blouse complemented by pearl earrings and necklace, placed the envelope into her black Louis Vuitton handbag.

"I have decided to retain Prentice and Aubert for our search," he said in French.

She projected a professional air of confidence and smiled approvingly of his offer.

"Thank you, Mr. Reiter. You won't be disappointed," she said in

French.

"Your reputation in placing top banking candidates is superb throughout Switzerland."

"I'll work on the search immediately."

"Wonderful. Perhaps we can discuss your search over dinner sometime?"

She didn't want to encourage the married banker to expect any additional benefits associated with an evening meal but knew she had a mission.

"Of course, once when we narrow it down to a handful of prospects, let's set up a dinner."

Reiter's face lit up into a big smile as he confidently tilted his head back, "Talk to you soon."

She left his office and took the elevator down to the lobby. When the elevator door opened, she stared at a man who looked familiar. The tall, slender man with the gray hair and mustache glanced at his wristwatch, looked at her momentarily, and then moved to the side to let her and two other people exit the elevator. She hoped the man didn't recognize her. She recognized him. His name was Sergei Ryzhkov, a former Russian KGB, and SVR (foreign intelligence) Colonel, who had just retired from the Russian Foreign Intelligence Service. He had been in charge of the European Continent when she had met him in Berlin at a diplomatic party. Caldwell, who was fluent in German and French, was not your ordinary executive recruiter in Geneva. She worked for the CIA as a clandestine officer and a non-official cover officer (NOC), a spy. She had no diplomatic immunity, and, if caught, she could be imprisoned in Switzerland

From July 2000 to 2002, she had worked at the American Embassy in Berlin. During that time, she had dyed her hair brown and gone by the name of Betty Nichols. She had attended the International Institute for Management Development (IMD) in Lausanne in 2005 under her current name and graduated in 2007 in the top ten percent of her class. Armed with an MBA, including banking and finance specialization, she joined a firm in Geneva.

After a year with a Swiss firm, she became manager of the Geneva branch operations of Prentice and Aubert, a New York executive recruiting firm and a shell company for the CIA.

Chapter Thirteen

The signage on top of the ten-story modern glass and steel office building in Jeddah, Saudi Arabia, read: *Al-Bustani Group of Companies.* The building sat on five acres of beautifully landscaped gardens with palm trees, exotic plants, and a waterfall. Their security cameras were positioned and installed at crucial placements throughout the building. The information desk on the lobby level was staffed by two armed security men, and posted at each entrance were more security guards.

In the large conference room on the ninth-floor with bay windows overlooking the Red Sea, Khalid Al-Bustani, a tall, heavy-set man in his late forties, with black piercing eyes, a trim beard, and dressed in an impeccable white robe and headdress, stood in front of the conference table. Sitting around the long rosewood conference table where the group's managing directors. Khalid raised his pointer at his colleague, who was holding the company's organizational chart.

"I expect at least a ten percent increase in revenues from each of your companies by June 30, 2009," Khalid said in English.

The managing director of Al-Bustani Construction Company raised his hand to speak. "We'll exceed our forecast by twenty percent once we officially receive the contract from the Ministry of the Interior for the new National Police Headquarters project."

"Don't count your camels until you can smell their presence." He looked around the table. "All of you are well compensated. However, if you don't reach these goals, I'll not only be disappointed, but you'll no longer be working for me."

The managing director of Al-Bustani Oil Exploration raised his hand. "Khalid, I would very much appreciate it if you would join me at the upcoming oil summit in Dubai this fall."

He moved closer to the man and asked, "What are the dates?"

The man looked up at Khalid. "September 15 and 16."

He looked at his male secretary and nodded his head to write down the date. He wore a massive gold nugget ring on the middle finger of his right hand with a raised 18-carat gold Arabian horse's head on it. The Arabian horse's head sat on a raised black onyx stone, with the best grade cut of diamonds on each side and etched below the horse's head in sterling silver, the inscription Falcon Dancer.

"I'll get back to you," he said, as he placed some reports in his burgundy leather portfolio. "Now please excuse me, gentlemen, I have another meeting, and I can't keep the Saudi Minister of the Interior waiting. I'll see you tonight at the restaurant."

———

HIS ROYAL HIGHNESS, the Minister of the Interior, settled comfortably down on a large chair facing Khalid. Behind his desk, located five feet above on the wall, stood a photograph of his favorite Arabian horse, Falcon Dancer. Both men were drinking tea.

"Khalid, I would have given you anything to own your marvelous Arabian," the minister said in Arabic as he leaned back in his chair.

"Your Highness, there are a few gems I could never relinquish; Falcon Dancer was one of them."

"I've known you and your family for most of my life, and without question, your construction firm is the best in the Kingdom. However, the new National Police Headquarters project is out for bid, and my older brother is pressuring me to award the project to one of his good friends."

He pressed the intercom. "Please have Mr. Bullock come in." A tall man entered in his late fifties, with wavy silver hair, a sun-tanned face, and alert, piercing blue eyes. Vance Bullock preferred to wear business casual clothes, a white short-sleeved custom dress shirt, blue slacks, and Ferragamo brown loafers in hot climates. He held the title of CEO and managing director of The Bullock Group in Beverly Hills, California. They had offices throughout the world. He bowed his head to his Royal Highness. "It is always a pleasure meeting you, Your Highness."

His Royal Highness smiled and nodded. "Mr. Bullock, I'm sure Khalid is deeply appreciative of your firm's architectural talents since your firm has been in collaboration on projects in the Kingdom for many years."

Bullock nodded to the prince, then turned to Khalid. "He has an affinity for perfection, and, in all fairness, Al-Bustani Construction Company workers exceed the highest level of quality craftsmanship in the world."

Bullock took another swig of water. "Allow me to show you this scale model of the new headquarters building project over here." He motioned to both men to follow him to the large table near the flat-screen television.

After ten more minutes of discussions on the merits of recommending Al-Bustani Construction for the project, Khalid said, "My new CFO has crunched the numbers for me," and pressed the intercom. "Have Ziad come in with the proposal." He leaned over his desk and stared at the minister.

Twenty seconds later, a handsome, clean-shaven man entered his office. Ziad exuded confidence as he made eye contact with the minister. "Your Highness, I would like to introduce you to Ziad Kabbani, my new finance manager."

He bowed before the minister of the Interior. "Your Highness, I'm honored to be in your presence," Ziad said, and then handed the proposal to Khalid.

Chapter Fourteen

I n the evening of April 2, 2009, outside General Mohammed Al-Jabr's residence in Riyadh, four bodyguards armed with MP submachine guns secured access to his home from a command and communications truck. As General Secretary of the National Security Council to King Abdullah, he could feel his responsibility to the King and the Kingdom, increasing his stress levels. He picked up his secure landline and placed a call from his palatial estate to Langley, Virginia.

"Hello, Mohammed," Sullivan said.

Al-Jabr glanced at the picture on the wall in his study of the Crown Prince and himself in his military uniform years before Crown Prince Abdullah became king.

"It has been a while since we last talked. I have some urgent intel to share with you from one of my deep-cover officers. He infiltrated an Islamic Jihadist terrorist organization called The Red Sea Brotherhood a few years ago."

"How secure is your phone?" asked Bill Sullivan, the Central Intelligence Agency Director.

"Don't worry; it's secure. I just want to inform you that this terrorist organization leader is a wealthy Saudi and plans a nuke attack on two American cities.

"What! Does he know where or when this is going to take place?"

"Sometime this year."

"How reliable is this information?"

"Quite certain. We trained our operative for this mission years ago, and the Al-Qaeda leadership holds him in high esteem."

"Al-Qaeda!"

"Bin Laden sent him to Iraq at the end of 2003 to fight along with the insurgents against the American and NATO forces."

"What are the chances he'll be able to provide us with the details?" asked Sullivan.

"I'll be meeting with him on Monday, May 18, in Zurich."

"Can you meet me in Lucerne the next day at the National Hotel?"

"For safety and security, I prefer a restaurant," Al-Jabr said.

"All right, can you meet on top of Mt. Pilatus at eleven o'clock on Tuesday, May 19?"

"That's fine. I almost forgot an important point. The mastermind is interested in acquiring a biometrics encrypted communications security system from EyeD4 Systems to manage operations with his sleeper cell leaders living in the United States. He heard their systems are classified and only sold to the intelligence community. Do you use it?"

"Yes, we do. Thanks, General, for the intel. See you on May 19."

This bastard is tech-savvy.

Sullivan picked up his landline and had his secretary connect him to the Agency's procurement director. "Sir, the main person we deal with at EyeD4 Systems in Oregon is Mark Ericksen. Their systems are still in a beta-test mode but are extremely reliable and deliver excellent performance. I've talked with several other people in the intelligence community, and they confirmed the same opinion. In fact, your chief of staff is picking up your new laptop computer with their classified suite of biometrics software and firmware next week."

"I assume he has a top-secret security clearance?"

"Affirmative, sir."

Deputy CIA Director Susan Norstad was walking out of the CIA cafeteria when her secure cellphone started ringing. "Hello, Director."

"This is urgent. Please get me background information on Mark Ericksen, an executive at EyeD4 Systems in Wilsonville, Oregon."

"Roger that, Bill."

Pete Geiger, the FBI director, sat at a table in a Tyson's Corner Starbucks coffee shop along with two members of his security detail. While he was drinking his French roast, his secure cellphone vibrated. Some people in the shop worked on their laptops, talked on their cellphones, and others carried on conversations. On Geiger's secure cellphone LCD screen appeared a text message: "Urgent, I need a dossier and a recent CV ASAP on Mark Ericksen, an Executive VP at EyeD4 Systems, a biometrics company located in Wilsonville, Oregon. Regards, Phantom."

Sullivan had selected the code name of Phantom because he felt it symbolized a master spy's journey into the shadows.

Chapter Fifteen

Ericksen ran at a six-minute-mile pace on a treadmill at his health club ClubSport, in neighboring Tualatin. After twenty minutes, he pressed cool-down and waited five minutes to proceed to his typical exercise regimen, where he pumped iron and stretched. When in town he usually worked out four times a week, alternating between his exercise routine and his forty minute lap swim.

EyeD4 Systems had hired him in September 2006, after having conducted an executive search for a top-level executive with a top-secret security clearance, a successful track record within the US intelligence and defense establishment, and an extensive knowledge of biometrics. His MBA from the University of Virginia helped him, but Jeb Templeton's recommendation sealed the deal, and he accepted the job offer.

He jumped into his new Porsche and drove to his Wilsonville, Oregon office. He served as executive-vice-president of marketing at EyeD4 Systems, a government defense contractor that designed, developed, and marketed biometrics technologies and AES-256 key length encryption software. Their technology products were used in sensitive physical access control environments requiring positive identification of the individual by their unique biological characteristics.

Their dual-systems consisted of the iris and palm subcutaneous vein patterns. The company responded to the clients' requests, whether their requirement was a single or dual biometrics systems approach. Currently, their palm subcutaneous vein pattern biometrics used for communications had entered into the last stage of the pilot program, funded to the tune of five million dollars by the United States Department of Defense and the intelligence community. Following one year of preliminary testing of five hundred units, they had transitioned into the beta-testing stage.

After spending two hours in his office, Ericksen walked over to the file cabinet and retrieved a file. He entered the hall, passed several departments, and approached a solid oak door that had an EyeD4 Access System control reader built into the wall next to the door. He leaned closer to the iris optical scanner, embedded in a camera-like apparatus, twelve inches away from his eyes, and looked straight into the mirror-like device, which sensed his presence and activated the optical scanner. The light source scanned his eyes, illuminated the patterns of his iris area, captured them in real-time, and did a pattern recognition match to his previously registered template in the database. Once they matched, and his identification authenticated, the process generated a Green LED: ID Confirmed.

Since their area was designated a Sensitive Compartmentalized Information Facility or SCIF by the Defense Security Services, they implemented both biometrics technologies to harden access to their SCIF. The first process took less than five seconds from the time Ericksen looked into the iris camera. The chance of a false acceptance, whereby a person not in the database could gain access, was roughly one in a million. Ericksen now placed his palm up, facing the palm subcutaneous vein recognition system's optical scanner. The motion from his palm activated the scanner in real-time and matched the live palm vein patterns to his previously registered template in the database. His identification was authenticated, and a Green LED appeared: ID Confirmed.

His palm vein pattern recognition system had a one in a million chance of false acceptance. Both systems were virtually impenetrable. This dual-biometrics system now activated the door electronics control switch and opened the thick door. The whole process took approximately twelve seconds. He entered the sensitive area where a vice-president of engineering, a senior software engineer, two software programmers, a hardware engineering manager, two hardware engineers, and two electrical engineers were testing four EyeD4 Comm laptop computer systems for the US government. The US government had approved ten employees at the company for a top-secret security clearance, including Ericksen.

These seven men and three women were the only employees in the company authorized to access the SCIF area. Should any other employee try to gain access without an approved top-secret security clearance and get caught, the company would lose its certification and clearances as well as be subject to federal prosecution.

The government integrated the company's encryption software's best features with their software because the company's algorithms were virtually impossible to defeat. They used the Advanced Encryption Standard (AES) using 256-bit keys, using the same key for encrypting and decrypting the data. Two of their engineers had previously worked for the NSA.

Ericksen approached the vice-president of engineering, a tall, thin, balding man with a full beard and handed him a file marked Top Secret. The top of the letterhead displayed The Central Intelligence Agency, and in capital letters printed The Golden Cypher Project.

The vice-president of engineering looked up at him. "We'll get back to Langley tomorrow morning."

Ericksen nodded, smiled, and left the building. He jumped into his Porsche and drove to Lake Oswego. His secure cellphone rang. His Bluetooth activated the incoming call, and he leaned toward his Porsche Command Console: "Ericksen speaking."

"Hi Mark, Fico Delgado. Don't hang up on me! I got your number from Templeton."

Shit. Do I have to talk to him? Ericksen didn't feel like opening up about his PTSD, his treatment, or his withdrawal from normal social activities over the past several years to an old comrade-in-arms.

"Please hold, Fico." He hadn't spoken with Delgado or anyone else from Special Operations Forces except Templeton in over six years. The former Delta Force sergeant had integrity and professionalism.

He pulled off the road and leaned closer to the Command Module, "Where are you?"

"I work in McLean, Virginia, for the national counterterrorism center (NCTC). Templeton told me you're planning a trip to DC on Sunday."

"Affirmative."

"Would you like to join me for dinner Monday night?"

"Fico, unfortunately, I'm tied up both Monday and Tuesday evening with procurement and technical staff meetings from the three-letter guys in both Langley and Ft. Meade."

"How long are you staying in town?"

"I take off Thursday morning back to Oregon."

"How about Wednesday evening, April 8?" Then silence. "Hello, Mark, are you still there?"

Shit, he was a witness that day.

He got back to the conversation. "Sure. That will work."

"Where are you staying in DC?"

"The Hilton McLean Tysons Corner. How about 6:30?"

"See you there, bro."

———

HE THOUGHT MEETING his former JSOC team member might bring him closure. He leaned back on a comfortable leather chair in his psychologist's office. The suite overlooked the Willamette River in Lake Oswego. He felt relaxed as he faced Dr. Ari Holtzman, a heavy-set man in his fifties, with a full dark brown mustache and bulbous round nose, who wore tortoise-shelled eyeglass frames. On the walls hung three surrealist, colorful paintings, photographs of Einstein and Carl Jung, and several impressive diplomas.

Ericksen had finally reached the decision to seek help for his PTSD. Having researched psychologists in the Portland area who worked with veterans who suffered from PTSD, he found Holtzman, who had some success in this field, and became his patient in September 2006. Over the past two years of Prolonged Exposure Therapy as well as various forms of meditation, Holtzman's approach enabled him to control his anger, guilt, fear, and anxieties. He still continued to keep his treatment a secret. The events of April 18, 2002, near Khost, Afghanistan, were always present, but not as painful as before.

He now wanted answers as to why his commander, Colonel Dawkins, had lied about Sadozai. The psychologist had heard his story countless times during treatment and encouraged him to accept that the real murderer was Colonel Dawkins.

"Mark, you served your country admirably, and you should be proud."

He stood up. "Doc, I'm grateful to you for providing me the tools and the confidence to manage my PTSD."

Dr. Holtzman shrugged his shoulders and nodded. "In the fog of war soldiers do things out of fear, confusion, and survival. You have the connections in Washington to conduct an under-the-radar investigation and find out the truth."

He nodded as he took out the picture of Sadozai's wife and daughters from his wallet. "Jannan told me last year his brother's wife and oldest daughter were murdered by the Taliban. Whenever I glance at the photo, I make a promise to myself: I must find a way to get his brother, his family, and Bashir's daughter Laila, out of Afghanistan." He sighed, and then looked at the doctor. "That would give me some measure of redemption."

Chapter Sixteen

CIA HEADQUARTERS

S ullivan's chief of staff entered his office and handed him both an FBI and a CIA condensed report with the heading: *Mark Niels Ericksen.*

Mark Niels Ericksen, born July 13, 1970, in Copenhagen, Denmark – Naturalized American Citizen. Raised on Mercer Island, Washington.

B.S. degree with major: Computer Science, Oregon State University, 1992.

NCAA All-American wrestler at OSU.

Commissioned Ensign in the U.S. Navy, 1992. October 1993, Completed BUD/S class 184

1993-1998, SEAL Team-8 operator. Clearance: Top Secret.

September 1997-June, 1998, Naval Post Graduate School, Arabic Language Proficiency.

August 1998-March, 1999, Completed SEAL T-6 training The Naval Special Warfare Development Group: DEVGRU.

May 1999, Promoted to Lieutenant.

Married in May 2000.

Classified missions in Yemen, Somalia, and Egypt 2000-2001.

Ericksen's wife, Karen Ericksen, was killed in a car accident in June 2001.

December 2001, platoon leader of ISAF, coalition joint special operations force in Kandahar Province (leading a team of SEAL T-6, Australian SAS, and Norwegian SOF). Dec-Feb 28.

March 1–May 7, 2002: Operation Ending Freedom. Part of JSOC Bagram Air Base, Bravo Team – Tier-One Missions. Received Silver Star in 2002 for bravery in Kandahar Province.

Purple Heart, North Africa-classified mission. Resigned commission May 10, 2002.

Employment Records:

September 2002–August 2004, Cambridge Defense Systems, U.S. military contractor. Project Manager. Clearance: Top Secret. Bethesda, Maryland. (Drones)

September 2004–August 2006, Avanti Biosystems, U.S. military contractor. Vice-President, military affairs, Vienna, Virginia.

Biometrics ID Integration Task Force in Iraq and Afghanistan. Clearance: Top-Secret Security Clearance.

Executive MBA, University of Virginia, 2006.

September 2006–Present, EyeD4 Systems, executive vice-president, marketing and sales, a biometrics technology firm, utilizing both the Iris and the Palm Vein patterns in access control and encryption communications. Wilsonville, Oregon. Clearance: Top-Secret Security Clearance.

"Find Ericksen and get him on a secure line immediately."
"Yes, sir."
Ericksen heard his cellphone ring and picked it up, "Hello."
"Mark, this is Bob at Three Letters, Virginia. The big boss requests your presence in his office at nine this morning. It's urgent."
"All right. I'll have to cancel my appointment with Three Letters Maryland this morning."
"The director will try to re-arrange your appointment after your meeting."
Ericksen was escorted into the CIA Director's soundproof conference room on the 7th floor.
"Hello, Mr. Ericksen, I'm sorry you had to break your appointment. This meeting is urgent. It concerns national security." Sullivan picked up his phone. "Please send them in."
The Deputy CIA Director, Susan Norstad, and the National Clandestine Service Director, Nate Sheridan, entered the office. Sullivan introduced Ericksen to them. Everyone took a seat facing Sullivan. Sheridan's eyes widened as he stared at Ericksen like a deer startled by the glare of high-beam headlights.
"Hello, Mark, good to see you again."
Sullivan looked at him. "I'll get right to the point. There is a Saudi

terrorist mastermind who's planning to attack the United States with nuclear suitcase bombs. We recently learned of his interest in acquiring your beta-tested classified biometrics systems to communicate with his sleeper cell leaders in the U.S. Frankly, we need your help."

"Sir, are you asking me to be a CIA contractor?"

"Exactly. This is a critical opportunity for us to not only prevent the attack but to destroy this terrorist organization."

"What do you want me to do?"

"Our assets reported the mastermind got wind of your Saudi distributor's upcoming showcase event where you'll be presenting the EyeD4 Access System, June 9–10 at the Jeddah Hilton. We believe he will contact you there."

Ericksen's eyes widened. "In other words, he will attempt to bribe me, and my task is to sell our classified encrypted biometrics systems to them and provide NSA with the back door?"

"Exactly, you summed up the mission in a nutshell. Your combat leadership experience in the SEALs and your employment history with several defense contractors is excellent. We'll brief your CEO in due time. We'll need you to report back on June 2."

———

ERICKSEN'S FACE lit up with a smile when he spotted Delgado in the Hilton Hotel's lobby in McLean. Delgado gave him a big hug. The former Delta operative wore a leather jacket, blue dress shirt, and khaki slacks.

"Mark." He hugged him again. "It's great seeing you."

They went to the bar and spent the next few minutes getting caught up. Delgado had a muscular build, black hair, large brown eyes, and stood five foot ten. He raised his glass of beer to Delgado's glass. "Cheers. How long have you been with the Agency?"

"Soon, it will be for three years. After I left the service in 2004, I went back to college, received my degree, and a few days later, the Agency knocked on my door. Their efforts were focused on hiring more former Special Ops guys with language proficiency in Arabic.

I've been working at the National Counterterrorism Center for the past year."

"Great. Are you married?" asked Ericksen.

"Yep. I am married to a real sweet Cuban-American lady. She's six months pregnant now."

"Congratulations!"

"How about you, Mark?"

"No, haven't found the right woman yet."

Delgado chuckled and slapped his back. "Playing the field, bro?"

"Fico, I wish I had the time to meet the right woman, but my primary focus is making our company successful. However, I do get lots of pressure from my mother and sister."

"Templeton told me about your tech company, and the future looks great."

"How is Templeton doing these days?"

"He's still working for the Office of the Secretary of Defense. He directs a group within the Resource Management Office. However, he told me he's tired of all the bureaucracy and is seeking a position with a high tech firm in California."

If it wasn't for Jeb's help, I wonder where I would be. Someday I hope to return the favor.

"He would be an invaluable asset, that's for sure," said Ericksen.

"I believe his wife is from Palo Alto, and all of her family is back there."

Delgado looked around the bar area and back to him. "You'll never guess who I ran into in Washington last week!"

"Who?"

"Remember Dex, the Agency Ops guy at Bagram Air Base?"

"Sure."

"He's still with the Agency, but on loan to the Treasury Department's counterterrorism and financial intelligence division in Switzerland."

"I thought his expertise dealt more with satellite intelligence and countermeasures."

"The Agency sent him to MIT in 2004 for a master's degree in computer science and encryption. He's quite busy monitoring private numbered accounts. Most of the monies are derived from illegal activities, corruption, tax evasion, terrorist financing, and arms dealing."

Ericksen shook his head. "I wouldn't be surprised if some of the reported billions lost in Afghanistan and Iraq wound up in offshore banks."

"I was on one mission back in February 2002, when we delivered thirty million bucks in packets of ten thousand dollars. They were shrink-wrapped in one hundred dollar bills and placed in footlockers. We delivered them to a warlord in Spin Bolak."

Ericksen leaned in and stared at Delgado. "Were you on any missions in Kandahar Province with Sadozai?"

Delgado nodded his head. "Yes, that's the one. Sadozai served as the interim government's intelligence officer and translator. Dawkins ran the mission."

"Dawkins!" Ericksen's eyes widened at the mention of his name, and shook his head. "Thirty million dollars."

"That's not all. Besides the money, Dawkins and the bigwig promised the warlord we wouldn't burn or confiscate his poppy seed fields if he cooperated."

"What did the warlord give in return?"

"He had to provide us actionable intel on Al-Qaeda and Taliban leaders."

He had heard about the DoD and the CIA giving large amounts of cash to prominent warlords and drug lords for their cooperation but didn't know Dawkins had any involvement.

"Who else participated in the meeting beside Sadozai, Dawkins, and the big shot?"

Delgado glanced back at Ericksen, "Pulaski."

"Dawkins claimed the Agency had proof Sadozai was a spy, but when I confronted Dex, he said they had no evidence. Dawkins lied to me!"

"That son-of-a-bitch," Delgado said.

Ericksen tensed up and made a fist. "Do you think the payoff came from the CIA or the DoD?"

"I don't know, but I heard that the bigwig knew the warlord from the Soviet-Afghan war period," said Delgado.

"Whatever happened to Pulaski after 2002?"

"Pulaski and I were part of Dawkins' JSOC operations during the Iraq invasion in 2003. In late 2004, Dawkins retired and joined Stealth Dynamics, as head of recruitment and training for a private security firm. Pulaski assisted him with the training. Stealth Dynamics worked under State Department contracts in both Iraq and Afghanistan through the end of 2008, and I believe it continued through the end of this fiscal year."

Ericksen raised his voice, "I'll bet whoever hired him has a checkered past."

"I wouldn't be surprised. The CEO of Stealth Dynamics helped arrange the meeting at Spin Bolak."

"Do you know his name?" asked Ericksen.

"Chuck Huntington. He died last June in an airplane accident in Alaska. However, another individual you know played a role, though it could have been a case of standard operating procedures."

"Who's that?"

"His name is Nate Sheridan. He's now the Director of the National Clandestine Service. You probably knew him as Clyde, the Agency's chief of station and head of Predator Drone Ops in Afghanistan."

He raised his eyebrows and shook his head. "Shit, I met him yesterday at Langley."

"I didn't make much of it at the time, but I saw Sheridan unload the footlockers from the aircraft to Dawkins and Pulaski. From my vantage point on the tarmac, I would swear on a stack of bibles, a few more footlockers were remaining in the cargo hold before they took off from Kandahar. However, you never know for sure when you work in the shadows," said Delgado.

Ericksen's thoughts charged into high gear like a warrior faced with a fight or flight decision.

Maybe Dawkins developed a kickback scheme with Huntington to pull it off with the warlord. If that were the case, Pulaski would also get a percentage, but Sadozai, being an outsider, couldn't be trusted to keep the information quiet from the interim government officials. He had to be killed, that's it! Nothing else makes sense. How does Sheridan fit into this plan?

Ericksen had an epiphany. *The dots connected. He now realized he had to get at the truth, even if it meant risking his life in the process. He took a deep breath and smiled.*

"Fico, you just solved a major problem that has plagued me for years. You provided me with Dawkins' ulterior motive for lying to me. Now I understand why Pulaski wouldn't serve as my witness when I threatened to bring this criminal matter to the Admiral."

Delgado gently slammed his hand on the bar. "Those fucking bastards!"

Ericksen asked, "Do you have his telephone and address?"

"Yes. Pulaski lives in Miami. I'll email you the information."

Chapter Seventeen

After dinner and a few drinks with an old high school buddy, Pulaski decided to call it a night. He returned to his seventh-floor condo on Ocean Drive. Entering the kitchen, Pulaski reached for his favorite coffee mug from the oak cabinets, then walked by the butler's pantry, reached up, opened the liquor cabinet door, and took out a bottle of Puerto Rican rum. He poured the rum into the coffee mug and took a good swig. It bore the inscription *Banque Matthias Reiter SA, Genève*, highlighted in red and blue fonts and a graphic of a Swiss flag.

He opened the sliding glass window that separated his living room from the patio, stepped out, and scanned over Biscayne Bay. He focused on the boats making bright patterns in their reflections. It was ten o'clock in the evening.

Pulaski went into his home-based office in his condo, sat down, and powered up his laptop computer. He punched in his passcode and waited for the images to appear on his high-definition monitor. While waiting for the desktop icons to appear, he glanced at the photo on the wall above the laptop. The picture showed eight men in full Special Operations Forces battle gear, giving a victory sign with an Afghan mountain range behind them. He nodded as in deep thought as he recognized himself in the photo. He had spent thirteen years in the US Army, advancing from Airborne Ranger to the 75th Ranger Regiment, and finally to the elite Delta Force. In Afghanistan and Iraq, he was part of JSOC. When he left the service, he spent three years as a private security contractor in Iraq for the State Department. Besides being a smooth-talker, he could also be rude, which at times got him in trouble.

Pulaski developed an interest in computers and started his own business. In 2008, he set up a military surplus internet business, where he sold military clothing, pistol and rifle accessories, body armor, equipment, and technology on his website.

Suddenly, a big man with broad shoulders as wide as an NFL linebacker approached him from the shadows. Surprised and shocked, he turned and faced the man. "Colonel, can't you knock like any other decent, respectful person?"

Dawkins looked like a man you never wanted to cross or meet in a dark alley. If looks could kill, they belonged to him. A three-inch scar ran across his forehead, along with a boxer's crooked, broken nose. He wasn't the type Hollywood would cast as a leading man. The former Delta Force colonel's ice-blue eyes locked in and stared at Pulaski, whose tense body sat behind the desk.

Dawkins moved a foot closer. "You fucked up! You took out a quarter-of-a-million bucks from our Geneva bank two weeks ago. I told you not to withdraw large amounts at a time."

Pulaski looked up at him. "I needed the capital to grow my internet business. What's the fucking big deal, sir? I flew to Geneva, spent three days there, withdrew the money, placed it in hidden bottom compartments of two of my hard-shell suitcases, and cleared customs in Miami without any problems."

He shrugged and shook his head, "Asshole, I thought you knew better than to possibly leave a money trail for the Feds to discover our numbered accounts."

Pulaski leaned back in his chair, his eyes wide open, and his arms and hands raised. "Colonel, you have my word I won't cause you any more problems."

Standing ten feet away from him, he spoke, "Really, Lech, we hacked into your computer."

"Hacked?" Pulaski said as sweat began running down his forehead.

Dawkins shook his head. "You're getting sloppy."

Pulaski's face turned ashen-gray as silence ruled his stone face.

He didn't like Dawkins' tone or the fact that he broke into his condo.

"Any of our old war buddies get in touch with you lately?"

"Yeah, Fico Delgado called last Friday and wanted to get together."

"Why would that fucking Cuban suddenly want to get together with you?"

"He's flying in on Thursday suggested we have some drinks in South Beach…you know, chew the fat about the good old times."

He got a little closer, his massive head sporting a military crew-cut anchored by a muscular neck, and asked in his booming voice, "Did any other old buddies call recently?"

"No," Pulaski said, as he looked away from Dawkins' eyes.

"You're lying."

Dawkins' face turned red. "Why did that fucking SEAL Ericksen call you on Saturday?"

Sweat poured down Pulaski's face, and his breathing became shallow. "He wanted to get in touch with you. He said it was something important. I told him I didn't know where you lived, and you were probably on a project somewhere overseas."

Pulaski reached for his mug of rum, spilling some on his shirt. Dawkins tightened his jaw, narrowed his eyes, and his bushy eyebrows looked like they were almost touching the bridge of his nose. He turned away for a moment and then stared at him. "Did you forget Delgado was the fucking machine-gunner on the Apache who escorted the helo to Assadullah's compound in Spin Bolak with the millions on board?" asked Dawkins.

"That had to be seven years ago, and besides, he wasn't aware of the deal you cut with the warlord because he was outside the compound with several other JSOC operators, weapons at the ready.

The only ones who knew were Sadozai, you, me, the warlord, his bodyguards, and Huntington."

Dawkins' large vein in his neck started bulging up and down, and Pulaski realized his life was in danger. He knew him well. They had been on several contract hits together, and Pulaski recognized the signs. He had to think fast. With some luck, he might be able to reach for the Colt .45 he hid in his desk drawer and shoot Dawkins before he got killed.

"You stupid shit, Fico is with the CIA and works at the National Counterterrorism Center. Who knows, he might be in touch with Ericksen. We can't afford to have Ericksen asking questions, especially about Sadozai."

Dawkins's voice was filled with rage as he slammed his fist against the wall and yelled, "That fucking former SEAL is the last person I want to meet again! If he pushes his luck, he'll meet the same fate as I have in store for you!" At that moment, he removed the 9mm Makarov pistol with an extended suppressor from his windbreaker and aimed it at Pulaski. Dawkins' eyes narrowed, and his face tensed up as he suddenly flew into the zone, like a leopard stalking a gazelle, knowing in a matter of seconds, death will be final.

Pulaski's adrenaline kicked in as his hand reached, opened the top right desk drawer, grabbed the Colt .45 handgun, and squeezed the trigger. His face turned ashen-white, his eyebrows raised in tandem to his wide-opened eyes and mouth, when he realized in a fraction of a split-second that his gun didn't have any bullets. He was in shock.

"Surprised? Goodbye, buddy," said Dawkins, as he fired two bullets into Pulaski five feet away. His blood oozed out of his forehead and chest. Brain tissue and skull fragments splattered on the carpet, the wall, and the desk, as his body slammed against the credenza before hitting the carpet with a thud.

He found a suitcase with ninety-five-thousand-dollars in packets of one hundred dollar bills after rummaging throughout the condo. He also opened up his wallet and took several hundred dollars in cash, a Rolex watch, a gold bracelet, and the Banque Matthias Reiter SA mug. The scene had the makings of a burglary gone badly. He placed a black wig over his head, put on a fake black beard, and aviator prescription glasses over his eyes. Then he closed the door to the condo, suitcase in hand, and entered the elevator.

After leaving the building, he walked two blocks, turned around to make sure nobody followed, crossed the street, went into an alley for a brief minute, removed his black wig and beard, took off his light jacket, and placed all of them in a laundry-type bag. He walked another block before he jumped into his parked Ford SUV, threw the laundry bag and suitcase in the back seat, and drove away. Shane Dawkins, ex-Delta Force colonel, had just added another murder to his resume. He picked up his Blackberry and made a call.

"Timberwolf, what's up?" Sheridan demanded.

"Raven lost his wings tonight. Check the worldwide airline reservation database for anything on Ericksen, especially international travel," Dawkins said.

"Affirmative."

Chapter Eighteen

GENEVA, SWITZERLAND

Ericksen finished breakfast, placed his laptop in security at his Metropole Hotel, and left for his scheduled meeting three kilometers away. He crossed the bridge from the old town of Geneva and walked along the promenade until he reached the *Musée d'Histoire des Science*. The park had beautiful botanical gardens, statues, trees, and trails alongside Lake Leman. He looked at his watch and walked one-hundred-meters from the museum to a bench under a tree.

Five minutes later, he watched as a man approached the bench and sat beside him.

"Hi, Mark."

Ericksen shook his hand. "Should I call you Dex or Dave Jacobson?"

"Dave will do for now. Fico informed me about the Spin Bolak warlord operation and why Dawkins ordered you to kill Sadozai. I heard the communications between you and Dawkins, but it would have been a no-win situation for both of us if I came forward. I'm terribly sorry."

"I understand," he nodded. "Fico indicated you could help me."

"Listen up. What I'm going to tell you must be kept in the strictest confidence; otherwise, our operations could be jeopardized."

"Go on."

"We are privy to a DoD criminal investigation involving four Army contracting officers who received kickbacks from defense contractors and some Iraqi ministry officials. We're talking about millions of dollars. We think Dawkins deposited the monies into a Swiss private numbered account in Geneva from 2003 through August 2004 while still on active duty. We believe he continued his agenda when he joined Stealth Dynamics. Anyway, the four men were murdered."

"Murdered?"

"Several witnesses claimed to have seen Dawkins and Pulaski with them on numerous occasions."

Ericksen shook his head and clenched his teeth.

"Dawkins has been seen in the company of Jurgen Reiter, the President, and COO of Banque Matthias Reiter SA, in Geneva. We're planning an operation to penetrate this bank's private numbered accounts and hopefully collect evidence to put him away for a long time."

"I wish I could help," said Ericksen.

"Have you sold any of your biometrics systems to banks yet?"

"No. Even if my distributor approached their security director and pitched our access control system tomorrow. It could take a year before they made a decision."

"We've also uncovered information on one individual who was formerly a high-ranking State Department official who works with Dawkins or is his boss. I'm not at liberty to reveal his name. Just be careful."

They stood for a minute and then walked away in different directions. Unbeknownst to them, a man in a jogging outfit partially hidden in the shadows of the brush near the museum took several photos of them from his telephoto lens camera.

Chapter Nineteen

BERLIN, GERMANY

A light drizzle fell on the city while the clouds overhead grew darker. At six in the morning, Ericksen wearing his jogger's outfit and a Seattle Seahawks wool skull cap, maintained a comfortable six-minute mile pace in the Tiergarten, the large urban park in central Berlin. He passed through the large beech and oak trees that hugged the path as he enjoyed his interlude with nature. After forty minutes, Ericksen slowed down as he passed the Brandenburg Gate. He felt exhilarated as his breath mingled with the chilly air. He wasn't concerned about his wet jogging outfit, or the brisk temperature, which read forty degrees fahrenheit, just feeling alive and rejuvenated because today held an excellent opportunity for his company.

After entering the Hotel Adlon Kempinski, on Unter den Linden 77, Ericksen picked up his laptop computer in hotel security, rode the elevator to the eighth-floor, and walked to his room. Diplomats, Heads of State, and foreign intelligence officers preferred staying at this elegant hotel. It was located one block from the Brandenburg Gate and two blocks from the American Embassy. Upon entering, he took off his wet outfit, opened the shower door, and enjoyed a long hot, steamy shower. After he had cleaned up, he put on his shorts and began his morning meditation ritual with his mantra, Mt. Olympus.

Thirty minutes later, his secure cellphone started ringing.

"I've changed your hotel reservation – you're booked at the Devonshire Hotel for two nights. I've arranged for a driver to meet you at Heathrow. After you clear customs, he'll hold a sign with the name Mr. Tisdale on it. The man will drive you to your hotel. In the morning, look for a black Jaguar, license plate number GB49 DSR. The driver will pick you up at 0800 sharp in front of the hotel and drive you to Vauxhall Cross," the voice said with a British accent and authority.

He heard another couple of rings from his hotel room phone, "Hello."

"It's Roger. How did your meetings go with the Swedish Ministry of Defense?"

"Quite good. I'll fill you in when I get back."

"Okay. Good luck with the German government."

"Thanks. See you soon."

He picked up his television remote, clicked on power, and scrolled down to the *BBC News channel*. Breaking news appeared on the screen as the BBC news anchor read the headlines from a teleprompter: "American Army sergeant charged with killing an innocent Afghan civilian."

Ericksen's face turned pale, his heart started racing, and he lost his composure. The headlines triggered a painful memory as his thoughts ran back in time to that terrible April day in 2002: watching Bashir on his knees begging for his life, and a second later staring down at him as his lifeless, bloody body lay on the ground.

I've killed many terrorists without batting an eye but killing Bashir numbed my heart and my soul. I feel as if my compassion for humanity lost its moral compass.

Ericksen inhaled deeply to the count of four, exhaled to four, and continued for four minutes. He said his mantra, Mt. Olympus, several times and regained his composure. Mt. Olympus had made a big impression on him while growing up in the Seattle area. During the summer, he and his best friend would hike the Olympic Mountain

Range, set up their tents, and camp at Elk Lake. Mt. Olympus's peak overshadowed the other mountains and generated inspirational feelings of tranquility for him.

After he had finished breakfast in the hotel dining room, he glanced at his sports watch, which read 9:00 am. He wrote his room number on the check, stood up, left the dining room, and walked to the lobby, where he put his laptop computer into security. Leaving the hotel lobby dressed in a casual sports shirt, a Columbia Sportswear windbreaker, sneakers, and jeans, he decided to spend the next five or six hours as a tourist in Berlin.

At four-thirty, as he exited the hotel door dressed in a conservative dark blue suit, tie, a khaki-colored trench coat, and carrying a leather briefcase in his right hand, the hotel doorman offered him an umbrella.

"Thank you," Ericksen said, walking under the red elongated hotel canopy, taking a deep breath and exhaling.

A black Audi sedan with Munich plates pulled up to the curb. The Germans must have inherited a gene dedicated to punctuality like a clock that never seemed to miss a beat. He recognized the big, burly driver with the large, full head of brown hair graying at the temples as Heinrich Kruger. Kruger gave him a nod as he got into the passenger seat, closed the door, and drove away.

A few minutes later, they pulled up to the well-fortified Bauhaus-designed German Federal Ministry of the Interior building at Alt-Moabit 101D. The imposing twin structures overlooked the Spree River. The complex had German Federal Police checking vehicles upon entrance to the main gate of the Ministry. Their car pulled over, and two federal police officers inspected it. After receiving a permit, they placed it on the dash, parked the Audi, and walked to the front of the government building.

A federal police officer asked for ID. He produced his American passport and Kruger, his German passport, a photo ID, and his German government's approved contractor ID. One of the officers waved Kruger to an iris biometrics device mounted on the wall next to the security officer's console. Kruger looked into the mirror-like optical reader, and the system scanned his iris. On the reader, the screen appeared the word: ID Bestatigt (German for confirmed). He then placed his palm up about three inches from the optical reader, held it for a few seconds as the scanner read his unique palm subcutaneous vein patterns. On the reader, the screen appeared the word: ID Bestatigt.

He smiled and gave Kruger the thumbs-up sign. He felt a sense of pride in observing his company's dual-biometrics access control system in operation at the Ministry. Ericksen thought to himself, *today might be my lucky day*. They signed in, received badges, and walked over to the metal detector. They took out all of their coins and keys and placed them in a bowl, along with their laptop computers, and proceeded through the metal detector. They were met by a well-dressed woman in her late forties, a senior administrative-type, who escorted them toward a bank of elevators. They entered an elevator and got off on the sixth floor.

Ericksen appeared cautiously confident that the German government would order a large number of EyeD4 Access Systems; otherwise, he thought, *why the invitation for the meeting, at least that's what Kruger had been telling him*. A woman approached the door to the conference center, placed her proximity card over the scanner, and the door immediately opened. Ericksen and Kruger walked into the conference room. Standing near the conference table were the same five men, all dressed in suits, that Ericksen had met a year earlier when he pitched his systems. The only addition to the group was a heavy-set, short man with bushy eyebrows and a beard, wearing a dark blue sports jacket.

At the head of the conference table sat a short, bespectacled slim man of sixty, with a gray beard and bald head. Ericksen remembered him as the key man he had met last year. His badge read: Dieter Hartmann, the director of procurement, German Ministry of the Interior. The other men's badges listed only their first names and their departments: BfV, for the protection of the constitution, the German version of NSA; GSG9, the counterterrorism and special operations unit of the German Federal Police; BPOL, the German Federal Police; and the BKA, German Federal Criminal Investigations, (German FBI).

The sixth man's badge signified he was the Ministry of the Interior's IT director. Ericksen thought these men were likely the heads of security for their respective departments. Everyone shook hands with Ericksen and Kruger before they took their seats.

"Sorry about the weather, Herr Ericksen," Hartmann said in English.

Ericksen and Kruger smiled at the remark. "Director Hartmann, Ericksen is used to the rain where he comes from," Kruger said. As EyeD4 System's distributor in Germany, Austria, and Switzerland, Kruger's company, Zugspitze Systems, had installed over one hundred EyeD4 Access Systems at several critical facilities a year ago on behalf of the Ministry of the Interior's pilot program.

On the table next to each person were a bottle of mineral water, a notepad, and a pen. Director Hartmann looked around and placed his hands on the table. The woman gave him several contracts written in English and took a seat next to him.

The German Ministry's IT director pointed to Hartmann, glanced at everyone around the table, and interjected, "Based on the input we received after our pilot program trials, the performance, accuracy, and reliability of your systems exceeded our expectations. The EyeD4 Access System has proven to be the most reliable biometrics system we have ever tested."

Ericksen and Kruger looked at the IT director and nodded in agreement. He pointed his finger toward Ericksen. "We tried many times to defeat your system and were unsuccessful. We have accepted your bid and are awarding your company the contracts."

An administrative assistant handed the contracts to Ericksen, who immediately looked at Kruger, nodded, and then looked approvingly at the director. "Thank you, sir."

"Let's focus on the key points so that we can hopefully agree," Director Hartmann said.

Over the next twenty minutes, they went over the contracts, which indicated that the installations were to be delivered in phases. The arrangements focus on the quantity of the EyeD4 Access Systems, their readers, intelligent controllers, software, and firmware, written in

German, and strict instructions stipulating the shipments would be picked up by the German government's contracted trucking carrier at EyeD4 System's facility in Wilsonville, Oregon.

Each department had budgetary control over their requirements, thus, the need for several contracts. "As you can see in the contracts, we'll have four-ship dates," said Hartmann.

Ericksen turned to Hartmann, who was sitting to his right, "Based on the numbers, I'm confident we'll be able to comply with the dates and have ample time to get things approved by the Department of Commerce as well as State."

He narrowed his eyes, "I must warn you, Herr Ericksen, there are penalties if your company doesn't make the ship dates on time."

He thought for a moment. "I understand, sir."

Kruger made a note of each order's dates, knowing that his company would be responsible for the training, installation, and technical support.

Ten minutes later, Ericksen signed all of the contracts and returned to the director for all of the key principals to sign.

"I'll FedEx the contracts overnight to your office. As soon as your CEO signs and returns the contracts, they'll be valid."

Kruger cut in and asked, "What are your plans for the EyeD4-Comm's palm subcutaneous vein security system?"

Hartmann placed the contracts in a neat pile and took a gulp of water. "We were impressed with the demo at the German Chancellery recently. Since it is still in beta-test mode, we'll wait and see. However, once your government officially endorses the system, we'll contact you and send a delegation to your office."

Ericksen sighed.

After the meeting, Ericksen and Kruger left the Ministry at 7:00 pm for their dinner appointment. The windshield wipers were engaged at full speed as the rain grew in intensity, generating a rhythmic beat on the car's windshield. His thoughts centered on his company's orders should be receiving next week: *Three years of busting my ass are starting to pay off.*

The car pulled up to the five-star Adlon Hotel Kempinski, where a valet approached. The valet handed Kruger a ticket with a number and took the car keys. At that moment, an armored Mercedes SUV pulled up, and a tall gentleman in his early forties, with close-cropped blond hair and dressed in an elegant, brown herringbone suit, greeted Herr Kruger. Ericksen spotted the man's handgun partially hidden under his suit. Two bodyguards got out of the car and followed Ulrich Genscher, the BND Director (German Foreign Intelligence Service).

"Heinrich," yelled Genscher. Kruger turned around and saw Genscher. The men greeted each other and entered the lobby of the hotel. Kruger turned to both men and motioned to follow him up the hotel lobby stairway to the second-floor restaurant. The Lorenz Adlon Esszimmer had a two-star Michelin rating. The restaurant epitomized culinary excellence in Europe. One of the bodyguards followed and found a seat outside of the restaurant entrance. The maître d' met them, handed them menus, and escorted them to a table by the fireplace. The entire restaurant was crafted in beautiful wood paneling. The other bodyguard sat at a small table where he could watch Genscher. Over the next ten minutes, the men enjoyed their mugs of premium Berlin beer.

"Herr Ericksen, you're fortunate to have appointed Herr Kruger. He happened to be one of the finest German foreign intelligence directors we ever had, and my mentor," Genscher said with vigor. Kruger sighed and lightly slapped Genscher's back.

"That's why I hired him," Ericksen said. He had realized some time earlier that if EyeD4 Systems was to be a significant global provider to foreign governments and their ministries, he needed to appoint the best distributors, those who had access to the key decision-makers and enjoyed excellent reputations.

"My friends at Langley shared with me how well the EyeD4 Comm has performed during the pilot program, and frankly, we need all the tools to fight global terrorism and cyber warfare, especially technology that is virtually impossible for terrorists and hackers to penetrate."

He nodded in agreement. He knew that EyeD4 Systems made the best dual-biometrics access control and computer communications systems and were virtually impossible to compromise. Having spent the past three years targeting, pioneering, and capturing the US government and defense business, he recognized that even though the orders were small initially, he built a solid foundation for the company to grow and be profitable.

The waiter walked up to the table and spoke in German, "Have you gentlemen decided?" The men all glanced at the menus. Ericksen smelled the roast lamb dish that was served to a man at the next table. "I'll order the tartare of smoked eel and the sea bass," Genscher said.

Then the waiter glanced at him. He looked up and said in English, "I'll go with the smoked eel and the roast lamb." Kruger ordered the smoked eel and the St. Patrick salmon. The waiter gave Kruger the wine menu, who pondered it for a few moments. "We'll have the Australian 1998 Tower Estate's Cabernet Sauvignon."

"When I was the director, I only wish we would have received information from the CIA on the two Al-Qaeda members who attended the Malaysian meeting and moved to San Diego. During that time, Mohamed Atta had been under direct surveillance by the German Federal Police. In fact, all three pilots of the hijacked American planes on that ill-fated day of 9/11, Mohamed Atta, Marwan Al- Shehhi, and Ziad Jarrah, were part of the Hamburg cell," Kruger said.

Genscher interrupted, "In hindsight, I'm convinced if all of the intelligence services had been aggressive in sharing actionable intel during that critical time, we could have arrested the entire Al-Qaeda cell in Hamburg."

Ericksen and Kruger nodded in agreement.

"The most unfortunate thing about the 9/11 tragedy had to be the lack of action on the part of senior FBI officials at headquarters who refused to respond to the warnings from their field agents in Phoenix and Minneapolis. This wouldn't happen in Germany," said Kruger.

Genscher shook his head. "That's for sure."

He felt uncomfortable with the men's critical condemnation regarding the failure of the American intelligence community. But he knew they made some excellent points.

"Hopefully, under the Office of the Directorate of National Intelligence, this tragedy won't happen again," Ericksen said.

The waiter approached the bottle of wine, uncorked it, and gently poured a little into Kruger's wine glass. Kruger brought the glass to his mouth, swirled it around, and, smelling its bouquet, took a taste. He nodded to the waiter and smiled approvingly. The waiter poured the wine into the three gentlemen's wine glasses.

Kruger studied Genscher, and in a serious tone, asked, "How can we persuade the Ministry of Defense to give us a meeting?"

"Please understand they're still heavily influenced by Handelsdorf Systems," he said, as he took a sip of his wine. Even though their biometrics technology doesn't compare to yours, the company has been in bed with the MoD for over thirty years."

Ericksen asked, "When can we expect some EyeD4 Access Systems business from your department?"

Genscher sighed and placed his hand on the table. "If you can deliver all of the Interior Ministry's orders on time and those systems perform well, I'm confident I can persuade the BND procurement director to place a purchase order."

Ericksen nodded and smiled, evoking a sense of confidence. He looked at Genscher and Kruger. "I would like to make a toast to you, Herr Genscher, for joining us and hopefully doing business with the BND someday." Everyone held their glasses up as they all toasted.

"Prost."

Chapter Twenty

Ericksen cleared customs at London's Heathrow Airport on Thursday, April 23, and entered the receiving hall at 7:45 pm. He spotted the man holding a sign with the name Mr. Tisdale. The driver took his bags, placed them in the car's trunk, and drove to the hotel.

After Ericksen had checked into the hotel in Knightsbridge, he took off his coat and suit jacket and placed his laptop computer on the desk in the room. Responding to a discreet knock, he opened the door, and the bellman entered the room with his luggage and the latest edition of the *International Herald Tribune*. He reached into his pocket and gave the bellman a two-pound sterling coin tip.

"Thank you, sir."

Ericksen pulled up a chair and glanced at the front page of the newspaper, which read, "The Taliban ambushed and killed six American soldiers last night on the road from Kabul to Jalalabad." He tensed up, clenched his fists and teeth. *At that moment, he thought of his last words to his dying SEAL friend Vinnie Goldman. "Extraction is minutes away, bro. You're going to make it."* He took four deep breaths, repeating his mantra "Mt. Olympus" and spent the next few minutes meditating.

He finally stood up, walked to the mini-bar, and opened it up with one of the hotel keys. He reached for a bottle of beer, took a swig, and regained his composure. Ericksen never forgot the *Daring Eagles Operation's* memory where Bravo Team had lost six of its brothers in a Taliban and Al-Qaeda ambush.

When you added Sadozai to that terrible day, the total reached seven brothers.

He felt his cellphone vibrate in his pocket. "Hello."

"Fico here. I have an update on the Pulaski murder investigation."

"Did they find the killer?"

"No. The only lead that turned up is a water bottle found in the trunk of Fico's car with the name of Banque Matthias Reiter SA, Genève, on it."

"What does that mean?" asked Ericksen.

"His most recent credit card statement indicated he spent three days in Geneva, two weeks before his death."

"Are you thinking the same thing I am? If Pulaski, Huntington, and Dawkins were involved in a kickback scheme with the warlord, they probably used private numbered accounts," said Ericksen.

"Precisely. I'll check my sources and find out what I can about this bank and their procedures for opening up an account."

"Good. Please keep me updated," Ericksen said.

"Roger that."

The next day's weather felt a bit chilly, but the skies were clear. He was running in his jogging outfit and a pair of Nike sneakers at a six-minute mile pace along the Hyde Park's trails. He passed Kensington Gardens and ran several times by Round Pound before heading up Broad Walk north to Bayswater Road. From there, he ran to Park Lane to Rotten Row and over the bridge. Once he passed the bridge, he dropped down to Serpentine Road, heading east. He was one hundred yards from the deli by Lake Serpentine, running in the zone like an Olympic runner focused on the finishing line when he felt a breeze a few feet in front of him and heard the sound of a bullet ricocheting off a tree to his left nearby. "Holy shit! Shots! What the fuck!" Ericksen immediately ran to the next tree and hid behind it. Then another shot hit the center of the tree. His heartbeat sped faster, and sweat poured down his face. *Where did the shots come from?*

He speculated the shots were fired from two hundred yards across the lake, near the Lido Café. He waited a few minutes until he instinctively felt the time was right to emerge. Running at a good pace until he came to Knightsbridge, he caught a glimpse of a lean, tall man about three or four hundred feet away, wearing a jogger's jacket with a hood, and carrying a large backpack. The man jumped into a black BMW with tinted windows and sped away. Ericksen crossed the street and walked three hundred feet back to his hotel.

After entering the hotel, he handed the bellman a receipt. Twenty seconds later, the bellman gave him his laptop computer from the security room. He opened the door to his room and saw an envelope on the bed. He closed the door and double-locked it. With raised eyebrows, he silently read the note: *"Hyde Park was a warning! If you treasure your life – stop this bloody journey."*

Ericksen stood outside the hotel entrance holding his laptop case, glancing at his watch. It read 0800 hours. Suddenly, a black Jaguar with the license plate GB49 DSR pulled up outside the Devonshire as if on cue. The driver opened the rear door, and he got in. The drive from Knightsbridge to the SIS Building at Vauxhall Cross took about fifteen minutes. The Jaguar pulled up alongside the entrance to the headquarters of the British Secret Intelligence Service, otherwise known as MI6. The impressive building had a strange and exotic looking structure, consisting of glass and aluminum, and overlooked the River Thames. Many people claimed it looked like a giant Legoland.

Ericksen got out of the car and walked up to the entrance. Once in the massive lobby, he spotted a well-dressed man in a navy blue three piece suit. Kevin Howden, a man in his early fifties, with thinning grayish-red hair and beard, greeted Ericksen with a hearty handshake. Howden had retired in 2005 as head of British Special Forces (SAS) as a brigadier general and had operated out of the Ministry of Defence's Whitehall location. He then joined a private security contractor providing access control and communications security systems to the

MoD and intelligence agencies. As Chief Operating Officer of Global Dynamics, Howden represented EyeD4 Systems in the United Kingdom as their distributor and systems integrator.

He registered Ericksen at the security desk, and they placed lanyard name tags around their necks. After going through security, they were met by an MI6 official who escorted them to the elevator. They spotted an EyeD4 System for access control on the wall and next to a thick door on the third floor. The MI6 official did the log-on, received confirmation, and entered a conference room equipped with large, hi-def flat-screen monitors, technology equipment, and a small kitchen at the other end.

Graham Moore, a handsome, rugged-looking man in his early forties, with brown hair, piercing light-blue eyes, and dressed like a member of the Royal Family, approached them. "Good day, Mr. Ericksen; General Howden told me all about your company."

"It is a pleasure to meet you, Mr. Moore," he said. As MI6's counterterrorism director, Moore had a lot of responsibility on his shoulders. With a Cambridge degree, six years as a SAS officer, and twelve years with MI6, he had the perfect background to run counterterrorism. His bright blue eyes were always on alert. He introduced Ericksen to several men and women from MI6, MI5, Defense Intelligence Service, and Government Communications-GCHQ, the NSA of Great Britain. They were a mixture of operational security chiefs, scientists, mathematicians, and procurement directors.

Over the next thirty minutes, he answered most of their questions on both the EyeD4 Access Systems and the EyeD4 Comm Systems. His professional sales presentation centered on why their national security interests needed to acquire his company's systems. He delivered a flawless cost-benefit analysis performance, highlighted EyeD4 Systems' performance, reliability, and solutions-oriented capabilities to address the challenges Great Britain faced today.

He continued to focus on his company's featured capabilities in the main battlefield today: cyber warfare, counterterrorism, sabotage, financial intelligence, and asymmetrical warfare.

After his presentation and a Q and A, several men and women

stood up, shook his hand, and left the conference room. A silver-headed gentleman in his sixties entered the room with two staffers. Moore looked straight ahead. "Good morning, Sir. This is Mr. Ericksen."

"I heard a lot about you and your company. Director Sullivan told me the intelligence community is quite impressed with the performance and reliability of your systems," Sir Derek Worthington said. He had received his appointment in 2008 as the new Director-General of the British Secret Intelligence Service.

"Our pilot program with your EyeD4 Access at MI6 has been operational for the past five months. Our people have expressed confidence in your system, and we should be placing a purchase order soon," said Moore.

"It has been six months since you last visited GCHQ and demonstrated your EyeD4 Comm System. The Director of GCHQ told me last week they still can't decode your communications. As you know, they're one of the best code-breakers in the world," said Worthington.

"Sir, the procurement director of GCHQ, told me they would like to send a delegation as soon as they hear back from the CIA and NSA that they officially endorsed the product. Then we'll be happy to set up a meeting and send a delegation of engineers and security officials to Portland," said Moore.

"Sounds good."

Howden cleared his throat and fixed his eyes on Sir Derek Worthington. "What do you think, Derek?"

"My God, Kevin, you were right." Worthington turned to Ericksen.

"I dare say, we're impressed with your systems."

While Ericksen spoke to Worthington, the MI5 Director joined them. Moore took General Howden aside and asked, "How did you find this amazing technology?"

"I met him in Iraq and Afghanistan when he was the vice-president for military affairs at Avanti Biosystems. He trained the American Special Operations Forces and SAS on how to enroll terrorists and download their biometrics ID templates: fingerprints, iris and facial recognition templates into the FBI Biometrics Database Center in West Virginia and the DoD. I was impressed by him and the technology, and we've kept in touch ever since he joined EyeD4 Systems."

Howden didn't mention Ericksen's military background when he served as a US Special Operations Forces platoon leader in Afghanistan under Howden's command from January through March 2002. They operated out of Camp Wolverine, their new headquarters base at Kandahar Airport. Ericksen had run a platoon of eighteen individual Norwegian, Australian, British, and Danish Coalition Special Operations Forces under the ISAF Joint Command and participated in *Task Force Iron Guts*.

They left MI6 headquarters and moved into a waiting Jaguar. "I'm looking forward to attending the international distributors meeting next month," Howden said, and added, "I'll send you the name of the dive shop."

"Thanks."

Howden asked, "Would you like to join my wife and me for a home-cooked meal tonight?"

He raised his eyebrows and sighed. "That's very considerate of you, but I'm looking forward to a quiet evening and a good night's sleep before taking my flight back to the States."

"How about a rain check?"

"You're on."

As the Jaguar pulled up to the hotel entrance, the hotel doorman opened the car door, and Ericksen got out of the back seat. He waved his hand at Howden. "I believe we're going to make a lot of money."

"I jolly well hope so," Howden said.

Chapter Twenty-One

T he bright, glowing morning sun blazed through the bay windows of his living room as the rays fell on Ericksen's face. His contemporary Northwest-style house sat anchored on a hilly slope, six hundred feet up 'on Rawhide Drive in West Linn, a suburb of Portland. His home had a majestic view of Mount Hood and was surrounded by beautiful Douglas fir trees and a manicured green lawn, providing him the serenity and space to unwind.

After completing his fifty minute morning jog at a seven-minute mile pace around the hilly area, he showered, spent ten minutes in meditation, got dressed, finished breakfast, activated his home security alarm, and took off for work. Ericksen arrived at EyeD4 Systems in Wilsonville at 8:30. After spending a few minutes in his office, he walked down the hall to the CEO's office.

Behind an oak executive desk with his phone to his ear sat Roger Hamilton, a sixty-year-old, tall man with thinning gray hair, wearing a drab gray suit, blue tie, and metal, aviator-type framed eyeglasses. Hamilton had started EyeD4 Systems in 2003 after retiring from a career at IBM. Ericksen knocked on the office door and gently opened it. Hamilton caught a glimpse of him, and both men's eyes met. He motioned for him to enter.

Hamilton put the phone down and raised his voice, "Welcome back. I wish I could give you good news, but I have some bad news. We can't count on our banks or our angel investors anymore. Our only choice is to bootstrap our growth through our revenues."

Ericksen shook his head, his body tense upon hearing Hamilton's remarks. "You must be joking. Our cash burn rate can't sustain itself if we intend to enter the commercial and industrial sectors for our biometrics and encryption software products."

Hamilton stiffened his lips. "Have you ever known me to joke about finances? Just keep delivering sales and let me worry about receivables," said Hamilton.

"What about our future goals in building an international sales organization, and also developing a miniaturized iris camera recognition system embedded within a laptop computer and tablet for mobile communications applications?"

"Mark, you're not hearing me."

Ericksen took a deep breath. "We'll receive contracts from the French and German governments shortly. Those orders will generate at least three-million in revenue over the next seven months. The Swedish Ministry of Defense and several government agencies will submit three orders soon for two million dollars. Their government purchased Eye Retinal Biometrics systems from Eyedentify back in 1986 and are quite knowledgeable and supportive of biometrics. We can expect another four million from our government in October when their new budget goes into effect. We could probably raise fifteen million with venture capital alone on those orders."

"Mark, I'm not going to do business with venture capitalists, and that's final!"

Ericksen leaned forward and wiped his brow. "Don't forget we'll be receiving an order from our government after the beta-tests next year, and by their comments to me, the systems are flawless. My old fraternity brother works as a partner for a VC firm in Menlo Park. I'm sure his group can help."

Hamilton leaned back and snapped. "I'm not interested in diluting our shares and being controlled by venture capitalists."

He pinched the bridge of his nose and closed his eyes briefly. He tightened his lips and leaned his head towards Hamilton. "When you recruited me from Avanti Biosystems, you made a commitment to me. You told me raising capital would never be an issue, even if you had to go the venture capital way."

Hamilton stood up, shook his head, and stared at him. "Sorry, but we have to be realistic. The whole country is in a major economic meltdown."

Ericksen's adrenaline shot up. His dreams of building a startup into a success story suddenly appeared hostage by a CEO who feared VC funding.

"Do you think Amazon, Apple, and Google would be where they are today without a major infusion of venture capital?" asked Ericksen.

Hamilton's eyes narrowed. "Let's drop the subject."

"I'm disappointed," he said, as he left Hamilton's office. He broke his word. Ericksen drove to Lake Oswego for his eleven o'clock appointment with his psychologist, Dr. Holtzman. He told the doctor about his recent meeting with Delgado and what occurred in Kandahar Province under Dawkins' command. "I believe Dawkins ordered me to kill Sadozai because he was a witness to their kickback scheme. What do you think?"

Dr. Holtzman nodded. "I agree. I admire you for being proactive in your search for the truth, but you need to be careful. The warning in London is proof Dawkins doesn't want you to pursue this path for fear it will lead to him and the group."

Ericksen nodded in agreement. "Delgado told me he suspected they murdered Pulaski." He sighed and shook his head. "I believed he could have led me to Dawkins."

Holtzman thought for a moment. "Who have you recently contacted?"

"Some business associates I've worked with at the State Department, the FBI, and the Office of the Director of National Intelligence."

Dr. Holtzman walked over to him and placed his hand on his shoulder. "The colonel betrayed the sacred honor of the American military command structure by his outright lies and duplicity in criminal behavior. He killed Bashir as sure as if he pulled the trigger."

"I'm going to find Dawkins, and I'm not going to stop until I find out where they stored their blood money. Then the Feds can prosecute his ass."

Chapter Twenty-Two

JEDDAH, SAUDIA ARABIA

Ziad, sporting a thick black mustache and wearing the traditional flowing white cotton robe and a headdress, enjoyed eating a hearty lamb and rice dish in a Jeddah restaurant. The smell of the spicy Indian curry and other exotic spices permeated the restaurant. In his right hand, he held a cup of Bedouin coffee.

He finished his meal, paid his bill, and left the restaurant. He walked down Falasteen Street, stopped occasionally, and glanced through the store windows at the merchandise displayed in the window. He wasn't interested in the products, only the reflection off the windows to see if someone had been following him.

He entered Jarir's Bookstore and immediately went to the history section. He went down a row of aisles and turned to the second shelf from the top, and saw a book about the history of Saudi Arabia. Ziad took the book down from the shelf, dropped his pen, bent down to retrieve it, casually looked both ways, saw one person at the end of the aisle, and their eyes met. He opened the book and put a tiny piece of paper with one sentence on the first page of the book, and closed it. He tapped on the hardback book twice, placed the book on the second shelf protruding three inches from the frame. Then he left the aisle. Ziad walked to another section of the bookstore slowly, aided by his cane. He picked up *BusinessWeek* magazine, paid the cashier, and left the bookstore.

An Arab man in his fifties with a large nose and beard observed him from the moment he entered the history aisle, saw, and notice Ziad tap on the book. Jamal Al-Kharusi walked down the history aisle, casually checking a few books on the same shelf, then picked up the book, opened the first page, and glanced at a sentence on the tiny piece of paper. He put the paper in his pocket, walked to the cashier, paid for the book, and left the bookstore.

Jamal entered his dental office, walked past his male receptionist, and continued until he reached the back of his office. He closed the door behind him and locked it. He took the piece of paper out of his pocket and read the sentence in Arabic: "One of the best scuba diving experiences in the Red Sea is off the coast of Hurghada, Egypt."

He slid his bookcase to the right, exposing a small hidden room. He opened a cabinet and retrieved a special viewer, and placed it over the word Egypt. This action brought the microdot into sharp focus. The sentence read: "Islamic terrorists plan to attack the conference at The Grand Beach Hotel in Hurghada on Sunday, May 10, at 0700 hours."

Jamal opened up a drawer, removed a USB flash memory drive, and inserted it into a USB port on his laptop computer. This drive had a built-in encryption software program. He scanned the decoded message on the printer, converted it into a PDF file as an attachment, and sent it to an overseas server that changed the IP address every second until it reached its final destination. A couple of seconds later, he deleted the sent email message.

General Mohammed Al-Jabr sat behind his cherry wood desk in the executive office adjoining the king's quarters at King Abdullah's Palace in Riyadh. He dressed in traditional Saudi attire and smoked a cigarette. With his right hand, he gently cupped his trim gray mustache. He coughed and coughed again. He put out the cigarette.

He heard a blip sound from his laptop computer on his desk. He clicked on the email and read the message with his eyes intently focused on the screen. Suddenly his mouth opened up, and his eyebrows rose with a shocked expression. I must warn the Saudi delegation. He wrote on the back of a business card, Sunday, May 10, 0700 hours, deleted the email, placed the business card in a letter-size pad holder, and abruptly left his office with it.

Three hours later, General Al-Jabr presided over a meeting at King Abdullah's Palace. In attendance were several government officials: Chief of Saudi's foreign intelligence agency, the minister of the interior, their staff, and Colonel Al-Gosaibi of the Royal Guard. They discussed the upcoming intelligence and counterterrorism summit meeting in Hurghada and the planned terrorist attack on the Grand Beach Hotel.

Colonel Al-Gosaibi, impeccably dressed, twitched his nose and scratched his dark, full mustache while glancing around the well-appointed conference room. He stared at General Al-Jabr and asked in Arabic, "General, I'm sure your sources are excellent but have you confirmed the veracity of this threat sufficiently?"

Al-Jabr's face briefly tensed, showing disdain for the colonel's question. He looked right at the colonel, raised his right hand, palm up, and thrust it forward.

"My operative has produced actionable intel before. He is connected to this Islamic terrorist group." The general thought for a moment: *This pampered prince has balls questioning me.* Al-Jabr looked directly at the General Director of Saudi Intelligence. "Immediately warn Egyptian Intelligence."

The Saudi intel chief nodded, "Consider it done, General."

Chapter Twenty-Three

At 1300 hours in Jeddah, Saudi Arabia, Khalid Al-Bustani, wearing the traditional Saudi robe and a headdress, sat in the back seat of his Rolls Royce limo as the vehicle drove through town. When he heard a couple of rings from his secure cellphone, he picked it up with his right hand and brought it to his ear, brushing the phone against his trim beard. On his middle finger, he wore a bright, large gold ring engraved with a horse's head and a small etched inscription, Falcon Dancer. "Hello," he said in Arabic.

Marwan Haidar spoke in English in a calm voice, "This is George. The birthday party has been moved to Cleopatra's Resort Hotel – same time."

"Give the boy my best wishes," Khalid Al-Bustani said in English.

THE RED SEA

A few minutes later, a 280-foot mega-yacht, *The Dolphin Prince*, had been cruising at fifteen knots when it slowed down and floated in the sea with a drift anchor, twenty-five miles southeast of Hurghada, Egypt.

In the main salon, Abdullah Al-Suhaimy's penetrating black eyes surveyed a map of the Red Sea. His satphone rang. "Hello," said Abdullah in Arabic.

"The party has moved to Cleopatra's Resort Hotel, same time," Khalid said in English.

Abdullah and a driver boarded a twenty-foot Zodiac speedboat alongside the mega-yacht. The temperature has reached one hundred degrees; they were wearing t-shirts, khaki shorts, and sandals. They waved goodbye to the crew and the captain of *The Dolphin Prince*.

The speedboat raced across the Red Sea and two hours later pulled up to the Hurghada Marina. He got out, and the speedboat driver took off. An Arab driver met Abdullah at the Marina, greeted him, opened the SUV passenger door, and invited him. They drove through the old section of Hurghada, past the sights and smells of bazaars, restaurants, and food markets.

Ten minutes later, they pulled up to a scrap iron yard. Abdullah got out of the SUV, walked up to greet seven Arab men, hugged each man, and planted a kiss on each man's cheeks. A slim Arab man with a thick black beard walked alongside him. As they passed a panel truck and a pick-up truck, they entered a storage shed. The slim man lifted a canvas cloth for him to gaze at the 1,600 pounds of C-4 explosives.

"Good work, my Saudi brother. This should be enough to send the infidels to hell. Praise be to Allah for this opportunity. Allahu Akbar!" Abdullah said in Arabic.

"Allahu Akbar," the slim man said.

Chapter Twenty-Four

Ericksen rested by the EgyptAir gate at Cairo International Airport and watched a British comedy show. At 1530 hours, He boarded his EgyptAir flight for Sharm El-Sheikh, Egypt, a one hour flight.

He arrived at the baggage area at the Sharm El-Sheikh International Airport with his scuba backpack, suitcase, and computer case, looking like a person who hadn't slept in a long time. He cleared customs and strolled into the reception area in his wrinkled blue short-sleeve shirt and tan khaki shorts, searching for the hotel driver. He spotted the hotel driver who held a sign with his name and continued with the baggage cart. The driver loaded the luggage into the parked van alongside the curb. The sign printed on the side of the SUV read: Regal Crown Resort Hotel. The drive from the airport to the hotel took thirty minutes.

The hotel van pulled up to the entrance to the hotel. The bellman took Ericksen's luggage out of the van and placed it on a luggage cart as he entered the hotel lobby. A panel truck and SUV drove slowly up the driveway to the hotel's front entrance, followed by a pick-up driven by Omar, a slim, Arab man with a baby face and a scraggly black beard. The panel truck, the SUV, and the pick-up followed the circular driveway and re-entered the highway.

The lobby of this luxury hotel was full of people. The desk clerk smiled as Ericksen approached the front registration desk.

The hotel desk clerk asked, "Welcome to the Regal Crown, sir... your name, please?"

"Mark Ericksen." He handed over his passport and visa to the hotel clerk to verify it and received the keys to his room.

Two minutes later, he entered a deluxe room with a view of the Red Sea and noticed a bottle of chilled French white wine in a bucket and a gift basket. He found a note by the gift basket and read it, "Welcome to Sharm El-Sheikh. Mona and I look forward to meeting you tomorrow morning at 7:00 am in the Aladdin Café. Get ready for a great day for diving. Ahmed."

———

THE GULFSTREAM G550 jet roared as it approached the Hurghada Airport runway. The aircraft taxied to the government gate, and eight men and two women walked down the airstairs to the gate area. The Director of the CIA Counterterrorism Center was the last member of the group to arrive at the military terminal gate. They were greeted by the Egyptian Secret Service. A senior secret service officer met Bill Sullivan. "Director Sullivan, Welcome to Egypt," the officer said. Sullivan nodded approvingly.

At that moment, three American men arrived from the gate area, armed and with earpieces.

Sullivan shook the CIA men's hands.

"Saudi intelligence uncovered a potential threat. We moved the conference to Cleopatra's Resort Hotel," the Egyptian security official said.

He seemed a bit surprised and suspiciously snapped, "Has the Saudi delegation arrived?"

"Yes, director."

He glanced at the Egyptian security officer. "Thank you." Sullivan didn't like surprises, and his instincts went on high-alert.

Chapter Twenty-Five

SHARM EL-SHEIKH

The weather off Sharm El-Sheikh on Saturday, May 9, 2009, turned out hot and sunny, not a cloud present. The scuba divers put on their dive gear. The dive boat captain moored the boat off a reef, and the buddy system swung into operation. A man and woman, both in their thirties, two women in their late twenties, Mona and Ahmed Kamel, Ericksen, Kevin Howden, and the divemaster, and his wife were all enjoying the pristine, tranquil turquoise waters of the Red Sea.

They were in thirty meters of water. The serenity of the Red Sea and its spectacular reef life made the dive rewarding. Ericksen and Howden turned and watched two large sharks swimming close by them. Ericksen took his eleven-inch SOG knife from its sheath, which was fastened to his right leg. The sharks swam toward them, and at the last moment, turned off in another direction. Ericksen nodded to him, and the divemaster motioned an okay sign with his hand.

After a few hours, the scuba divers were back on the boat. The deckhand started serving lunch while the dive master's wife served drinks. Ericksen, Howden, and Kamel drank beers.

Two young women joined Ericksen's table. Ericksen extended his right hand and shook both women's hands as he introduced himself. "I'm Mark, and these are my friends, Mona, Ahmed, and Kevin."

The taller, more attractive woman with the sparkling blue eyes and auburn hair replied, "I'm Rachel, and this is my friend Ava – we're Canadians."

"We won't hold that against you, neighbor," Ericksen said and smiled.

At seven o'clock in the evening, Mark, Kevin, Mona, and Ahmed sat down at a dinner table in the hotel's Magic Carpet Restaurant. Off to the side near the bar, a pianist, played soft, romantic music.

"How many people do you expect to attend the two-day conference?" Ahmed asked.

"About thirty from Europe and the Middle East," Ericksen said, as his eyes shifted to two women as they entered the restaurant.

Suddenly, Rachel and her friend appeared. She wore a beautiful blue and white dress, highlighting her curvaceous figure.

"Hi, Mark, good to see you again."

"Would you like to join us?"

"Thanks," she replied as she and Ava pulled up chairs. The waiter came over. "Would you like a menu?"

"No, thank you."

The waiter asked, "Would you like something to drink?"" Rachel smiled, "I would like a martini."

She turned to Ericksen, "Where are we going tomorrow?"

"A secret location. Lots of beautiful sea life, reef sharks, sea turtles, barracuda, dolphins, a famous sunken old Spanish ship, and a few tiger sharks to check out."

"Everything sounds exciting except the tiger sharks," as she gave him a warm smile.

He thought Rachel was a lot like Karen, warm, kind, and with a sense of adventure. It had been more than three years since he had been in a relationship. She hailed from Vancouver, British Columbia, a ninety-minute flight from Portland. Perhaps this could be my lucky break.

HURGHADA, EGYPT

At eight in the evening, four Egyptian secret service men, wearing earpieces, their handguns holstered, checked for proper badges. Adlib chatter, laughter, and drinking occupied the government delegations in the Pyramid banquet hall at Cleopatra's Resort Hotel. Sullivan enjoyed a conversation with three men, Sir Derek Worthington, Graham Moore, and Ulrich Genscher. His Director of Counterterrorism stood by his side.

Worthington asked, "Does President Porterfield allow you to express your views directly on intelligence, or does Campbell have the honors?"

Sullivan chuckled. "Derek, I can't comment officially on bullshit."

"Bullshit or not, I'm sure you let your opinions on critical matters be heard regardless of diplomatic civility," said Worthington.

"There are risks in being assertive with the facts in Washington, and bureaucrats and politicians don't like to hear the truth."

"Would you like another Scotch?" Moore asked.

"No, thanks, Graham. I need to get back to the room and go over my speech."

"That's not neighborly, Bill," Worthington said with a smile.

As Sullivan left the banquet hall escorted by two bodyguards, he walked by an Arab man, Abdullah Al-Suhaimy, dressed in business casual western attire. They both stared at each other in passing. Sullivan thought there was something curiously strange about the man. *Have I seen him or his photo before?*

Little did he realize, at that moment, the man was one of the most dangerous Islamic Jihadist operators in the world.

Sullivan's two-bedroom suite had two CIA men, one outside and one inside, for protection. He sat down by the desk, powered up his laptop, removed a portable device from his briefcase, and placed it on the desk. The optical scanning area measured two inches by four inches with a USB cable connected to one of the ports.

Then he took out a USB flash drive and inserted it into the other port. The USB flash drive stored his original registered palm subcutaneous vein template. Then he placed his palm face down, and the motion of his hand on the optical scanner activated a scan of his palm. It took less than five seconds to match, in real-time, his live-palm biometrics patterns to his previously registered template in the database.

His identification was authenticated, and a Green LED appeared: ID Confirmed. EyeD4 Comm Systems' biometrics and email software used top-level encryption.

This authentication process gave the intelligence agencies and the DoD employees a sense of security in protecting their laptops because passwords were vulnerable to hackers.

Up came a document with the letterhead of the Central Intelligence Agency.

Top Secret

Government Counterterrorism Summit
Date: Sunday, May 10, 2009, 8:00 am
Speaker: CIA Director William "Bill" Sullivan
Topic: Actionable Intelligence and Counterterrorism

Chapter Twenty-Six

SHARM EL-SHEIKH

Ericksen opened his eyes and felt Rachel's right arm on his chest. He smiled to himself, reached over, and kissed her cheek. She awoke and moved closer to him. He turned to the side and glanced at the digital clock radio. The time: 5:45 am. Ericksen gently touched her head, got up, went into the bathroom, and turned on the shower.

Five minutes later, he reappeared by the bed, rejuvenated after his three-minute shower. Rachel opened her eyes and smiled. "Mark, where are you going?"

"It's 5:50 am. I'm going back to my room and get ready." He put his clothes on. "See you downstairs in the lobby in an hour."

They both smiled, their faces glowing like rays of light.

HURGHADA, EGYPT

The Muezzin's call to prayer was emanating from the mosque's minarets. Six Arab men were praying next to their vehicles on prayer rugs and wearing black jeans, t-shirts, and headbands. It was 6:00 am. In the lead pickup truck were two men, a driver and a man seated in the passenger seat armed with an AK-47. The panel truck and the SUV followed, loaded with C-4 explosives hidden behind the seats and covered under a black canvas cloth. Motorcycles were driven by Abdullah, and his right-hand man trailed behind. The time was 6:10 am.

At 6:59 am, five armed Egyptian soldiers planted in front of the entrance to the driveway exchanged fire as the pickup drove up to the hotel with the two armed terrorists. Bursts of shots killed three soldiers, as the pickup ran off course and crashed. The panel truck loaded with one-thousand pounds of explosives slammed into the front entrance.

The terrorists yelled, "Allahu Akbar, Allahu Akbar." At that moment, Abdullah pressed the remote detonator from the hotel's parking lot. The thunderous sound of the explosion sent smoke billowing over the hotel as the city shook. The SUV loaded with six hundred pounds of explosives slammed into the other side of the building as Abdullah pressed the detonator button, bringing down a portion of the hotel. Fire erupted. The sound of the massive fragments of brick, marble, cement, glass, and steel was deafening. He and his assistant sped off on their motorcycles. A soldier took aim and fired several shots, killing Abdullah's assistant.

SHARM EL-SHEIKH, EGYPT

At 7:00 am, Ericksen brought his scuba equipment to his hotel room's door, opened the door, and stopped when he heard the phone ring. He bolted back to the bed stand and picked up the telephone. "Hello."

"Mark, Roger here. I have good news for you. Today we received the German government's signed contracts with their purchase orders."

"Now, all we need is venture capital to accelerate our growth plans," Ericksen said. A panel truck loaded with eight hundred pounds of C-4 explosives rammed the front entrance to the hotel lobby outside the hotel. The terrorists yelled, "Allahu Akbar, Allahu Akbar."

Wolfgang Beltermann, a former Stasi intelligence officer and terrorist in the Red Sea Brotherhood's employ, pressed the remote detonator button from the parking lot, one hundred meters from the entrance.

Within one second, the line went dead. The force of an explosion suddenly hurled Ericksen against the wall, knocking him unconscious. The blast knocked out all the glass windows in his room. An SUV loaded with eight hundred pounds of explosives slammed into the side of the hotel. Fires erupted as part of the structure of the Regal Crown Resort Hotel started tumbling down.

Beltermann and Omar jumped onto their motorcycles and rode down El-Salam Road to Maya Bay. They got off and bolted to the twenty-foot speedboat by the jetty. Once they boarded the speedboat, the driver took off. The time was 7:10.

Abdullah reached the Safaga Marina at 7:20 and ditched his motorcycle. An Arab speedboat driver pulled up near the dive shop and kept the twin engines idling as he jumped into the boat. They took off for the open seas as Abdullah put on a baseball hat and changed his shirt and shorts.

Back at the Regal Crown Resort Hotel, police and firemen arrived on the scene. They entered the hotel wearing oxygen masks and searched room by room for any sign of life. They broke down the door to Ericksen's room as smoke began filling up. He lay on the floor with soot and blood all over his clothes and body. One of the firefighters yelled in Arabic, "Hurry, this one is still alive! Bring the stretcher." A few minutes later, they carried Ericksen to an awaiting ambulance.

At Cleopatra's Resort Hotel, people ran screaming, crying, and bleeding as they fled the hotel. The sounds of police and fire engine sirens howled as part of the hotel structure crumpled to the ground. Firefighters entered the hotel wearing oxygen masks and searched room by room.

Two hours later, the authorities' cordoned off what remained of Cleopatra's Resort Hotel as people assembled and watched the destruction. The Hurghada police chief's cellphone started ringing. He picked it up.

"This is the US Ambassador. Any word yet on the status of the American delegation?"

"Mr. Ambassador, unfortunately, the only Americans we found alive were CIA Director Sullivan and four members of his delegation."

"I've dispatched a medical team, and once they're on the ground, I'll have them contact you. Please get them flown immediately to Landstuhl Regional Medical Hospital."

"Of course, Mr. Ambassador."

Abdullah, Beltermann, and Omar arrived on *The Dolphin Prince* within thirty minutes of each other. They let their speedboats drift from the mega-yacht. When they were two hundred feet away, they fired their AK-47s and watched the small boats disappear from the surface.

Viewing the event from his periscope forty-meters under the Red Sea and one mile from the mega-yacht was an Israeli Navy captain aboard a submarine. The sub had monitored *The Dolphin Prince* for the past twenty-four hours. The captain held the radio phone and spoke in Hebrew, "Sir, we're about 100 kilometers due east of El Quseir... coordinates are 26 degrees 18'21.28" North, 34 degrees 50'31.83" East. We'll follow the ship."

Chapter Twenty-Seven

On May 11, outside of room 311 at Landstuhl Regional Medical Center in Landstuhl, Germany, stood two armed US Army MPs. Inside, a nurse and a doctor attended to Sullivan.

"How does it look, Colonel?"

"Director, you have some nasty lacerations and bruises, but you're fortunate."

"You're damn right, colonel. Over 300 people were killed, Ulrich Genscher, Derek Worthington, the Director of Counterterrorism, and several of my staff. We're going to find those bastards and give them a one-way ride to hell!"

"Death is the only justice they deserve." The colonel nodded in agreement. The US Ambassador to Germany and the CIA station chief entered the room. They updated Sullivan on the Regal Crown Resort Hotel terrorist bombing in Sharm El-Sheikh.

"Most of the hotel guests killed were tourists and businessmen. Two American tourists, a former British head of SAS, and Mark Ericksen, an Oregon businessman, were flown to Herzliya Medical Center in Israel," the CIA station chief said.

Sullivan's eyes widened with the mention of Mark Ericksen.

"Keep me updated on any breaking news. And keep me informed on Ericksen's status."

"Yes, sir."

Director Sullivan focused on the two major terrorist attacks and suspected they had to be the work of Al-Qaeda or a new Islamic Jihadist group, perhaps the group General Al-Jabr mentioned. Sullivan had an uncanny ability to evaluate both raw empirical data and human intelligence collection. Once he and his staff confirmed the facts, he activated a course of action. If he had a target in mind in the final analysis, he never gave up until they were captured or killed, like a baseball pitcher in the zone programmed for strikeouts.

HERZILYA MEDICAL CENTER, ISRAEL

Doctors hooked Ericksen up to an IV while they examined the imaging results from the MRI. He opened his eyes and felt groggy. The nurse entered the room and placed her hand on his shoulder.

He moved slowly and whispered, "Where am I?"

"You arrived last night. You're at Herzliya Medical Center in Israel."

"What!"

"Please, Mr. Ericksen, take it easy. You have a traumatic brain injury."

He started to get lucid. He gripped the side of the bed and pushed hard to sit up.

"What happened?"

"Terrorists bombed your hotel yesterday."

She picked up a copy of the *International Herald Tribune* newspaper and gave it to him. The headline read: *"Islamic terrorists blew up two Egyptian hotels, The Regal Crown Resort Hotel in Sharm El-Sheikh and Cleopatra's Resort Hotel in Hurghada. Over four hundred people were murdered, and six hundred were wounded."*

He put the newspaper down. "Please check and see if Rachel Bos, and Mona and Ahmed Kamel are okay."

"I'll find out. Now get some rest."

The Israeli nurse, a young woman with dark, long black hair, hazel eyes, and olive skin, left the room.

He looked toward the window. He could see the Mediterranean Sea from his hospital bed. He remembered the last time he had spent time in Israel, doing a six week joint-training exercise in 2000 with Israel's version of the Navy SEALs – Shayetet 13, their elite naval commando force. The training had served him well on future missions.

His thoughts raced back to April 2002:

Bashir removed a photo from his vest pocket. "Please, I have a wife and two daughters. Please, I'm telling you the truth. I beg you," cried out Bashir, as the sound of two shots pierced his body.

The nurse entered the room and noticed his gown soaked with sweat and his face wet. He shook his head. "It's Afghanistan."

The nurse wiped the sweat off his face with a towel.

"What branch were you in?"

"We were part of a joint special operations task force in 2002. I was a platoon leader."

"Mr. Ericksen, I can only imagine how painful those memories must be for you."

The nurse placed her hand on his hand. "I'm sorry, but I have bad news. Rachel Bos, Mona, and Ahmed Kamel were all killed."

Ericksen placed his hands on his face and rubbed his head several times. He began feeling alive again, and then this tragedy struck. He was captivated by Rachel's stunning beauty, grace, and charm. He thought she might have been the one. *Why me...why did my friends die and I survive? These monsters deserve to burn in hell.*

Chapter Twenty-Eight

At the National Intelligence Directorate Headquarters in McLean, Virginia, leaders of the intelligence community and their staff were seated in a high-tech, bug-proof, and SCIF conference room. They were surrounded by large hi-def, flat-screen television monitors. Several people sat down around the conference table. Their name and title badges on their clothing read: Regis Helms, Secretary of Defense; Pete Geiger, FBI Director; Steve Campbell, Director, National Intelligence; Hank Lucas, Secretary of Homeland Security; Susan Norstad, Deputy Director of the CIA; the National Security Advisor; plus several senior heads of NSA. Their eyes were glued to the TV monitor.

Suddenly an Al-Jazeera anchorman spoke, "The Red Sea Brotherhood claimed responsibility for the attack on Cleopatra's Resort Hotel and The Regal Crown Resort Hotel. This is the first time we've learned of this terrorist group. Their brief communiqué made no mention of their motive. The world is in shock as to the magnitude of the violence perpetrated on the hundreds of innocent people who lost their lives the other night."

Campbell clicked the remote and shut off the television monitors. Norstad stood. "All of the participants registered under aliases and the meeting on the hotel reader board listed the organization as Global Warming Symposium."

"Apparently, they targeted the intelligence chiefs," the square-jawed Geiger said.

"Most of you witnessed President Porterfield's anger in the Situation Room today. Our number one objective is capturing or terminating these terrorists. Does anyone have anything on the Red Sea Brotherhood?" Campbell asked as he adjusted his rimless glasses.

"We have nothing, sir. We identified Aladdin Oil and Gas Exploration as the registered owner of *The Dolphin Prince*. Last night, Saudi time, our satellites located the mega-yacht anchored a mile from Yanbu," Norstad said, as she pressed a few buttons on the remote to activate the monitors. She continued, "Satellite thermal imaging showed a Zodiac boat brought three people to the Yanbu Marina. An SUV picked them up and drove them to the Yanbu airport. A couple of private jets took off over the next several hours."

Campbell asked, "Any ID on the aircraft?" "No."

A staffer knocked on the window to the SCIF and motioned for Geiger to come out. He stood up and left the room. A staffer handed him a secure landline portable phone.

"Geiger here."

"It's Sullivan."

"Thank God you're still alive. We're in the bubble at ODNI." He turned and whispered into the phone, "Campbell scheduled a meeting with the Saudi Interior Minister and General Al-Jabr for Monday, May 25, in Riyadh."

"Pete, let me talk to Campbell. Patch the call into the bubble and place it on the secure speakerphone."

A few minutes later, Geiger motioned to Campbell. "Bill's on the line. He wants to speak with you."

Campbell adjusted his glasses. "Happy to hear you're okay." Sullivan asked, "Any new developments?"

"Nothing yet. Pete probably told you that we'd scheduled a meeting in Riyadh."

"I've developed good relationships with both men over the years, and nothing productive will be gained."

"We just left the Situation Room, and the President wants action now."

"They're not going to level with us. The Saudi Government can't risk any more embarrassment," Sullivan said.

"What do you mean?'

"How many Saudis do you think are sympathetic to Bin Laden and this new terrorist group?"

"Bill, you might have a point, but I'm sorry, I'm overruling you on this issue."

"You're making a mistake; A big mistake." The line went dead.

Geiger scanned the room and looked directly at Campbell.

"Sullivan has a good point. The meeting in Riyadh wouldn't generate any meaningful information because our relationship with the Royal Family is based on lip service and cash for oil."

Chapter Twenty-Nine

General Al-Jabr greeted the interior minister in the palace's national security conference room. "Those cowards, murderers, they'll pay a high price for killing the prince and members of our delegation," Al-Jabr said in Arabic. "If they're captured alive, I will personally have their heads meet the blade of my sword."

The general nodded in agreement. "I don't know what Campbell expects to accomplish with our upcoming meeting."

The interior minister's face turned red with anger. "I can't understand why the National Intelligence Director needs to see us unless he thinks we're involved in this shit."

———

Campbell reviewed a top-secret report on the Hurghada terrorist attack with Lucas, Geiger, and two staffers. A "ping" sounded, and Campbell clicked on his secure computer and opened the email. Campbell glanced at his screen.

"Director Campbell, we won't be able to meet you on May 25. However, we would like to reschedule sometime in July at your office. Best regards, General Al-Jabr."

He slammed his fist on the desk, his face flushed. "Damn it! The general just canceled our meeting. Those fucking assholes."

Another "ping" sounded from Campbell's computer.

He opened the email.

"My sources have informed me that the mastermind of the Hurghada and Sharm El-Sheikh attacks is now planning a nuclear suitcase bomb attack on American soil. I'm going to Switzerland next week to pursue these leads with Saudi Intelligence. Please keep a lid on this until I get back to you. Bill."

Campbell slammed his fist again on the desk. "I would love to fire his ass. He acts as if I work for him."

"There's no way the President will be making any changes at the Agency," Lucas said.

"Hank, you and Defense Secretary Helms pushed for Sullivan over my objections when President Ridgeway considered him for the job last year. He has been a fucking thorn in my side throughout his CIA career. In Switzerland, he didn't follow my orders when he was station chief." He took out a handkerchief and wiped the sweat from his brow.

"How many station chiefs listen to their ambassadors?" asked Lucas.

Campbell's eyes narrowed and his face got red.

"Let's drop it." "

"Steve, you have to give him credit. Over the past three years, Sullivan delivered results as the director of clandestine operations. I trust his judgment," Lucas said.

Deputy Director Norstad coughed and interrupted them, "Upon the monitor is a photo of a man who got off *The Dolphin Prince* and entered the airport terminal at Yanbu. We identified him as Omar Al-Naima, an Al-Qaeda terrorist from Yemen. We couldn't find a match for the other two men. We ran checks throughout our global database and came up with nada."

Chapter Thirty

S ullivan entered the hospital lobby dressed in a blue blazer and a pair of khaki slacks and carrying his laptop. He greeted his doctor. "Colonel, thanks for everything."

"We're going to miss you, sir." Sullivan's security detail stood nearby.

His CIA and military security detail escorted him into a black Hummer. One Hummer rode in the lead and another behind Sullivan's vehicle as they left Landstuhl's hospital for the short drive to Ramstein Air Force Base.

The Air Force's security guards waved Sullivan's security detail past the exit gate. His Hummer approached the CIA Gulfstream G550 by the hanger. He got out of the vehicle and walked up the airstairs to the jet, receiving a welcome greeting by the CIA pilot, an aide, and two jet assistants.

He walked into the luxurious accommodations, slumped down on one of the executive-type leather seats, removed his laptop computer from the case, opened it up, and started the biometrics security log-on. He heard a ring on his secure cellphone.

"Hello."

"Swordsman speaking. A major meeting will be held tomorrow between the mastermind of the Red Sea Brotherhood and his principal terrorists at Al-Bustani Group of Companies headquarters in Jeddah. It will be in the chairman's office on the tenth floor. See you in six days."

Chapter Thirty-One

W olfgang Beltermann, a tall, muscular German with a salt and pepper beard and hair, approached the large oak door that led into the chairman of Al-Bustani Group of Companies' office in Jeddah, Saudi Arabia. The bodyguard stood ten feet from the entrance with his pistol holstered and waved him to enter.

Abdullah, Omar, and Beltermann sat on a large, dark brown leather sofa. Khalid's oldest son, Faisal, his chief security director. Ziad walked by the window overlooking a parking lot a few hundred yards away. He rubbed his eyes with his hand, turned, and strolled to a leather chair and slumped down in it.

A minute later, a Hummingbird robot drone maintained a holding pattern directly outside Kalid's office window. Equipped with a video camera and zoom lens, the drone transmitted images back to the CIA's unmarked van three hundred meters from the office. Another Agency shot a laser ear microphone to the chairman's tenth-floor suite window from their parked van on street two hundred meters away. The system transmitted an invisible infra-red beam to the window, causing a slight vibration from the window panel and generating a modulated sound converted into electronic signals by the receiver in the Agency's van, and started recording the meeting.

Khalid sat behind an intricately designed rosewood desk. His expensive oil paintings and Persian rugs adorned the room. On the wall behind his desk hung a photograph of a beautiful, chestnut-colored Arabian racehorse in a gold-etched frame. On the bottom of the frame was laser-engraved the horse's name, Falcon Dancer.

"Good morning," Beltermann said in Arabic.

Khalid asked, "Any new information on the American company's classified biometrics system?"

The forty-seven-year-old former East German Stasi spy had served in Dresden as a junior counterespionage intel officer for the East German Government until their government fell in 1990. Beltermann leaned forward, "George said the CIA and NSA's beta-tested systems from EyeD4 Systems were flawless. George also claimed that NSA designed the encryption software so that no foreign intelligence agency could hack into it."

Khalid thought *Al-Gosaibi said the same thing.*

"I think it's better to keep it simple. Don't forget 9/11," Abdullah said.

He shook his head in disbelief. "I know what I'm doing. The Americans monitor and profile anyone who looks like an Arab." He continued, "George and Wolfgang believe the next attack demands stealth technology."

Khalid thought Abdullah looks disappointed.

Abdullah folded his hands together. "I respect your point of view, but how do you expect to acquire a classified American intelligence covert security system?"

Khalid smiled. "Abdullah, leave that up to me. The Hurghada and Sharm El-Sheikh bombings have put the Red Sea Brotherhood on the map. The CIA Director got lucky this time."

He stood and raised his hand in a fist and continued. "We will strike the American Satan in his homeland and teach the infidels a lesson for their invasion and occupation of Muslim countries, and exploiting our oil resources."

Abdullah stood and raised a fist. "The rivers will flow with the infidels' blood."

Ziad yelled, "Inshallah."

Everyone joined in: "Allahu Akbar."

Khalid excused the group except for Abdullah, Ziad, Faisal, and Beltermann.

Faisal directed the command center on the first floor, with two guards protecting access at all times. Within the heart of the security operation was television monitors that observed everything within the facility and the external building complex. When Khalid entered his office, the video cameras shut down for security reasons. Whenever he wasn't present, Faisal would press a device under his desk that activated three security cameras. This action enabled the security department to monitor any movement within his suite.

Khalid walked by the large photograph of Falcon Dancer. He slid the picture to the right, exposing a medium-sized wall safe with a fingerprint scanner. Khalid placed his right index finger on the tiny optical scanner. Within five seconds, the system read his fingerprint and matched it with his computer's stored fingerprint template. He opened the safe. From a distance of thirteen feet, bundles of cash, watches, passports, and several envelopes were visible. Khalid reached into the safe, pulled out a large envelope, and opened it. It contained two hundred thousand dollars in one-hundred-dollar-bill denominations. He gave one hundred thousand dollars each to both Abdullah and Beltermann.

"In time, you'll meet with Casino and Cowboy. They both are the Red Sea Brotherhood's sleeper cell leaders. Soon, you'll activate them in Las Vegas and Houston for the upcoming nuke attack. I trained both men in Afghanistan during the Soviet occupation. Casino is an Albanian, and Cowboy is a Chechen. They emigrated to the USA in 1990."

He turned back toward the safe and closed it. "Each man is willing to die for our cause. They know they'll be notified soon to meet and expect to take their orders from you."

Abdullah looked at Al-Bustani. "Who else knows about our mission?"

Khalid walked toward a map of the world and pointed to the USA.

"Our operations are highly compartmentalized for obvious reasons. Ziad will have a role in our initial planning phase, which will be defined soon. You'll get the information promptly. Any questions?"

"I hope they can be counted on," said Abdullah.

He glanced at Abdullah. "This operation will not fail. Over the past year, I've been to both Las Vegas and Houston twice, coordinating it. You can trust them to execute your orders."

"Your word is good enough for me," Beltermann said.

Khalid looked at Beltermann and Ziad. "Please excuse me, but I need to talk with Abdullah and Faisal." The two left his office.

The Hummingbird drone had three minutes left on its battery life.

"I have made an appointment for you and Abdullah to meet Dr. Raja Gull. He is a nuclear physicist who works at the Nuclear Research Institute in Pakistan. He is interested in working with us. He will be with Hafiz Tariq, a top advisor of the Pakistani Taliban, and your old Al-Qaeda friend, Saad Al-Fulani. I've booked both of you into the Burj Al-Arab Hotel for two nights, May 26–28. They'll meet you for breakfast on May 27 in your suite. Sweep the suite before the meeting. They'll advise you two hours before dinner that evening at the location of the meeting." He pointed his finger directly at Faisal.

"Of course, Father."

"You'll make a proposal to purchase one tactical nuclear warhead with at least an eight-kiloton yield for fifteen million Swiss francs, and not a franc over that price. If they agree, we'll work with them on preparing the container shipment from Karachi to Jakarta. One of the key factors to discuss is adequate shielding of the warhead so no radiation signature can be discovered at either departure or arrival ports," Khalid said.

"When can they deliver the nuclear warhead container to a secure facility and ready for shipment?" asked Abdullah.

Khalid glanced out the window, then turned back and faced Abdullah. "We need the nuke shipped from Karachi, the first week of December. Once the container arrives at our secure warehouse in Jakarta, we'll unload the nuke and load it into another container filled with furniture. The departure date from Jakarta will be set for the first or second week in January for its final destination: Port of Los Angeles."

They smiled and raised their voices. "Allahu Akbar!"

"If anyone determines that we should seriously have a backup plan if furniture isn't available at zero hour, then we must choose between coffee, rubber, or tea. The key point is the Indonesian products must cover the nuclear warhead inside the container ship. We have big plans for the Red Sea Brotherhood," Khalid said.

They smiled and yelled, "Allahu Akbar."

The Agency case officer powered the Hummingbird drone back to the parked van.

Chapter Thirty-Two

Otto Steiner, a bald, middle-aged Swiss banker, dressed in a custom-tailored three-piece suit and wearing horn-rim glasses smoked his Cuban Churchill cigar as he sat at the head of the mahogany conference table in his sizeable grand room. Steiner lived in a luxurious condominium near Kilchberg, overlooking Lake Zurich,

Khalid, Beltermann, Ziad, Abdullah, Sergei Ryzhkov, and Oleg Kupchenko sat down around the conference table. Ryzhkov, a slender man in his mid-fifties, with a military bearing, gray hair, a mustache, deep-set blue eyes, and Kupchenko, a short, muscular man his forties, were there to get the best deal for their nefarious agenda.

"We will need four suitcase nukes, each containing three kilograms of fissionable Plutonium and highly enriched Uranium. What size and weight do you recommend?" Khalid asked, looking directly at Ryzhkov.

"We can provide a standard, hard-shell suitcase, roughly twenty-four inches by sixteen-inches by eight-inches. It weighs about fifty-five-pounds," said Ryzhkov.

Khalid stared into his eyes, "What about the explosive yield?" "At least one kiloton."

"Good. I also need sixteen-hundred-pounds of C-4 explosives, like before."

"When do you need them?"

"It has to arrive at the Port of Houston no later than August twenty-eighth. Is that possible?" asked Khalid.

Ryzhkov laughed and shook his head, "Maybe."

"Can you?"

He turned to Kupchenko and, in Russian, asked, "Do you think we can get the nukes out of Russia by the end of July and shipped from Europe in time to arrive and be cleared at the port by August twenty-eight?"

"Probably, but it won't be easy," Kupchenko said as he nodded his head.

Khalid slammed his fist on the desk. "Well, what is it, yes or no?"

Please wire transfer twenty-two-million-dollars to my numbered account in my Geneva bank, and give me eight million in cash tomorrow," Ryzhkov said.

"Not so fast! Twelve million wired and three million in cash tomorrow. After it arrives and passes through customs, we'll wire you seven-million-dollars. You'll get the remaining eight million after you set the clock timers."

Ryzhkov glanced at everyone sitting around the table and looked at Khalid. "All right, but I want to communicate directly with only one person from your organization."

"Wolfgang will be your contact. Do we have an agreement?"

"Yes," the former Russian intelligence colonel said.

Khalid rose from the table, "We'll advise you seven days before the actual date of the attack with their locations, so you have adequate time to set the clock timers."

Steiner stood up, placed his table napkin neatly on his placemat, and glanced at the party, "Gentlemen, I have made lunch reservations for all of us. Khalid, Sergei, and Wolfgang, please come to my private office. Everyone else, please wait in the living room." He enjoyed being Senior Vice-President in charge of wealth management. His area of responsibility for the bank focused on wealthy Arabs from the Gulf Kingdom.

Ryzhkov gave Beltermann a piece of paper that read rzbear4@swisscom.ch. "That's my email address. Send me an email with your cellphone number from an internet café."

Beltermann asked, "You must have a code, don't you?"

"Affirmative, Wolfgang. Use numbers for the code to replicate the alphabet, like 1 is A, 2 is B, etc., and a period is a period and @ is still @."

"When the container is on the vessel ready for departure, I'll provide you with the SED, markings, bill of lading, commercial invoice, and all particulars, along with the arrival date at the Port of Baltimore."

Caldwell, dressed in a business casual outfit, seated in the rear passenger seat of a van parked two hundred feet from the condo, held her digital camera with an attached telephoto lens, and took photos of the men leaving the lobby to their chauffered cars. The driver started the van as Caldwell tapped Jacobson's shoulder. Jacobson was sitting in the front passenger seat, maintaining a watchful eye. "Get these downloaded to Langley," she said.

Listed as a senior economics attaché, Jacobson worked out of the US Embassy in Bern. For the past two years, he worked on special assignments for the Department of the Treasury and on loan from the CIA Counterterrorism Center at Langley.

ON LAKE ZURICH

Khalid, Beltermann, and Shane Dawkins stood on the top deck of the DS Stadt Zurich boat cruising Lake Zurich. Standing thirty feet away was Khalid's personal bodyguard, Oskar Moritz, a former Stasi intelligence officer.

"I heard you're still at Stealth Dynamics."

"True. However, I'll be leaving soon."

Khalid asked, "How's Pharaoh doing these days?"

"I ride Pharaoh whenever I get a chance to visit the stables in Virginia."

"Shane did some moonlighting for me a few years ago, and, in appreciation for his efforts, I gave him one of Falcon Dancer's colts."

Beltermann nodded his head. "My Russian intelligence friends are impressed with your unique talents."

"Being under the radar is critical in this line of work. I'm sure the SVR (the Russian Foreign Intelligence Service) resorts to the same modus operandi, too," said Dawkins.

Beltermann nodded.

Khalid glanced at Dawkins and turned back to Beltermann. "I'm sure we can use his services in the not-too-distant future." He handed Dawkins a gift bag from an upscale retail store. "You'll find a large envelope in there with 10,000 Swiss francs in cash. Think of it as a down payment for future services."

"Thank you," Dawkins said. He shook Khalid's hand.

"You know you can count on me for anything at a moment's notice."

Chapter Thirty-Three

ZURICH, SWITZERLAND

Monch and Schneider Private Bank's headquarters building was established in 1906 on the Bahnhofstrasse in Zurich's financial district. In Steiner's office, a well-dressed man in his mid-thirties, Hans Christian Scharz, stood with confidence as he handed Ziad his business card.

"If Herr Steiner is not available, please contact me," Scharz said. Steiner interrupted. "Herr Scharz is one of our best wealth managers, and you can be assured of his dedication to serving both you and Mr. Al-Bustani. As his financial advisor, we've set a limit for you to conduct wire transfers of up to ten-million-US-dollars per day."

"That should be sufficient, sir. It's been a pleasure to meet both of you."

Scharz escorted Ziad to the elevator, and once in the elevator, rode to the lobby level and exited the bank.

General Al-Jabr sat comfortably at an inside table and watched people walk by Springli's café on Paradeplatz. He picked up his espresso from the table. Seated two tables away were his three security detail, dressed in blue jeans and thin jackets. He spotted Ziad as he walked down the street thirty-meters from the café entrance. Something caught his eye, perhaps an inherent survival instinct many intelligence operatives acquire after years of experience in black operations. He took out his secure cellphone and made a call.

Ziad, walking at a comfortable pace, felt his cellphone vibrate in his pants pocket. He picked up his secure cellphone. "Hello."

"You are being followed by a slim, Arab man with a straggly black beard," Al-Jabr said in Arabic.

"I bet it is Omar Al-Naimi."

"Do the double-back routine, then turn around and head toward the Bahnhof. Walk until you reach the Schweizerhof Hotel at Bahnhofplatz 7. Do a jog through the lobby to the back entrance by the bar. Look for a white BMW 4-door with license plate number ZU69737. Meet me in the lion house at the Zurich Zoo."

Thirty minutes later, two Saudi security men stood outside the lion house at the zoo. Ziad walked up to General Al-Jabr inside the lion house and greeted him with a kiss on each cheek. A lion roared as the zookeeper threw several pounds of horse meat inside the cage. Several adults and children watched as the lion started biting into the horse meat.

"It's good to see you, General."

"You've been in the shadows too long."

"Yes, I'm afraid you're right."

"We can never be too comfortable in this business," General Al-Jabr said.

"Faisal Al-Bustani's thugs have been tailing me. I suspect they're also monitoring everyone's emails and cellphones."

"If they are on to you, make a dental appointment with your colleague, and we'll exfiltrate you at once. Any more details on the plan?"

"The royal operation won't be discussed in depth until after the American attacks," Ziad replied.

"I don't understand how an educated and successful Saudi businessman, whose net worth is about half a billion dollars, can plan the overthrow of the government that sustains his lifestyle and business."

"Khalid is a paradox. He has a scorched-earth hatred for the infidels while enjoying the fruits of wealth and power derived from his business relationships approved by the Kingdom."

"Keep me updated on any news on this conspiracy, and stay safe."
"Unfortunately, it's not easy when you're surrounded by a pack of Hyenas," said Ziad.

"You've sacrificed your life for our country, and we will never forget it. Soon, you'll return to Riyadh and enter our foreign service. There's a new assignment which should emerge within the next six months as a commercial attaché in our embassy in Australia." They both smiled.

"Remember, my brave warrior, always have the gaze of a lion, and you'll have no fear of anything,"

"God willing (inshallah)."

Chapter Thirty-Four

The next day, Sullivan and his security boarded the Lake Steamer from Lucerne to the port of Alpnachstad and rode the cog railway to the top of Mt. Pilatus. He entered the restaurant and saw the general seated by a table accompanied by his security detail. Sullivan walked over to the table and greeted Al-Jabr with kisses to each cheek.

The top of Mt. Pilatus offered fantastic views of Lake Lucerne and the Swiss glaciers. The Agency detail was a few tables away from Sullivan.

"Just about every week, there's a suicide bomber who detonates himself and kills innocent Muslims throughout the Middle East."

"I believe our greatest challenge today is stopping the spread of radical Islam. We need to reach out to the hearts and minds of this young generation before it's too late," Sullivan said.

"How do you propose to reform our system when we're exposed to global news 24/7, focused on Americans killing Arab Muslims and innocent citizens?"

Sullivan raised his right palm. "Your government has no choice."

"Bill, your government's invasion and occupation of Iraq haven't helped, especially the CIA's torture campaign of waterboarding and renditions. The worldwide media exposure of torture at Abu Ghraib is a good example."

"I agree, you're right on both of those disasters." Sullivan's face tensed up, and he shook his head. "I disagreed with the administration's campaign of torture, but several of us at the Agency were overruled."

"Bin Laden's forecast is coming true to form. Your former president, and now the new president, continues to bleed your treasury while your soldiers lose their lives. For what?"

"I'm afraid we've already burned those bridges." Sullivan changed the subject. "What have you found out?"

"Our spy works closely with Abdullah Al-Suhaimy, the Saudi terrorist leader who led the operations in both the Hurghada and Sharm El-Sheikh bombings."

"One hour, that's all I need for that fucking Abdullah to beg me to kill him," Sullivan said, as he grasped his hands in a choking motion.

"We want his head," the general said. "The Red Sea Brotherhood has a mole in your government."

"How do you know?"

"Abdullah received a call from Khalid Al-Bustani on *The Dolphin Prince* and had been informed of the hotel changes a few days before the attack. The spy's name is George," the general said.

"Believe me; we'll check it out. What makes a wealthy Saudi businessman become a mastermind terrorist?"

The waiter appeared with the Bratwurst lunch special and Swiss beer.

"Khalid apparently was radicalized during the Soviet-Afghan war but kept his intentions under the radar."

"I remember him. He owned an Arabian horse breeding business."

"He still does." Al-Jabr picked up his glass of water and took a swig. "They made a deal in Zurich with Russian arms dealers to buy four weapons-grade nuclear suitcase bombs and sixteen-hundred pounds of C-4."

"Any new intel on the cities targeted?" Asked Sullivan.

"Las Vegas and Houston."

"Please provide me with Khalid's dossier and all of his communications numbers."

"Of course!"

They both shook hands and departed from the restaurant.

Sullivan and his security detail took the cable car down to Lucerne, where the limo met them.

CAFÉ IN GENEVA

Caldwell sipped some coffee and grabbed the *International Herald Tribune*. Her secure cellphone rang and picked it up on the third ring. "Hello."

"Phantom speaking," said Sullivan, using his code name. "You're right. The man is Sergei Ryzhkov, the former KGB, and SVR Colonel. He's an expert on nuclear weapons, and we believe he still is in contact with the Russian foreign intelligence agency. We've identified the other man. He is Oleg Kupchenko, a former colonel in the Spetsnaz, with links to organized crime."

Caldwell took another sip of her coffee. "Ryzhkov has a private account with Banque Matthias Reiter in Geneva. Dave can provide you with more information on those transactions."

"I'll be going to Bern on Wednesday to meet the Swiss Federal Police Director."

Caldwell asked, "That was your old tennis partner when you lived in Bern?"

"Yes. As a matter of fact, we'll be playing tennis at his club. We'll talk again soon."

"Goodbye, sir."

———

JACOBSON WAS STROLLING along a stretch of Lake Zurich when his secure cellphone rang. He stopped and pulled the phone from his pocket, "Hi."

"Phantom here. Any new developments on the Russian's bank account at Banque Matthias Reiter?"

"Sergei Ryzhkov received two wire transfers from the Monch and Schneider bank in Zurich over the past year, totaling eight million dollars. However, yesterday he received a twelve million dollar wire transfer."

"We must stop these bastards at all costs."

"Sir, I will be in touch with my counterpart tomorrow and get back to you."

"I need you to fly to Dubai and hook up with our chief-of-station there on May 26. Book a suite in the Burj Al-Arab Hotel for three days. Faisal Al-Bustani and Abdullah Al-Suhaimy are meeting with Pakistanis, who want to sell the Red Sea Brotherhood an eight-kiloton nuclear warhead. We'll provide more details soon. Take care."

———

THE EIGER TENNIS Country Club in Bern has one of the best tennis courts in Switzerland. At two in the afternoon, Bruno Muller, a tall, tan, athletic man in his late fifties, and Sullivan finished their last tennis set. Muller beat Sullivan. They walked over to the courtside bar, plopped down, and ordered drinks. Sullivan's security detail was close by watching him.

"I can't believe I beat a former UCLA tennis player."

"Bruno, I played baseball, not tennis. But I must say your tennis game has improved."

Muller shook his head, "That's the first time I ever beat you."

"You played like a forty-year-old pro."

Muller laughed. "Flattery must come at a steep price. What do you need, Bill?"

"David Jacobson works for the US Treasury's Office of Counterterrorism and Financial Intelligence at our embassy in Bern. He's working with one of your undercover intel case officers, Hans Christian Scharz."

"What's the name of the Swiss bank?" asked Muller.

"We believe Banque Matthias Reiter provides terrorist and arms financing to major Russian Intelligence operators and organized crime figures."

"How can I be of assistance?"

"I want you to empower Mr. Scharz to run a black ops job for us at their headquarters in Geneva."

"On one condition, we agree to review the collected intelligence together to determine if there are any Swiss laws broken."

The waiter walked over to their table and served the men their drinks. "Here are your Eichhof Lagers gentlemen," the waiter said in German.

Sullivan and Muller raised their beer glasses. "Cheers."

"We're interested in those bankers who deal with terrorists and their illegal financial transactions," Sullivan said.

"Our country has a great reputation for safeguarding bank privacy, and we don't tolerate any terrorist financing, money laundering, or arms dealing."

"You didn't mention tax evasion."

"Director Sullivan, your sense of humor hasn't changed."

Chapter Thirty-Five

NATIONAL COUNTERTERRORISM CENTER

The American flag flew at half-staff outside the large, well-fortified complex that employed the best security systems money could buy. The NCTC Ops Center employees came from many government branches and departments: FBI linguists/translator staffers, NSA, CIA, DIA, and other intelligence agencies. They maintained their computer work stations amid an array of flat-panel HDTV plasma monitors.

Campbell, Geiger, and other directors were present. Marwan Haidar, an FBI linguist, and translator wore an NCTC badge and was by his terminal.

Campbell approached the podium. "Ladies and gentlemen, we've picked up actionable intel over the weekend, indicating the Red Sea Brotherhood plans to attack two American cities soon."

Haidar felt a sudden surge of pain in his stomach. His forehead began perspiring. Fear racked his mind, almost paralyzing him, freezing his thoughts.

Later in the evening, he entered his Falls Church home, kissed his wife, and rushed into his study. He plumped down into his plush chair by his desk. On his wall hung a large painting of an Arab warrior with a raised sword, leading men into battle. He shouted out in Arabic, "Death to the infidels!" He started his email in English:

TO: fdancer@swisstelecom.ch
FROM: grodriquez@comcast.net
"Our good friends learned about our exciting plans. We need to find a new singer for our church choir. George."

Haidar's parents had come from Baghdad, Iraq, in 1967, after the Israeli-Arab war. He was born in Detroit in 1968. Every few years, he, his siblings, and parents traveled to Iraq to visit relatives. Those visits helped shaped his views of Arab life in the Middle East.

With a degree in political science with honors, a clean record, and fluency in Arabic, he was recruited by the FBI. The American invasion of Iraq in 2003 planted the seeds and began to influence his loyalties away from his country. Still, the torture, humiliation, and physical abuse of Muslim prisoners at the hands of Americans at the Abu Ghraib prison cemented his conversion. In 2007, he gained the trust of Khalid Al-Bustani and became a spy for the Red Sea Brotherhood.

JEDDAH, SAUDI ARABIA

The Dolphin Prince anchored in the Jeddah Marina with Khalid, Abdullah, Omar, Ziad, Beltermann, and two bodyguards huddled in the salon. Khalid slammed his fists onto the conference table and yelled in Arabic, "Our plans have been discovered. We have a traitor in our group!"

Ziad placed his right hand into his pants pocket and pressed a programmed number on his pre-paid, doctored cell phone. A phone rang. After three rings, the men began checking their cellphones.

Omar lifted his cellphone out of his pocket, punched in his code, glanced at the LCD, and immediately pressed End.

A minute later, people heard a phone ringing again. Everyone picked up their cellphone, checked, and then turned toward Omar's direction. They noticed him shut off his cellphone.

Abdullah chuckled and asked, "Omar, it's your phone. A girlfriend calling?" Several sounds of laughter followed in the salon.

Omar's voice quivered. "No, it's a wrong number."

"Come up here and show me," Khalid said.

He moved slowly toward where Khalid stood, his face tense with fear. Omar gave the cellphone to Khalid, who activated the cellphone. Seconds later, a message symbol appeared on the LCD. Beltermann and Abdullah stood up and were now on each side of Omar.

Khalid pressed number one and looked at the screen. The caller ID appeared. On the LCD, the display read American Consulate, Jeddah. "American Consulate!" Khalid said in a rage. His eyes focused on Omar.

"I have never spoken to anybody at the American Consulate," Omar said nervously. Sweat ran down his cheeks. He tensed up, visibly shaken, and appeared in fear of his life. Khalid pressed the start button on the cellphone and listened to the recording:

"Hello, Omar, it's urgent. Please meet me at the Jeddah Hilton tomorrow morning at 0700 hours. We have some more cash for you. Please be careful. Cobra."

Beltermann and Abdullah held each of Omar's arms tightly.

Omar yelled, "No! No!"

Khalid pulled out a large knife and plunged the knife into Omar's heart. He gasped for air, bleeding, and hit the deck. A few seconds later, he died.

Al-Bustani turned to the captain. "Start the engines and take the boat fifteen kilometers out. He pointed to Beltermann, "In an hour throw this pig overboard."

He turned back to his men. "Our future is soon to be in our hands. Praise be to Allah for guiding the Red Sea Brotherhood on the path to re-establish the caliphate to rule the Arabian Peninsula."

"Allahu Akbar."

Chapter Thirty-Six

Adjoining the Portland International Airport on the south side is the Oregon Air National Guard's Portland facility. Two men escorted Hamilton up the airstairs and into the CIA G550 Gulfstream Jet, next to the hangar. He took a seat and faced a 30-inch, flat-screen monitor attached to the bulkhead. A few moments later, Director Sullivan appeared on the screen.

"Good morning, Mr. Hamilton. Have you been briefed on the subject of this meeting?"

"Yes, Director. If Mr. Ericksen left at this time, our business would be severely impacted."

"This mission is critical to our national security. Most of your company's sales revenue is generated from government contracts, and I'm sure you want to continue with that revenue stream."

Hamilton's face turned pale as if he got spooked by a bear while on a hiking trail in the forest.

"Yes, sir."

"I'm glad you understand the gravity of his mission to our country. His employment status hasn't changed, only his cover. This mission is classified as top secret."

"We'll do whatever it takes to support the mission, sir."

A senior CIA man, in his late-forties, sat next to him. "My staffer has some additional comments for you to consider. Thanks for your support."

"Mr. Hamilton, we would like to provide you with the name of a major venture capital group in Silicon Valley. Some of the companies they invest in do sensitive work for our agency. The lead partner of the firm would like to meet with you to discuss investing a substantial amount of money into your company." The staffer gave Hamilton a four-page report on Jefferson and Schonfeld Ventures.

"I appreciate the interest, but I don't want to bring in any venture capital."

"You might want to seriously rethink this opportunity because when this mission is completed, Ericksen will resign from your company unless you get funding."

Hamilton's face turned ash-white. "Ericksen told you he would resign?"

"Yes, he did. He is the driving force of your company. Ericksen maintains excellent credentials, top-secret security clearance, relationships with the procurement officers of our U.S. agencies, the DoD, and international governments. What I'm saying is your company might not survive another six months if he resigned."

Hamilton stood and walked toward the airstairs.

"Mr. Hamilton, EyeD4 Systems is your company; however, you might want to explore an opportunity with Cyberburst Communications out of Palo Alto, California. The company generates a significant amount of business within the intelligence community." He gave him the CEO's business card and continued, "Poul Kastrup has confided in us an interest in possibly acquiring EyeD4 Systems. We recommend you explore this opportunity. It might be in your best interests."

Hamilton descended the airstairs and glanced at Ericksen, approaching the jet, carrying two suitcases. They looked at each other without a smile. Hamilton finally spoke, "Good luck."

Chapter Thirty-Seven

E ricksen was escorted to the CIA Director's Office on the 7th floor. An Agency psychiatrist, Deputy CIA Director Norstad, Director of the National Clandestine Service Sheridan, and Ericksen sat facing CIA Director Sullivan.

"After you left the Navy, did you ever experience PTSD?" asked the psychiatrist.

"Yes, being tormented by nightmares. The majority of the incidents revolved around a JSOC mission called *Daring Eagles*. In April 2002, under orders from my Deputy Task Force Commander, he claimed, based on Agency intercepts, that our Afghan intelligence officer, Sadozai, was a Talib. He ordered me to kill him. When I returned to the Bagram Air Base, Dex, an Agency Special Operations Group Officer, told me the deputy task force commander lied to me. Nate Sheridan can confirm that meeting."

Sullivan turned to Sheridan. "Affirmative."

Ericksen continued, "I have been living every day with the memory of knowing I killed an innocent Bravo Team member."

"I understand how you feel," said Sullivan.

"After I left the Navy, I knew if I divulged my PTSD, I wouldn't be hired for the two defense contractor positions offered to me."

"True. Who was the commander who ordered you to kill Sadozai?" Sullivan asked.

"Colonel Shane Dawkins."

Sullivan shook his head and sighed. "He served as our military attaché in Riyadh when I was chief-of-station. The last I heard, he ran Stealth Dynamics' recruitment and training."

"That's the same guy."

"Did your psychologist, Dr. Holtzman, treat you?"

Ericksen tensed up. "Sir, you spooks amaze me. Yes, he did."

"We need to know all about you," Sullivan said, as the intercom on his desk rang, and answered, "Yes."

"Ms. Caldwell has arrived," the chief of staff said.

"Have her come in."

Caldwell entered the room. "Elizabeth, I would like to introduce you to Mark Ericksen, our agent for this mission."

Caldwell and Ericksen glanced at each other, nodded, and shook hands. She nodded to the other executives in the room.

"Please take a seat next to Mark," Sullivan commanded.

The psychiatrist asked, "Tell us about your treatment, please."

"In 2003, I went to a shrink in Virginia, who provided me with several experimental drugs and therapy. After five months, there wasn't any improvement."

"When did you start receiving treatment from Dr. Holtzman?"

"I started in 2006 after I joined EyeD4 Systems. Dr. Holtzman provided me with Prolonged Exposure Therapy treatment, and I began to improve."

"Have the treatments alleviated your PTSD?"

"Sometimes, an incident might trigger my memory of those events; however, it hasn't had any detrimental effects on me."

Caldwell leaned toward him and asked, "Really, what kinds of events?"

"Flashbacks. Bashir on his knees, begging for his life."

She moved closer to Ericksen. "We'll be working together in Switzerland."

"Elizabeth is a non-offical-cover CIA officer. She has no immunity from prosecution if caught as a spy in Switzerland," Sullivan said.

He handed her a large envelope. "This is the information you requested for my company."

Sullivan cracked his knuckles, interrupting the flow of their conversations. "Tomorrow, you'll start a three-day refresher course at the Farm. We have high regard for SEAL Team-Six members, so your refresher course shouldn't be too difficult. The focus will be on surveillance detection, close-quarters combat, tradecraft, and some weapons training. We'll plan on seeing you back here on Friday morning at nine."

Ericksen nodded.

Caldwell chuckled, "They placed you under Clint's care in close-quarters combat. Be careful; he sometimes gets too rough with recruits."

Ericksen didn't know in what capacity he would be working with her in Switzerland, but he felt her smart-ass antics would be a challenge for him. He thought she had a remarkable resemblance to the actress, Elizabeth Banks, who played Laura Bush, in the Oliver Stone movie W, he saw recently. It was hard not to glance at her stunning beauty, a real ten. Sullivan walked Ericksen to the door, where he was met by a CIA security guard who escorted him back to the elevator.

Sullivan glanced back at Caldwell, the psychiatrist, and the other senior executives of the Agency. "What do you think?"

The Agency psychiatrist leaned forward. "The challenges he deals with every day from PTSD and the recent traumatic brain injury he suffered in the hotel bombing are a concern, Sir. However, as they say, 'every cloud has a silver lining.' I believe the treatment he has received over the past three years has significantly helped him. He strikes me as an intelligent and mentally tough individual. SEALs are trained to compartmentalize missions. I believe Ericksen can perform the task," said the psychiatrist.

"We're up against the clock. He's our best bet!"

Caldwell leaned toward Sullivan, "I hope you're right, sir." The red phone rang, and Sullivan picked it up.

"This is Mohammed. We wiretapped a call in Jeddah at approximately one pm on May 7; it came from Columbia, Maryland, to Khalid's Swiss satphone. The phone number was from area code (301) 730-8976."

"That would be about six o'clock in the morning here. Thank you, Mohammed."

———

Off THE GREENS from a safe distance of fifty yards stood two security guards who kept a watchful eye on their boss at the River Creek Club Golf Course in Leesburg, Virginia. Campbell adjusted his swing and teed off on the fourth hole with a two hundred yard drive. Dawkins came up to the tee, concentrated on the ball, swung, and drove it two hundred sixty yards.

"Great shot!"

"I was lucky, sir."

"We'll follow up."

As they got into the cart, Campbell turned to Dawkins. "When will you begin your security consulting business?"

"I just leased some space in Alexandria and will launch the business in September."

"You did very well at Stealth Dynamics."

"Thanks to you, sir. We consummated a lot of contracts. I would like you to share some of those profits from the last two contracts."

"Shane, once I accepted Ridgeway's offer to become Director of National Intelligence, I didn't dare to take any more payoffs without becoming a visible target for the Agency. I could never embarrass and jeopardize my friendship with my old college buddy."

Dawkins walked to the next hole. "Understood, sir." He lined up his ball and drove it two hundred fifty yards. Campbell squared off and hit his shot into the sand trap.

"In fact, the Treasury Department's new efforts are putting the Swiss banking industry under a watchful eye. They're demanding the banks cooperate and release the names of Americans who have secret numbered accounts. Tax evasion is a serious crime. If the banks don't comply, the Feds will impose heavy fines and threaten criminal prosecution. We must be more careful now," Campbell said.

"Don't worry; our assets are protected by Reiter's bank. We're fortunate our Defense Department cannot conduct reliable audits in Iraq and Afghanistan."

"At least ten billion dollars of US government cash has been airlifted to Iraq and Afghanistan over the years to pay ministries and contractors, and our government doesn't even know where it is. Auditors working for the Iraqi and Afghanistan Reconstruction efforts are still conducting an investigation to try and find the cash."

They arrived at the sand trap. Campbell got out of the cart. He walked to his ball and then turned to Dawkins. "How reliable is Reiter?"

"Reiter enjoys his lifestyle and knows what would happen if he jeopardized our privacy," Dawkins said.

Campbell had heard rumors about how Dawkins terminated people who created problems for him. He measured the distance and hit the ball out of the sand trap. It rolled within ten-feet of the green.

"Good shot."

"If we're smart, we should transfer our accounts to the Grand Caymans or some other safe offshore haven."

Dawkins smiled. "Don't worry. We'll be fine."

The men got back into their golf cart and drove to the next hole, followed by Campbell's security guard detail.

Chapter Thirty-Eight

The interrogation of Evan Chiu, a Chinese-American, had begun several hours earlier at FBI Headquarters. Chiu had sweat running down his face. A small table separated Chiu from the FBI agent. "We have the information you made a call at six o'clock in the morning on May 7 to Saudi Arabia."

"No, not me! A club member asked if he could use my cell phone to call his wife. Naturally, I gave it to him since he said it was a local call. The next day, while checking my cellphone, I noticed someone called Switzerland."

"Can you give me his name and address?"

"Of course; his name is George Rodriquez. The club has a photo of him too."

"Fine."

Four hours later, an FBI SWAT team knocked on the door with their weapons drawn. A man about seventy-five-years-of-age, dressed in pajamas, answered the door. The SWAT team barged into the home. The old man, struck with fear, yelled in broken English, "I don't understand."

"Is Mr. Rodriquez here?"

"He doesn't live here."

"Where does he live?"

"I don't know. George gave me his cell phone number to call if I received any of his mail."

Growing impatient, the FBI SWAT commander barked an order, "What's the number?"

"703-555-0088. Is anything wrong?"

"Can't discuss it. Now get dressed – you're coming with us." The FBI SWAT commander picked up his secure phone. "Run this cellphone number down 703-555-0088."

At FBI Headquarters' communications center, a tech operator inputted the number 703-555-0088 and highlighted it on the monitor. Rapid scrolling of cell phone numbers displayed the 703 area codes on the computer.

Twenty seconds later: "We have a hit. The number belongs to Marwan Haidar. I'll get some background on him right now," said the FBI Counterterrorism Center IT supervisor.

"Good work," the FBI SWAT Commander replied.

A few minutes later, the IT supervisor placed a call. "Sir, this is unbelievable. Mr. Haidar works for us. He is the FBI Arabic language linguistics/translations group manager at the National Counterterrorism Center."

At two o'clock in the morning, the telephone rang at the Georgetown home of FBI Director Geiger. He and his wife were sleeping. After five rings, Geiger awoke. He tossed a few times and reached for his secure landline phone on the seventh ring. "Hello!"

"Sorry to bother you, Sir, at this hour. His real name is Marwan Haidar. He is with the FBI's Arabic linguistic desk at the NCTC."

"Holy shit!"

Chapter Thirty-Nine

OFFICE OF THE DIRECTOR OF NATIONAL INTELLIGENCE

C ampbell, Geiger, Lucas, and Sullivan, and their staff sat around a conference table in a secure, bubble room at the ODNI headquarters. "Apparently, a member of our delegation contacted the NCTC from Hurghada, and somehow Haidar got wind of the change of hotels," Geiger said.

"An FBI Arab linguist! Pete, the president is going to go nuts on this one. I hope you're dusting off your resume," Campbell said.

Sullivan cupped his hand on his chin and glanced at Geiger. "All is not lost. The Saudi spy who works for General Al-Jabr has been right-on with the Intel."

"We'll place Haidar on 24/7 surveillance and conduct wiretapping."

Campbell stood up and gestured to his staff, waving his right hand. "I would appreciate it if everyone would leave the conference room now. I need to talk with the principals in private."

Everyone left the room except Geiger, Lucas, and Sullivan. "I went over Ericksen's dossier, and I'm quite impressed with his background and current experience for this urgent mission," Lucas said.

His endorsement didn't surprise Sullivan or Geiger. They knew Hank Lucas had a special admiration for special ops warriors. Lucas had spent twenty-seven years in the US military, retiring as a major general, and many of those years were in Special Forces command posts.

Campbell, always prone to contrary views, had a sour expression on his face. "I seriously doubt if Al-Bustani is going to swallow Ericksen's pitch, given his mental state."

Sullivan turned and faced Campbell. "Steve, he is the only one that has the credibility to this mission. Khalid Al-Bustani has already determined his operation needs this level of communication security."

Sullivan thought, *Why can't this jackass comprehend intelligence operations' rationale when the task of the mission serves our allies and the principals in the White House?*

Chapter Forty

E ricksen, Caldwell, Norstad, and the CIA psychiatrist sat across from Sullivan in the SCIF Conference Room. Caldwell stood up and clicked on the PowerPoint slide presentation: a photo of Khalid Al-Bustani.

"Khalid Al-Bustani is the mastermind. He is forty-nine, a graduate of King Abdul Aziz University in Jeddah, with a B.S. in petroleum engineering and an MBA from the University of Texas at Austin. He played soccer at the Al-Thagher Model School in Jeddah with Osama Bin Laden, a schoolmate, who was two grade levels ahead of him."

"The next slide shows Khalid in Afghanistan alongside his boyhood friend, Bin Laden, fighting against the Soviets from 1985 to 1987."

"It was at this time we believe he became an Islamic Jihadist," the psychiatrist said.

"The next photo was taken at Ghazi Al-Bustani's funeral in 1987. His father suffered a fatal heart attack and the control of the company went to his older brother Nabil. However, six months later, Nabil was killed in a car accident in Marbella, Spain," Caldwell said.

Sullivan chuckled. "What a surprise. Who is next in line to run Al-Bustani Group of Companies?" Sullivan asked.

"His younger brother Nayef. He is the head of Al-Bustani Geological Exploration Company and is married to one of the Royal Family's daughters. There are no indications he's involved in terrorism or any criminal adventures."

"Our team has concluded Al-Bustani is a sociopath who exhibits a conflicting struggle between material wealth and being the leader of the holy jihad. You'll never find him living in a cave," the psychiatrist joked.

Sullivan walked over to the refrigerator and retrieved three bottles of mineral water. He gave each one to Ericksen and Caldwell and took a swig.

"Our mission will be called *Operation Avenging Eagles*. Please show Mark, his inner circle."

Caldwell activated the remote. A slide of Ziad Kabbani appeared. "Ziad is a Saudi government spy. He proved his loyalty by his years as a bomb maker in Iraq for Al-Qaeda. Now he's Khalid's financial advisor and savvy computer security guru. The next slide features the head of their terrorist operations: Abdullah Al-Suhaimy is a Saudi and Al-Bustani's top operative. He led the Hurghada bombing operation," Caldwell reported.

She clicked the remote for the next picture. "The next key guy is Wolfgang Beltermann, the former East German Stasi intelligence spy. He is another major operative and a computer expert. Beltermann has conducted a couple of terrorist missions to his credit."

Sullivan interjected, "Mark, your code name will be Gold Eagle, like during your SEAL days. Elizabeth's Venus and mine is Phantom. Khalid spends most of his time from July through mid-September in Switzerland. It is during this period where your covert operational activities might come into play by appointing Elizabeth's firm to conduct an executive search for a European Sales Manager."

Caldwell pointed her index finger and thumb at Ericksen. "If all goes as planned, Khalid will offer a sizeable amount of money to buy you off. Don't accept his initial offer. He'll respect you for your stance.

If he is serious about acquiring your systems, he'll negotiate a counteroffer. Once you agree to his offer, make sure to open a private numbered account only with Banque Matthias Reiter in Geneva. It must be this bank. Understand?"

"Affirmative, Ms. Caldwell." *This is the bank where Dawkins probably has a private account, thought Ericksen.*

Ericksen and Caldwell shared many positive organizational leadership skills, except one: He had killed many men in combat. She had never killed a person. However, both had strong analytical abilities, were self-motivated, goal-oriented, and had a track record of delivering results. Her experience focused on analyzing, evaluating, and selecting the best potential candidates for senior wealth asset management positions within the Swiss banking industry. When she recommended a potential asset to the bank, and the candidate was approved, she would contact the senior Treasury department's counterterrorism and financial intelligence officer in Bern, David Jacobson. Then he began turning the asset.

Ericksen handed Sullivan the photo of Bashir's wife and daughters. He pointed to Laila. "Laila survived a Taliban attack two years ago. Her mother and oldest sister were killed. I met Jannan in 2005 in Kandahar. He works for the Afghan government and has been raising Laila along with his kids." He continued, "He called me recently and asked if I could help him and his family get out of Afghanistan. The Taliban has threatened him several times, and he feels it's just a matter of time before they kill him." Ericksen stared into Sullivan's eyes. "Director Sullivan, can you help bring them to America?"

"I'll have someone look into this and see what we can do to help get them to the States."

"Thank you, sir."

The psychiatrist leaned in. "Mr. Ericksen, I believe if the director can accomplish your request, seeing them in America would certainly give you some sense of redemption."

Ericksen nodded.

Sullivan stood up. "Clint contacted me from the hospital. He told me you kicked his ass."

"I didn't intend to hurt the guy, but he tried to beat the shit out of me."

Sullivan smiled. "We should have given Clint a heads-up on your black belts in Okinawan karate, Brazilian jujitsu, and your expertise in Krav Maga."

Sullivan heard a sound emanating from his desktop computer and glanced at the upcoming email. It was from Wolverine: Khalid Al-Bustani wired fifteen million Swiss francs from Monch and Schneider Bank Zurich two days ago to Tariq Cement Company's private account at Waldmann and Tessier Bank S.A. Luxembourg. Hafiz Tariq is the chairman of the company."

Chapter Forty-One

Two hundred Saudi corporate and governmental security people arrived on June 9th to attend Massoud Trading Company's two-day show in conference hall B at the Sheraton Hotel in Jeddah to view several vendors' products on display. Ericksen spent one hour delivering a PowerPoint presentation on how each of EyeD4 Systems' access control biometrics technologies worked. He then demonstrated with several individuals whom he had already enrolled, having them approach the units one at a time and match in real-time their live-iris or palm vein to the previously registered template. He hoped the presentation would generate more business for his Saudi distributor.

After the presentation, he walked away from the podium. The CEO of the company and Saudi distributor for EyeD4 Systems approached the stage and announced, "Gentlemen, lunch will be served in the Oasis room in ten minutes."

Khalid, Beltermann, Faisal, and Ziad greeted the CEO, who stood next to Ericksen. "Khalid, let me introduce you to Mark Ericksen. Khalid Al-Bustani is one of our best customers in the Kingdom," the CEO said.

Both men shook hands, and Al-Bustani introduced Ericksen to

Ziad, Faisal, and Beltermann. Khalid turned to the CEO and, in Arabic, said, "Would you please answer some questions for my men while I talk with Mr. Ericksen privately?"

"Of course."

He and Ericksen walked toward the lobby. In the hall were many Arab businessmen and foreigners talking amongst each other. There were also some Arab women with their husbands. They all wore an abaya, a long outer garment covering their bodies, arms, legs, and heads. Some of the women were covered entirely, where all you saw were their eyes.

"Do you have any dinner plans tonight, Mr. Ericksen?" he asked in English.

"No."

"Good. I would like to discuss some opportunities with you over dinner. I'll have my driver meet you in the lobby. What time is best for you?"

Ericksen looked at his Omega Seamaster dive watch, "How about seven?"

"See you tonight."

———

THE CHAUFFEUR-DRIVEN Rolls Royce arrived at the Jeddah Marina and pulled up to the dock. The chauffeur opened the rear passenger door, and Ericksen got out. He walked up the imposing *Dolphin Prince*'s gangplank, where an attendant greeted Ericksen as he reached the top.

"Please follow me, sir," the attendant said. He escorted him into the dining room, where Ziad and Khalid greeted him.

"My financial advisor is joining us."

They sat down at the dinner table. The head waiter approached the table and filled the glasses with water.

"Can I offer you some beverage – orange juice or wine, sir?"

"I would like a glass of your Pinot Noir."

"Get him our best Pinot Noir, the Elk Cove Vineyards, La Boheme 2003, and orange juice for us," Khalid said.

"Thank you."

"Having lived in Austin, Texas, for a few years, I became more acquainted with your American culture and the more informal ways of enjoyment. May I call you Mark?"

"Of course."

"I run several diversified companies throughout the world. Everything from oil and gas exploration, hotels, construction companies to consumer electronics," Khalid said with enthusiasm.

"That's quite impressive, Mr. Al-Bustani."

The waiter entered with a Pinot Noir bottle and poured some wine in Ericksen's glass for his approval. He glanced at the bottle, checked out the wine's color in the glass, swirled it, smelled the bouquet of the wine, and drank it.

"The wine is splendid," Ericksen said as he nodded his head and smiled. The waiter then filled the glass of wine and handed glasses of orange juice to both Ziad and Khalid.

"I own forty percent of a Houston company. We believe our competitors are involved in industrial espionage. We are interested in purchasing your EyeD4Comm System's palm vein biometrics and encryption software systems."

Ericksen dropped his jaw and appeared startled. "The EyeD4 Comm System is classified. It is only available to the US Government and currently has been in beta-testing for over a year."

"I understand. However, I'll make an offer worthwhile to you. Can you provide me with the same capabilities you offer the CIA?"

"Mr. Al-Bustani, you can't be serious."

"Please call me Khalid."

He raised his eyebrows, and his face tensed up. "Khalid, you certainly have a good sense of humor. I enjoy my freedom, and what you're proposing will guarantee me a one-way ticket to a federal prison for a long time."

"I'll give you one million dollars for four systems, five hundred thousand now, and placed in a private numbered account in Switzerland of your choice. The balance upon delivery at a US location."

"Thanks for the offer, but I'm sorry I must decline."

The waiter brought in the appetizers: jumbo prawns, yellowfin tuna with Asian cucumber salad, escargots à la Bourguignonne, and Arabic unleavened bread.

"Please think it over tonight, and if you change your mind, call me in the morning."

"Here's my business card," Khalid said.

"Please don't take this personally, but if I'm going to take all the risks, I need to have at least two million dollars for the four systems. One million upfront and one million upon physical handoff to a trusted representative of your company."

"You drive a hard bargain. I'll think over your offer. In the meantime, let's enjoy the appetizers. The entrée is our chef's delicacy – Saudi lamb."

DURAB, SAUDI ARABIA

Khalid leaned against the white fence and watched several Arabian horses at the auction in Dirab, Saudi Arabia. Colonel Mustapha Al-Gosaibi approached him. They both walked toward some men who also showed interest in the horses. Khalid and Al-Gosaibi spotted General Al- Jabr and his four-man security detail. "General Mohammed, good to see you," Colonel Al-Gosaibi said in Arabic.

General Al-Jabr smiled. "Colonel Mustapha, are you buying or just here to observe?"

"Khalid's the one who is in the market."

Al-Jabr faced Khalid. "I can never forget your Arabian Falcon Dancer, the year he won the King's Cup. He was fast and furious like the desert wind."

Khalid nodded and smiled, a sense of pride suffusing his face, in appreciation of the recognition voiced by a warrior about his Falcon Dancer. "God willing, I'll find another someday – maybe today."

"Congratulations on being awarded the national police headquarters project. Perhaps Colonel Mustapha will get a larger office when you've completed the job."

Al-Gosaibi's mouth tightened with a half-smile as he pondered Al-Jabr's meaning. "I'm confident the interior minister will be pleased when we're finished."

After Khalid and Colonel Mustapha had moved on, General Al-Jabr turned to his aide, "Place the colonel under surveillance."

Chapter Forty-Two

Ziad joined Steiner and Ericksen in the Banque Matthias Reiter's elegant conference room off to the side of the lobby.

"Do you want them shipped to Houston?" asked Ericksen.

"No, we'll test them and take delivery in Oregon," Ziad said.

"Where and when?"

"We will get back to you with the location and the dates."

"Fine."

Steiner handed the briefcase to Ericksen as Jurgen Reiter approached.

"Herr Reiter, Mr. Ericksen will be opening an account with your bank for one million dollars. I think he will become a valuable client to your bank."

"Excellent."

"Gentlemen, please excuse us, we'll be on our way," Ziad said, as both men left the room and strolled toward the lobby.

"Mr. Ericksen, please follow me to our fifth-floor conference room." They both entered the elevator and rode up to the fifth floor.

"Would you like some coffee?"

He escorted him into the conference room and pointed to a seat close to the front of the table nearest to a large painting of Bellagio.

"Please excuse me for a minute. I need to get some forms for you to sign."

Ericksen nodded. He marveled at the stained-glass painting with its majestic mountain vistas surrounding Lake Como and the homes and buildings of Bellagio. He noticed the painstaking effort the artist demanded of himself to accomplish such a masterpiece. The sun's rays illuminated the painting.

A few minutes later, Reiter explained the instructions and procedures for conducting deposits, wire transfers, and withdrawals on his private numbered account at Banque Matthias Reiter. Reiter handed him a Banque Matthias Reiter credit card to use for any purchases he wished to make.

"Your numbered account starts with the letters BMR, which stands for Banque Matthias Reiter, and the numbers 0534986JR/1. After the seven-digit number, you'll see JR, my initials, the forward slash, and the number 1. The number 1 references the Geneva location, the headquarters of our bank. Future deposits must be made by you in person or by phone. We can also wire transfer funds into your account from another account holder or another Swiss bank account holder.

"Do you have any questions?" asked Reiter.

"No."

"What is your passcode?"

"VikingMercerIslandDK."

"What is your date of birth and place of birth?" "July 13, 1970, Copenhagen, Denmark."

"We're almost finished. My employee number is 045, and my grandmother's maiden name is Keller." He pointed to his business card on the table. "Please call my direct line. I believe that covers our standard operating procedures. Your access code is Klosters. Do you have any questions, Mr. Ericksen?"

"Yes. What if you're not available?"

"Ask for Lorenz Reiter. He is the CFO of our bank and my nephew. I'll get his direct number for you. Lorenz's employee number is 060 and use "Keller."

Thank you."

"Welcome to Banque Matthias Reiter."

A woman entered and gave the receipt to Ericksen. "Mr. Ericksen, this is your receipt for your one million dollar deposit today."

Jurgen glanced upward at his administrative assistant. "Please give Mr. Ericksen Lorenz's business card."

"Will do, sir," she replied in French.

———

LOCATED on the third floor of an ornate building on the Rue de Rive is the office of Prentice & Aubert. Ericksen entered the lobby, and the receptionist greeted him. "Can I help you, sir?" she asked in French.

"I have an appointment with Ms. Caldwell," he said in English.

"Your name please?"

"Mark Ericksen."

"One moment. Please have a seat."

The receptionist called Caldwell. "Madame, Mr. Ericksen is here for his appointment."

He stood up and met her in the lobby. She wore a beautiful, stylish blue skirt, a camel suede sports jacket, and a white blouse with a pearl necklace. She looked gorgeous. Her eyes sparkled, and her smile radiated as she greeted him.

"Hello, Mr. Ericksen, please follow me." Caldwell escorted him to her office. She opened the door, and he noticed Jacobson seated in a chair.

"Dex?"

Jacobson stood up and extended his hand to him. "Hello, Mark, it's been a long time. My alias these days is 'Dave Jacobson.'"

They shook hands as Caldwell interjected, "Dave works at the US Embassy in Bern. He's with the Agency, but on loan to the Treasury Department."

"Write down my secure phone number in Bern, 31-909-6868. My code name is Wolverine."

Ericksen took out his cellphone and entered the number into his contacts. He looked up and noticed Caldwell's MBA framed on the wall.

"Nice job."

"I have to admit, the MBA from the IMD in Lausanne was an Agency perk."

"Elizabeth is a great recruiter. She even placed my Swiss counterpart. I'm sure he had other things on his mind when she interviewed him," Jacobson said jokingly.

Caldwell shook her head, rolled her eyes, and frowned at Jacobson. "That's bullshit. Hans Christian is a gentleman."

"Where's your sense of humor?"

She shook her head again. "Dave's such a character."

"When I tried to turn him into an asset, he told me he worked undercover for the Swiss Federal Police to investigate Otto Steiner and Monch and Schneider Bank. To this day, he doesn't have a clue about you being a NOC, just an executive recruiter in the Swiss banking industry," Jacobson explained.

Turning to Erickson, He asked, "Do you have any plans later this afternoon?"

"No. How about meeting me at three o'clock at the boat ramp? We can take a lake cruise and enjoy the scenery."

"Sounds fine."

Caldwell turned to Ericksen, "Mark, are you hungry for lunch?"

"Yes, I am."

"I've made reservations for lunch at one of my favorite places in Geneva."

"Make sure she picks up the tab."

She shrugged her shoulders, "Don't worry. They take plastic." Fifteen minutes later, Caldwell drove her BMW up to the valet at La Perle du Luc restaurant on the Rue de Lausanne. She gave the valet the keys to her car. She and Ericksen walked into the restaurant. The maître d' handed them menus and escorted them to an outside table on the open-air terrace with a beautiful view of Mt. Blanc and Lake Leman.

The waiter approached their table. "What would you like for lunch?" the waiter asked in French.

"I'll have the lobster bisque and quiche Lorraine," she replied in French as well.

"And you, sir?"

"I'll have the trout and a Carlsberg beer," He said in English.

"What would you like to drink, madam?"

"A cappuccino and Evian water, please." Elizabeth gave the menus back to the waiter. "Don't worry, I'm picking up the tab," she said and smiled.

He filled her in on his meeting with the Jurgen Reiter and his newly acquired private Swiss numbered account. It was Caldwell who insisted on the bank. He explained to her what transpired during his time in Jeddah and his dinner on *The Dolphin Prince*. "It was like having dinner at a five-star resort hotel on the water."

He recognized Caldwell's professional dedication to detail and her ability to fit into the Swiss culture as a seamless modus operandi. Her French impressed him, along with her ability to pull off her role as an executive recruiter in the banking industry. He wondered if she was in a relationship, married, or just too busy as a professional career-oriented CIA officer.

Ericksen arrived back at his hotel to check for messages. At three o'clock, he left and walked to the boat ramp. Ericksen thought about the four tragic events in his life: his wife's death, killing Bashir Sadozai, PTSD, and the terrorist hotel bombing in Egypt. From the moment of his Navy discharge to the present, he had found it difficult to develop any long-term relationships with the women he dated. He realized he refused to let go of his wife's memory, but most importantly, both his PTSD and his dedication to becoming a successful businessman had prevented any potential relationships from blooming.

During his first year at Cambridge Defense Systems, he had experienced periodic bouts of depression. On some weekends, he either got drunk in Georgetown bars or his apartment. A few times during this period, he would wake up in bed surprised to find a woman lying next to him. At the time, being drunk and engaged in one-night stands erased the depression and anxieties he tried to repress. It didn't take long for him to realize his actions were stupid.

Ericksen began to focus his energies at work, and on his next performance review, his supervisor recommended he explore the Executive MBA program at the University of Virginia. Six months later, he only had time for work and grad school. During the night, his nightmares would occupy his mind.

Once he accepted the position at EyeD4 Systems and returned to the Pacific Northwest, his sister Mia and his old alumni friends from Oregon State tried to fix him up with women who were interested in marriage. His objectives focused on working with Dr. Holtzman and building a successful company. After a year of therapy, he started feeling better.

His thoughts came back to the moment – Geneva. Tomorrow evening he would again be with Caldwell.

Ericksen heard footsteps, turned to his right, and spotted Jacobson. They greeted each other and boarded a steamer for a lake cruise to Nyon. A few minutes later, Jacobson handed a photo for him to see. "This is the photo linking Dawkins to the Banque Matthias Reiter."

Ericksen's eyes zeroed in on the photo of Dawkins being escorted by Reiter into the Banque Matthias Reiter lobby. He nodded, "We're going to nail this son-of-a-bitch!"

Chapter Forty-Three

Campbell and Sullivan played racquetball at the exclusive Olympic Gold Racquetball Club in McLean, Virginia. At fifty-six, the five-foot-ten, medium-build Campbell lacked athleticism, but he enjoyed the gentry sports: tennis, golf, racquetball, and horseback riding. He had grown up in Kansas, not far from Wichita. His family was wheat growers, and money had never posed any problems for them. His parents had sent him off to Phillips Exeter Academy in New Hampshire. He enjoyed the friendship of many of his fellow students, who later became successful businessmen and politicians.

He spent four years at an Ivy League university in New England, majoring in political science. His fraternity brother, Bentley Ridgeway, shared the same interests: parties, football games, and their primary course of study, political science. Campbell displayed a streak of arrogance, intelligence, and opportunistic tendencies that bordered on shrewdness and greed. His fraternity brother later became President of the United States. In April 2008, President Ridgeway appointed Senator Campbell to the position of Director of National Intelligence. Campbell had an insecurity problem, though his overtly egotistical presence masked it.

He had been married for over thirty years to a woman from Boston who taught elementary school. She had quit her job to raise their children. She complimented his appetite for social climbing within the political establishment. Being an ass-kisser in Washington appeared to be the norm. Their rocky marriage produced two children. They spent their weekends on their hundred-acre-plus estate in Virginia, where they maintained a stable of thoroughbreds. During the week, they lived in an upscale condo in the Watergate Hotel in DC.

Sullivan had grown up in Columbia, Missouri, where his father was a professor at the University of Missouri, and his mother taught music. He won a baseball scholarship at UCLA, posted thirty wins as a college pitcher, and enjoyed fraternity life as a Sigma Chi member. He took Air Force ROTC and, upon graduation in 1972, was commissioned a second lieutenant. After four years as an Air Force intelligence officer, he was recruited by the CIA. He spent close to thirty years with the Agency, which included service as a Special Operations Group officer in Pakistan, from 1983 to 1985, then promoted into the former Directorate of Operations. In 2003, he became Director of the CIA's Counterterrorism Center; in 2005, Director of the National Clandestine Service; and in July 2008, President Ridgeway appointed him to be the new CIA Director.

Sullivan enjoyed good relations with his three adult children from an early marriage, which ended in divorce in 1998. His son, US Marine Captain Ryan Sullivan, had been killed in 2005 by an IED in Iraq. In 2006, he remarried a woman who worked for a Public Relations firm in Washington DC. Sullivan allocated much of his spare time to being active in sports and physical exercise. At six-feet-even, the lean, muscular, and handsome director played a good tennis game and participated in triathlon events. Being intelligent, loyal, trustworthy, objective, and results-oriented, he had a difficult time working for Campbell, who he thought didn't deserve any measure of respect.

After playing for an hour, they both walked back to the locker room and headed for the sauna. When the two were alone, Sullivan informed Campbell, "One of our case officers received a hot tip from the Swiss Federal Police on Banque Matthias Reiter in Geneva."

Campbell's face stiffened up, and in a serious tone, he asked,

"Listen to me. The Russians and Al-Bustani do their banking in Zurich, correct?"

"True. Ryzhkov also has an account at Banque Matthias Reiter." Campbell nervously rubbed his fingers with his thumb.

"Just focus on Monch and Schneider."

"Don't you want us to explore the Russian arms dealers' activities in Geneva?"

"It isn't critical at this time," Campbell snapped.

———

GEIGER AND SULLIVAN left the marina on the FBI's eighty-foot yacht *Blue Knight* and cruised down the Potomac River, off Quantico. Four FBI heavily armed security officers were on the boat, while two Coast Guard gunboats provided protection alongside. Sullivan had on a tan short-sleeve sports shirt, khaki shorts and wore Sperry Top-Sider shoes. Geiger wore a blue sports shirt, white slacks, and sneakers and navigated the yacht's steering wheel down the river.

"What did Campbell say to you?" Geiger asked.

"His behavior is quite bizarre," said Sullivan.

"In what way?"

"He doesn't want us to monitor a Swiss bank in Geneva that we suspect is involved in arms dealing and terrorist financing."

Geiger called one of the FBI supervisors who co-captained Blue Knight and asked him to take over. They both stepped downstairs to the salon. "Bill, what I'm going to tell you must remain in the strictest of confidence because the Justice Department has an ongoing investigation into both Campbell and Dawkins' alleged fraud, corruption, and money-laundering operations, covering the period of 2003–2006. Additional charges are pending for Dawkins – murder."

"Murder!"

"I'll explain. We're the lead agency investigating. This period covered when Campbell exerted lots of influence on various committees and contacts within the State Department. During his time in the Senate, he served on three significant committees: Senate Appropriations, Department of State and Foreign Operations; and the Senate Select Committee on Intelligence."

"Pete, you can't be serious. Do you have any proof?"

"We believe Dawkins deposited monies into a private numbered account in Liechtenstein and Switzerland during 2002 through August 2004, while still on active duty. The trail continued shortly after Dawkins joined Stealth Dynamics. Being privy to upcoming bids in Iraq and Afghanistan, including Campbell's influence with State, cemented the contracts," Geiger said.

Sullivan took a swig of Apple juice. "Dawkins is a piece of work. When I was chief-of-station in Saudi Arabia, Dawkins served as a military attaché at the embassy. I worked with him briefly before he transferred to Cairo. The man was aloof, unreliable, and as cold as ice."

"This is where it gets interesting. Four senior Army contracting officers in Iraq received millions of dollars in cash to disburse to private contractors and ministries. There were hardly any records on how the money had to be spent, allocated, and distributed. Several soldiers swore under oath having seen Dawkins with these men, and later those contracting officers turned up dead."

"When were the bodies discovered?" asked Sullivan.

"Sometime around the summer of 2004."

"Do you have any witnesses?"

"Not a fucking one."

"Where do you think the money wound up?" "Liechtenstein."

"Have you been able to get cooperation from their bank?"

"No. However, a former Liechtenstein banker claims to have seen over twenty million dollars deposited into Dawkins' private account. Then last year, he closed his account."

"Any more on Dawkins or Campbell?"

"Well, two months ago, our agents took several photos of the Swiss banker, Jurgen Reiter, with Campbell at the Mar-a-Lago Golf Resort in Palm Beach."

"I think we might be able to get enough evidence to hang both of them. Our case officer in Geneva took a photo of Dawkins and Reiter together in the bank lobby recently."

"How are you going to get it?" asked Geiger.

"Our man in Switzerland and his Swiss counterpart are developing a plan of action as we speak."

Chapter Forty-Four

PORTLAND, OREGON

Campbell's Horizon Air Lines flight arrived in Portland at 4:45 pm from Spokane on July 15. After getting off the plane, she waved to Ericksen outside of the security area.

He greeted her with a formal handshake and took the escalators to the baggage area downstairs. After the thirty-five minute drive, they arrived at his West Linn home. He escorted her to one of the guest bedrooms. His cellphone rang, and he picked it up. "Hello."

"The NSA engineer will meet you at your office at six in the evening tomorrow. Elizabeth will keep Z occupied while you're in the meeting. After the meeting, bring Z with his toys to the engineer, and he'll fix them," Sullivan said.

"Why do you want Elizabeth to stay at my home?"

"Come on; you're both adults. I believe you need to bond, so get with the program."

Ericksen had acquired a culinary interest since moving to Portland. He first decided to purchase Giada De Laurentis' tri-ply clad cookware set and other chef-endorsed appliances and recommended cookware. Ericksen had remodeled his kitchen the previous year, putting in custom Brazilian cherry cabinets and granite countertops. For this evening's menu, he placed the cast-iron Dutch oven on the burner to prepare a side dish of Angel Hair Pasta. Ericksen decided to treat Caldwell to his seafood specialty – Baked Halibut with Arugula Salsa Verde. To top everything off, he went down to his wine cellar and retrieved a prized Stag's Leap Chardonnay from the Napa Valley, placing it on the dining room table. He took out two Royal Copenhagen plates and Sheffield Viscount cutlery. The white tablecloth was from Belgium.

"Can I help?" Caldwell asked and smiled. "Are you trying to spoil an Idahoan who grew up on a ranch?"

Ericksen now transferred the halibut fillets onto each plate and spooned the Arugula Salsa Verde alongside. "It's not often I have house guests here; however, I sincerely hope you enjoy the dinner." He smiled as he opened up his china cabinet, took down two Waterford crystal wine glasses, and filled both glasses.

At 3:40 pm the next day, the Amtrak train arrived at the Portland train depot downtown. Ericksen and Caldwell were there waiting to pick up Ziad. A few minutes later, he appeared, dressed in a casual set of clothes, carrying a large suitcase and a backpack. He shook his hand and introduced Caldwell to him. After he had placed his luggage in the back of the rented Cadillac Escalade SUV, they drove off to Lake Oswego. They pulled up into the parking lot of the Fairfield Inn in Lake Oswego.

Ziad provided the front desk clerk with his credit card and received the key to his room. He placed his luggage on his bed, transferred the cellphones from his suitcase into his backpack, and had fifteen pre-paid cellphones, each with two hundred minutes of talk time. They all got back in the SUV and Ericksen drove them to his office.

————

AT 6 PM, Ericksen pulled into the Wilsonville, Oregon headquarters' parking lot. He opened the front door with his key and proceeded to his office. Ericksen told Caldwell and Ziad to use his office for their meeting while he walked down the hall to Hamilton's office. He knocked on the door, and Hamilton said,

"Come in."

Seated in a chair facing Hamilton was an NSA engineer. The slim, long-haired engineer couldn't be more than thirty-years-of-age. He wore jeans and sneakers. Ericksen had met the engineer at Ft. Meade on two previous occasions with his vice-president of engineering.

"I need a few minutes with Mark, and then he'll join you. Just make yourself comfortable. If you want any refreshments, let me know."

The engineer shook his head. "No, thanks."

"I'll have Mark bring the box in shortly," Hamilton said. He buzzed his executive assistant.

"Please escort the gentleman to the conference room." Hamilton sat down and faced Ericksen.

"I've made up my mind. I'm accepting Kastrup's offer." Hamilton cleared his throat. "I'm selling the company. You're right. Without serious capital, the chances of success are remote."

"I'm glad you made that decision."

"Kastrup is sending the documents today for our signature. Starting November 1, you'll be President and CEO of the company. They told me you would have a great compensation program, including twenty-five-thousand-shares of stocks. He only had one condition: you have to hire his daughter to be your new chief financial officer."

"What's her background?"

"Her name is Sofia Kastrup. She worked for a big-eight accounting firm for six years in Silicon Valley, handling a few major software companies. She took a year off when her son was born and moved with her husband to Lake Oswego, where he accepted a law firm position in downtown Portland. She has a Harvard MBA in Finance and is a certified CPA."

"That's fine." Ericksen gave the victory signal. "Wow!"

The joy of hearing the news made his heartbeat pulse a lot faster, like a marathon runner passing his closest rival with a few yards to go. He stood up, smiled, excused himself, and headed for the conference room.

Ericksen opened the two boxes, removed four laptop computers, and placed them on the table. "I've embedded four powerful GPS tracking software systems into these rugged, tempest-shielded laptop computers. The terrorist IT expert will expect some level of shielding, but this is the lowest level," the NSA engineer said.

"What are the chances of detection?" Ericksen asked.

"It's virtually impossible." The NSA engineer kept a straight face. "We've covertly inputted your palm vein template and matching live-biometrics verification algorithm signature recessed into the bowels of the CPU. They reside on all four laptop computers, and we registered them as the 'real systems administrator.' Your agent, Ziad, will enroll Abdullah, Beltermann, and himself before he departs from Portland. He needs to provide you with each of their biometrics ID on USB flash drives. You'll send them to Ft. Meade. When he enrolls Khalid, you'll make arrangements for the USB flash drive to be sent to my attention at Ft. Meade."

"At what point does my biometrics template and matching 'real-live' authentication ID buried within Echelon II enable NSA to intercept their email communications?" he asked.

"Good question. Here's a typical scenario, Abdullah inserts his USB flash drive into the port, performs the biometrics log-on program in a city in the USA. It confirms his ID, and Khalid does the same process from Switzerland or Saudi Arabia. Then Khalid inputs his sensitive email message and clicks SEND. His message is encrypted with the same key as Abdullah's key. Both of their laptop computers will immediately recognize each other by their symmetrical keys. Their encrypted emails and computer IP addresses, and other tags will be routed to our referenced master protocol within nanoseconds – your biometrics ID, which resides within our Global Information Grid – using Echelon II. Once there, our Vortex Interceptor locks on and decrypts their communication."

"Why do you need my biometrics ID?" "Extra insurance."

"I'm impressed. If this works, we should all be congratulated," said Ericksen.

"Don't worry, Mr. Ericksen, it's a slam dunk!"

"How long will it take you to decrypt their communications from Arabic into English?" he asked.

"I believe our fastest supercomputers can reach five petaflops per second, that's five quadrillion floating-point operations per second. My best guess – probably crack it within five minutes. With Echelon II, we can handle approximately five hundred exabytes of global Internet traffic this year. To put it in perspective, Eric Schmidt, Google's CEO, once estimated back in 2003 that the total of all human knowledge created from the dawn of man to 2003 totaled five exabytes."

"Nothing like an American Trojan horse," Ericksen said and took a swig of water. "What type of countermeasures might they use during the tests?" he asked.

"Typical equipment...digital multimeter, picket RF field detector, spectrum analyzer, or any other professional gear. Nothing to worry about." The engineer coughed. "Do you have a soft drink?"

"Yes." He nodded, went to the refrigerator, and pulled out a Coke. "I'll be back with the pre-paid cellphones in a minute."

Ericksen went back to his office to retrieve Ziad's fifteen pre-paid cellphones. He returned to the conference room and gave the engineer the phones. He watched as the NSA man began configuring each cellphone's SIM card with NSA's intercept software algorithm routines. When activated by one of the cell carriers, each cellphone generated its location area identity, authentication key with the IMSI from the SIM card, and a local cellphone number. When the engineer completed his task, he walked back to Ericksen's office and gave Ziad the fifteen cellphones, who placed them into his backpack.

In the evening, he called an order of pizza from Bellagio Pizzeria and Chinese food from Wong's, both in Wilsonville Town Center. After dinner, Ericksen drove Ziad back to the motel. During the drive, Ericksen wanted some answers on Saudi Arabia's role with Al-Qaeda in Iraq. "How does it feel to kill innocent Americans?"

Ziad felt uneasy and appeared in a trance. "I never lost focus on my mission: To infiltrate Al-Qaeda and later, the Red Sea Brotherhood. I built and planted many IEDs. Killing Americans and

NATO soldiers enhanced my credibility with Al-Qaeda. It didn't take long before my actions started to numb my senses. I became one of them."

"I hate you for what you did, but I hope you can help us stop these attacks and cripple this terrorist organization."

"I hated myself for what I did, and whether I lived or died, my mission was to help defeat Khalid Al-Bustani and his Red Sea Brotherhood."

They pulled up to the motel, and Ziad got out of the vehicle. "I'll call your cell tomorrow and let you know the address of the Lincoln City rental."

As soon as Ziad entered his room, he noticed a flashing red message light on his bedside telephone stand. He picked it up and dialed the room of Juan Garcia, the alias of Abdullah Al-Suhaimy. They connected and spoke in Arabic.

Abdullah explained how he had arrived in Nogales, Arizona, through a tunnel from Mexico with one of the drug cartel members' help. He told Ziad, a Saudi student who studied at one of the local universities, would pick them up tomorrow at twelve-noon and drive to a motel near the rental. "The Saudi student knows nothing except that we're two businessmen from the Kingdom mixing business with pleasure, and will be staying on the Oregon coast for a few days of relaxation."

———

CALDWELL AND ERICKSEN went into the great room and watched *CNN* news, and later, a segment of the Food Network with Emeril Lagasse. Caldwell asked to see his master bedroom. The few times he had company, other than his relatives or very close friends, he had refused to have anyone see his bedroom. "Why do you want to see my bedroom?"

"I am just curious," she said. "Is that an unusual request?"

She followed him into his bedroom, noticed the Scandinavian-designed furniture and some seascape paintings. Then she saw the wedding photo of Ericksen and his wife. "She was beautiful. What was her name?"

"Karen." He looked at Caldwell and extended his hand and escorted her out of his bedroom.

She looked at him for several seconds. "Thanks for everything."

On the next day, Ericksen and Caldwell took off early for the drive to Lincoln City. She drove the rented Cadillac SUV, and he followed in his Chevy Silverado. He placed two surfboards in the back of his pickup. On the backseat were laptop computers and duffel bags.

Two hours later, they arrived at the Inn at Spanish Head, registered for two rooms, and brought up their luggage and laptop computers. After changing into their wetsuits, they drove to the beach. The waves were now about six to seven feet high.

They both paddled out three-hundred-yards, turned around, and began paddling toward shore. Ericksen and Caldwell matched the waves' speed when the swell caught them, got up, did floaters, and rode the wave almost to the beach before falling off. They continued for another two hours of surfing before calling it quits.

In the evening, Ericksen and Caldwell were dining out at a seafood restaurant when his cellphone rang. "Hello."

"Z speaking. Please arrive at the house on Sunday at one o'clock. The house sits on the right side of the 3600 block of Coast Drive, on a hill overlooking the ocean. Look for a tall oak private driveway sign with a bear painted on it. It will be at the bottom of the entrance leading up to the house. There is a large Oregon Duck flag hoisted alongside the front door of the house."

Caldwell took out her cellphone and called her FBI contact in Portland with an approximate address, and told them she would get the exact address in the morning. Once the task force had the address, they would implement plans for surveillance and eavesdropping.

On July 18, Caldwell returned the rented Cadillac SUV and departed from Portland to Washington, D.C. Monday morning, the 20th, she briefed Director Sullivan and Deputy Director Norstad on *Operation Avenging Eagles*. Later in the evening, she took a direct flight from Dulles to Geneva.

Chapter Forty-Five

Beltermann arrived Saturday afternoon at Portland International Airport on a flight from Houston. He reserved a Lincoln Towncar from Viskin Limo Service to drive him to Lincoln City, where he booked a room at the Chinook Winds Casino.

At 10 am Sunday morning, he called a taxi to pick him up and drive him to the executive rental home. When the driver arrived at the vacation rental, he carried two pieces of luggage to the front door, received a big tip, and drove away. Beltermann punched in the code on the lockbox outside the residence, retrieved the key, and opened the door.

Five minutes later, he took out several security detection equipment pieces and conducted a security sweep of the entire house. The house consisted of five bedrooms, a dining room off the kitchen, three bathrooms, laundry room, two-car garage, living room off the dining room with sweeping views of the ocean, and a large sitting area off the master bedroom on the third floor. He finally finished at one o'clock.

Over the past twelve hours, the FBI discovered which homes near the rental were vacant, as well as the owners' identification. They convinced the property owner next door to allow them to use his house and told him they would compensate him for lost rental revenue. They told the owner to come up with a plausible excuse for the renters from California and pay them for the inconvenience. The owner agreed to cover their expenses and put the tourists up at the Inn at Spanish Head. The FBI concurred to protect the owner's rental fee. The FBI technicians passed the house in a van and moved into the rental property.

Two FBI men were seated in the bedroom on the third floor with a view of the second-floor dining room window. They set up their laser beam technology, enabling them to lift the sounds from the house sounds next door as it bounced off the windows. The sound waves would be captured by their light-sensitive receiver, process the vibrations, and translate them into sound. Both agents were proficient in Arabic.

Ericksen arrived and parked his pickup truck along the fence. Affixed to his Chevy Silverado were stickers for the Sierra Club and the Oregon State Beavers.

He knocked on the door. Beltermann answered and greeted him. Ericksen carried a large box from the backseat of the vehicle and brought it into the house. He carried the box up to the second floor and placed it on the dining room floor next to the long table. Ziad introduced Ericksen to Abdullah.

Ericksen opened the large box and removed four laptop computers. Beltermann set up the test equipment and began testing each of the laptop computers. He removed its core components and examined them. He also ran an instrument device connected to a spectrum analyzer and glanced at the display screen. A few minutes later, he said, "All your laptops passed my test."

He looked directly into Ericksen's eyes. "How good is your encryption software program?"

"Our encryption consists of over one billion codes and uses a 256-bit classified encryption standard developed by our government with input from EyeD4Systems."

"If hackers attempt to break into your system, how secure are the templates?" Beltermann asked.

"The templates are encrypted in software and reside on one USB flash drive. When the USB drive is inserted into the USB port, the biometrics matching recognition software prompts the user to do a live palm vein optical scan log-on." He continued to explain the process to him.

Beltermann looked at Ziad and Abdullah. "Mr. Ericksen, please give us a sound understanding of your EyeD4 Comm System's full operational capabilities and levels of security so we can all understand it in depth."

"Okay." Over the next fifteen minutes, Ericksen demonstrated the system, the encryption, answers to false acceptance and false rejection rates, and the uniqueness of everyone's palm subcutaneous vein patterns.

Beltermann stood and moved closer to Ericksen. "While a person is engaged in the operation, what is to stop someone from hacking into the system?" Abdullah stepped closer to the table.

"Good question," Ericksen said. "We have built-in MILSPEC firewalls, robust intrusion and detection software, and high-level communication encryption. A hacker can't penetrate our communications."

"When the user ends their program, where does the live biometrics signature reside?"

"The templates are immediately backed up to the USB flash drive along with the encrypted files. You just put them back into your pocket or in a safe."

"Wait a minute. What if a terrorist organization or government with supercomputers attempted to penetrate the firewall?"

"Built into the firewall are powerful sensors which can calibrate the strength of an attack. If the intrusion attempts were executed by a very high degree of talent, the system would shut down."

"Excellent." Beltermann appeared to be pleased with the answers to his questions. "Wait, who made this customized laptop computer?"

"Even I don't know the manufacturer by name except I know it is made in the USA."

The doorbell rang. Abdullah answered it. The local pizza delivery person arrived at the door with two large mushroom, onion, and cheese pizzas. Abdullah brought them up to the second floor.

Everyone began eating pizza.

Twenty minutes later, Ziad enrolled Beltermann on his new laptop computer and enrolled Abdullah on his new laptop computer. Ziad functioned as the systems administrator. Unbeknown to him, Ericksen's biometrics template and authenticated ID also served as a systems administrator. It was layered deep within the NSA's Echelon II grid's bowels along with his biometrics ID signature buried within each of their encrypted USB flash drives.

Abdullah slapped Ziad's back. "Beltermann and I are going to shoot some billiards downstairs in the garage; do you want to join us?"

He looked at both men and said, "No, I need to remove your templates from your laptops and place them on your USB flash drives."

They turned and went downstairs. Ziad immediately backed up the template files to both their USB flash drives and made two additional copies each, one for Khalid and one for Ericksen.

Ziad went downstairs and gave each man his USB flash drive. "Don't lose this." He turned and looked at Ericksen. "Do you want to go for a walk along the beach?"

"Sure." When they were well out of sight of both Beltermann and Abdullah, he reached into his pocket and gave Ericksen a copy of each of their flash drives.

He turned to Ziad. "Who is Wolfgang Beltermann?"

"He served as a Stasi intelligence operative in Dresden, East Germany. He is an expert on IT security and is a major terrorist operative for Khalid."

"Once you enroll Al-Bustani's templates into his computer at his Swiss home, load them on a USB flash drive, and also get impressions of his fingerprints. Seal all of them into a package and contact Caldwell in Geneva. She'll advise you where to make the dead drop."

"I have an excellent excuse to go to Geneva. There is an Arabian breeder near the city."

"Good. What cities are they planning to hit?"

"Las Vegas and Houston. They have kept the actual targets in strict confidence. Only Khalid, Beltermann, Faisal and Abdullah know them."

I'll bet Sullivan received the targeted cities from Saudi intel and kept it on a need-to-know basis. Ericksen thought.

He studied Ziad's facial expressions. "I'll need Abdullah and Beltermann's fingerprints. Can you get them for me?"

"I'll leave their water glasses in a bag in the trash."

"How will I know who they belong to?"

"I'll mark the letter B on one and A on the other," Ziad said. The temperature reached into the high seventies with blue skies.

Ziad stopped and looked out at the ocean. "You probably don't think much of me, do you?"

"My mission isn't to pass judgment on you, but of course, I hate what you did."

"When you work for years in the shadows with the scum of the earth and are tasked to infiltrate Al-Qaeda, it is difficult at times to separate reality from fiction. All you know is to survive, provide your country with actionable intelligence to prevent attacks, and destroy the enemy."

"You've been dealt a tough hand, but now you have a chance of saving thousands of American lives."

They jogged back to the house and walked on the deck where Abdullah stood.

"When can I expect my money?"

"The second installment will be in your Swiss account tomorrow."

Ericksen nodded. "Fine."

"Khalid would like you to join him as his special guest in Gstaad on August 28 for a few days of leisure. He has another opportunity he would like to discuss with you."

"Please tell him thank you. I'll make the necessary travel arrangements soon."

Four hours later, Ericksen went downstairs, opened the front door, and noticed a black plastic bag next to the empty pizza cartons. He picked the bag up, placed it in the back of his Chevy Silverado, and drove back to the hotel.

The next morning, Ziad passed out seven pre-paid cellphones each to Abdullah and Beltermann. "You'll be using these pre-paid phones throughout the mission. All communications will be in English," Ziad said in Arabic.

"When will Khalid issue the instructions?" Abdullah asked.

"All I can tell you is Wolfgang's codename is Watchmaker, and yours is Black Stallion."

Ziad got into a taxi for the drive to the Portland International Airport.

That afternoon a town car from McDonald Custom Limo Service arrived to pick up the two terrorist leaders. Beltermann had the driver load up the luggage and place it in the trunk. He looked at the driver. "Tell your dispatch people our destination is The Marriott by the river. Would you like to make an extra three hundred dollars?"

"Of course," the driver said.

The FBI surveillance teams followed in two unmarked vehicles on the road back to Portland. One of the FBI agents heard a ring and picked up his cellphone.

"Hello. What did you find out?" The agent said.

"McDonald Custom Limo told me their destination is the Marriott Hotel on Front Street," an FBI agent said.

"Thanks."

An hour and forty-five minutes later, the driver went several blocks out of his way and pulled up to the Benson Hotel's front entrance. The driver unloaded their luggage, and Abdullah and Beltermann carried it in themselves. They went directly to the elevators and punched in the lower level floor. When they got off the elevator, they turned right and walked down the parking garage corridor.

One FBI agent called the front desk and confirmed two men entered the hotel with their bags and walked directly to the elevators. "Teams two and three, get to the Benson immediately," the FBI lead agent said.

Abdullah spotted the blue Ford SUV with Nevada plates and the driver from the Nevada sleeper cell, who stood alongside the vehicle. Beltermann noticed a gray Chevrolet SUV with Texas plates and the driver from the Texas sleeper cell inside behind the wheel. They entered the SUVs with tinted windows, changed shirts, put on baseball caps, left the garage, and drove to the I-5 ramp heading south towards Salem.

The FBI agents finally entered the hotel lobby and checked with the registration desk. Recognizing that the men hadn't registered, they went down to the parking garage. But it was too late for the FBI Counterterrorism squad. A missed opportunity.

Thirty minutes later, both Beltermann and Abdullah arrived at the La Quinta Hotel in Wilsonville. They entered the cell operators' rooms, shaved their beards off, and changed clothes. Abdullah's secure cellphone rang. "Hello."

"When I email you the date for the meeting place with your contact, the actual date will be the day before. Tell Watchmaker too," Khalid said.

The sleeper cell operators paid for their rooms with two counterfeit credit cards. Both men and their respective drivers left the motel and headed south on I-5.

Ziad checked in for his American Airlines flight to Houston and placed his new custom-designed laptop computer in baggage along with his personal luggage. Khalid's laptop computer was a carry-on. Upon arrival in Houston, he would transfer to another flight to Zurich.

GENEVA, SWITZERLAND

Ziad walked to the Botanical Gardens near the lake. After viewing the various plants and flowers, he saw an empty bench not far away. Caldwell monitored his movements and waited for his next move. He took a sandwich out of his brown paper bag and orange juice to drink. Ten minutes later, he finished his meal and threw the bag into a trash bin next to the bench. Ziad looked both ways, gently opened his briefcase, placed a sealed zip-lock bag containing an empty glass and a

USB flash drive into a paper bag, and hid it behind a large rock next to the bench. He stood and left, taking a stroll along the promenade.

Caldwell strolled over to the bench, sat down, looked to see if anyone was in sight, retrieved the paper bag, and placed it in her backpack.

Chapter Forty-Seven

MARBELLA, SPAIN

On a hillside overlooking Marbella, Spain, in the Sierra Blanca section of town, Khalid stood on the veranda of his fifteen thousand square foot mansion, enjoying the ambiance and tranquility his Spanish vacation home offered to him and his family. His mega-yacht, *The Dolphin Prince*, was docked only a few miles away at the marina in Puerto Banos.

Quite a few celebrities, artists, wealthy jet-setters, and aristocrats spent their summers frolicking in this sun-drenched resort town in the Andalusian Province on the Costa del Sol. The whitewashed buildings dotted this area, a remembrance of the Moorish architectural influence dating back to the Iberian Peninsula invasion in 711.

Khalid had spent every summer of his youth at his family's villa near here, achieving Spanish proficiency. The mansion was built in 2005. It had two levels, ten bedrooms and bathrooms, two game rooms, an indoor and a large outdoor pool, a large gymnasium, kitchen, living room, dining room, family room, cinema room, five fireplaces, and a beautiful garden on ten acres of land.

On this day, Khalid had brought two of his three wives to spend all of August at the mansion. Their six children, from two of his wives, ranged in age from eight to thirty. They enjoyed all kinds of activities, notably horseback rides at a nearby stable. His favorite wife, Mona, had celebrated her twenty-fifth birthday a week earlier. She had two children from him, ages two and five, back in his Swiss summer home in Zug. Khalid had two of his Arabian horses boarded at an Andalusian ranch owned by an old friend. He loved to ride one of the Arabian geldings whose sire was Falcon Dancer.

The temperature rose to a comfortable eighty-five degrees, and the mild wind came from the northeast. The refreshing, sweet aroma from the jasmine trees had a calming effect as it blew onto the veranda and filtered into the large living room.

Khalid picked up his secure cellphone and called.

"Hello, Iron Fist here," Dawkins answered.

"I need someone to take care of a little business for me. My friend lives in Falls Church, Virginia. He needs to leave this world."

"Where and when?" Dawkins asked.

"He'll be traveling south on Highway 95 on August 28 for a birthday party, somewhere near Fredericksburg, Virginia. I'll provide you more details soon." Khalid then hung up.

Sitting down on a large couch upholstered in leopard skins were three men, all dressed casually. They were all flag officers of the Saudi Army, Navy, and Air Force. His chief asset, Colonel Al-Gosaibi, sat near the fireplace. Silence permeated the room for several seconds while their eyes were all glued to Khalid's face as he spoke in Arabic.

"Within the next seven weeks, another major event will devastate the Great Satan – we will no longer tolerate the West's exploitation of our oil resources or culture. Nor will we ever tolerate their obsession with any future occupations of Muslim lands. Soon, we will begin a plan to overthrow the Royal Family, thereby eliminating their corrupt and nepotistic ways."

Everyone responded, "Allahu Akbar. Allahu Akbar."

Chapter Forty-Seven

Abdullah opened up his laptop at a table in Seattle's Best Coffee Shop within a Borders Bookstore in Las Vegas, Nevada. He loaded his USB flash drive in the port and started the palm vein pattern biometrics log-on at ten in the morning. He heard a ping denoting the arrival of an encrypted email from Khalid.

Go to the Venetian Hotel's coffee shop on Friday morning at ten-thirty, and look for a man wearing a New York Yankees baseball hat. The man will hold a gold coin in his left hand. Ask him if the seat next to him is taken. He'll say no. You say Muchas Gracias. The man will say Falcon Dancer, and you'll say Black Stallion. His authentication reply will be Casino. He is your Las Vegas lead operator. Over the next several weeks, he'll help you survey the targets with his two Alpha team members and get you essential maps and schematics. You'll also meet his two Bravo team members, who'll also provide you information on our other target. Keep your eyes open like the Falcon. Best regards, Falcon Dancer.

Abdullah sent a reply to Falcon Dancer. "Confirmed, Black Stallion."

BELTERMANN TOOK a sip of his coffee at the Starbucks Coffee Shop in Houston's Galleria. He looked at his cellphone, which read twelve o'clock in the afternoon, August 3, opened up his laptop, placed his USB flash drive in the port, and activated his log-on with his live palm vein pattern biometrics in real-time to match the template. He heard a ping and clicked on the encrypted email.

Go to the Deerbrook Mall on Friday at 10:00 am and get a cup of coffee at Borders. Look for a man wearing a University of Texas baseball hat. He'll hold his eyeglasses in his right hand. Ask him if you can sit down at his table. He'll reply – only if you're a Longhorn fan, and you'll say, Watchmaker. He'll answer with his code: Cowboy. He's your lead operator in Houston. Over the next several weeks, he'll help you survey our two targets. He has two teams, Charlie and Delta. Keep your eyes open like the Falcon. Best Regards, Falcon Dancer.

Beltermann sent a reply to Falcon Dancer. "Confirmed, Watchmaker."

NATIONAL SECURITY AGENCY, FT. MEADE, MD

The NSA, the computer engineering manager, keyed in the message on his computer screen:

Subject: EYES ONLY – TOP SECRET!

TO: Directors Campbell; Sullivan; Geiger; and Secretary of Homeland Security Lucas.

"Captured the I.P. address of Abdullah's and Khalid's laptop computers. Activated backdoor operations. A few minutes later, we received Beltermann's and Khalid's biometrics templates, their key encryption software, and decoding the encryption. Will send you the completed intercepts within the next ten to twenty minutes."

MCLEAN, VIRGINIA

Geiger, Lucas, Campbell, Sullivan, and staff were at the National Counterintelligence Center.

"We've identified the cities: Las Vegas and Houston," Campbell said.

"We updated drawings of what Abdullah and Beltermann might look like without their beards," Geiger said.

Campbell leaned forward. "GPS revealed Abdullah used his laptop at a Borders bookstore in Las Vegas, and Beltermann received his email at Starbucks in the Galleria Mall in Houston."

"I've alerted the FBI's HRT (the Hostage Rescue Team). Homeland Security and the Department of Energy will begin preparations. Once we get intel on the targets in those cities, we'll be able to move in fast."

"Steve, any luck with the Kremlin on Ryzhkov and Kupchenko?" asked Geiger.

"They claim they are rogue operators, and there isn't a trace of them anywhere," Campbell said.

"Sure," countered Sullivan sarcastically.

Chapter Forty-Eight

Ryzhkov bribed one nuclear physicist and two lab technicians in order to smuggle plutonium and uranium out of the nuclear power station in Novosibirsk, Siberia. The particles were packed into lead-lined steel pipes and fastened in a trigger mechanism within each of the four suitcases. Each suitcase had enough fissionable material when activated by a clock to generate about one kiloton of TNT.

They were carefully transported by truck to Minsk. They arrived on August 8 at an offsite location where Kupchenko's men unloaded the truck and placed them on another vehicle on August 9 to Leipzig, Germany. They arrived at the Duppelstein factory on August 10.

Four employees tied to Kupchenko's organized crime group received the goods that evening and worked into the early hours packing them. The suitcases were loaded into four ice chest-freezer cartons. Each carton measured 61" L x 29" W x 35" H and weighing 225 pounds. When adding each 55-pound suitcase, plus the lead and other materials to throw off any explosive detection machines, the total weight listed on the carton label on the outside was 308 pounds. The C-4 packed into the other twelve ice chest-freezer cartons was also protected by lead, steel weights, and other materials that matched the weight of the four ice chest-freezer cartons loaded with the suitcases.

They were part of an order calling for sixteen ice chest-freezers and ten side-by-side deluxe refrigerators measuring 36" L x 30" W x 72" H. Each weighed 285 pounds, was loaded on a pallet, and were placed on 40" x 48" pallets with the designated bill of lading and shipping manifests and loaded onto a forty-foot ocean container. On August 12, they were placed on a railcar headed for Hamburg harbor with the arrival of August 13. Their ultimate designation on the documentation listed Schultz Furniture and Appliance Store in New Orleans, LA.

Chapter Forty-Nine

BANQUE MATTHIAS REITER

Jacobson and Scharz approached the entrance to the entrance to the building at 6:00 pm on August 10.

"Please slip your IDs through the slot," said the security supervisor in French."

Their IDs listed them as employees of Berthier Les Services de Conciergerie. After reviewing their IDs, he opened the front door to let them enter and gave their IDs back.

"Your manager said you replaced Pierre and Dominick. Where did they go?"

"They were transferred to one of the watch companies in Bienne." They walked down the hall and picked up some janitorial supplies, a vacuum cleaner, a small ladder, dusting cloths, and a cart to collect waste material. They worked their way up to the fifth floor via the service elevator and entered Reiter's office. Jacobson first installed a key logger. He stood on the ladder and mounted a covert video camera with an audio recorder inside a recessed section of the vent in the ceiling. It had a clear view of Reiter's desk and computer. He also managed to place another covert video camera in a vent in the corner that faced Reiter when he sat in his chair.

Just as Jacobson climbed down from the ladder, they heard someone walking down the hall. They started to empty the trash into a bag connected to the cleaning cart. They closed the door and locked Reiter's office.

They saw the bank security supervisor wave his hand, walk down the hall, and push the elevator button. Jacobson and Scharz continued to clean the remaining offices and left at eight-thirty.

TWO DAYS LATER

Scharz and Jacobson re-entered Reiter's office. Jacobson powered up Reiter's desktop computer. The computer screen asked for a password, and he keyed in Matterhorn 55. The desktop icons appeared. He clicked on programs and scrolled down until he reached BMR client accounts and clicked. A file listing of private numbered accounts came up, the first three letters BMR, seven numbers, the JR/1 designation of wealth manager who manages the account at that bank office. Then came activities, balances, and dates in Swiss francs, and in parentheses appeared the word File plus a number symbol and the number.

A review of the folder showed that Reiter apparently had responsibility for 250 private numbered accounts with total assets of two billion US dollars. He had ten assistants who managed most of the accounts, leaving Reiter personally handling fifty, with total assets of $750 million. The bank's total revenues exceeded over thirty billion dollars.

Jacobson downloaded the information onto the flash drive. He removed the video camera and audio recorder from the vent. Then they cleaned the rooms and left the bank one hour later.

Chapter Fifty

Sullivan and Lucas sat in box seats two rows behind first base at the Orioles Park at Camden Yards, and seated behind them were four members of their security detail. The game, featuring the Oakland Athletics against the Baltimore Orioles, started at 7:05 pm. Another security detail was one hundred feet behind their box seats. The teams were part of the Agency's Special Activities Division.

Director Sullivan had spent the last twenty-nine-years with the Agency. Lucas developed a friendship with Sullivan in 2002 when he became the Under Secretary of Defense for Intelligence, after retiring from the Pentagon, as the Defense Intelligence Agency Director.

The temperature was enjoyable for the start of the night game, seventy-five degrees. In the top of the fourth inning, the Athletics' Landon Powell hit a home run.

"Thatta boy," said Lucas. He gave Sullivan a jab at his right arm. "Maybe the Athletics will win this game."

Sullivan chuckled. "We'll have to see, won't we?"

Lucas's secure cellphone vibrated. He pulled it out from his pants pocket. "Hello."

A few seconds later. "Sure. I'll tell Mom you'll be home next week. I'll call you a little later."

"Must be your son."

"He graduates next year from North Carolina and still hasn't made up his mind what he wants to do."

Sullivan said, "You shouldn't worry. He'll figure it out one of these days."

"I wanted him to take ROTC and become an officer like your son Ryan, but he told me he has no interest in fighting stupid wars." He looked at Sullivan and placed his hand on his shoulder. "I know how proud you were of him."

Sullivan nodded. "There's not a day that goes by without thinking about him. It's been four years since Ryan and his teammates were killed by an IED in Anbar Province." He tensed up. "IEDs killed over 1,000 American soldiers and wounded over 13,000 because we sent them into combat with unprotected Humvees. My son was one of them. One of the gutsy things Secretary Helms demanded when he took office was the production of the Mine Ambush Protected Trucks (MRAPs) in 2007. But the invasion and occupation of Iraq will go down as one of the dumbest foreign policy decisions ever made by an American President and his administration."

"Bill, you're wrong. We had to get rid of Saddam because he threatened the flow of oil throughout the Persian Gulf, and stability in the region."

Sullivan rolled his eyes and shrugged his shoulders. "Give me a break. You know our intelligence assessments proved Saddam had no ties to Al-Qaeda or possessed nuclear weapons. The administration fabricated the intelligence and perpetuated this propaganda so the mainstream media would buy into it and sell it to the American people. Their actions became a game-changer after they occupied the country and dismantled the government's ministries and military. It caused the resurrection of Iran, the leader of terror in the world. Besides Iran, the real winners were China and Putin's Russian Federation."

Lucas motioned with his right hand, "I agree with you on one point, Saddam had no links to Al-Qaeda. But the administration wanted to establish a democratically-elected government in Iraq to encourage other Arab governments that democracies can be attainable."

"Hank, sorry, but that is pure bullshit! The administration at the time didn't understand tribal rivalries. Shi'a versus Sunni." He lifted his Bud Light beer and took a swig. "The two reasons the administration pushed for the invasion and occupation rested on the stupid belief regime change would strengthen the US Middle East policy position, and assist the military-industrial complex with very lucrative business contracts."

"I disagree," Hank said.

Sullivan took a deep breath. "We need to cut the bullshit, relax, and enjoy the ballgame."

Chapter Fifty-One

R yzhkov propped his body up against the headboard at the Brenner Guesthaus in Hamburg, Germany. He took a drag on his cigarette and put the cigarette back in the tray. The room had a musty odor. He thought *what does one expect when staying in a seedy guesthouse near the harbor?*

He held his secure cellphone to his ear and spoke slowly: "Watchmaker, the shipment is on the *Gudrun Maersk*, departing Hamburg Monday, on August 17. The arrival date at the Port of Baltimore is Tuesday, August 25. The international freight forwarder, Bach and Tittl, prepared the shipping documents: commercial invoices, shipper's export declaration, and a bill of lading. You will find two cartons of ice chest-freezers on each pallet, eight pallets total. Another order called for ten refrigerators packed on pallets. The best brands are ice chest-freezers. I'll email you the information."

"The BIC code is JARZ 362859. The manufacturers' code is outside the forty-foot container: Duppelstein GmbH, Leipzig, Germany. The destination is Schultz Furniture Store, New Orleans, LA. The customhouse broker has a storage facility near the harbor called Dundalk Marine Terminal. All containers can be subjected to portal screening monitors that employ sensors to pick up Gamma radiation." He coughed and continued, "Once customs clears the contents of the load, they'll place the containers in the storage facility on Thursday, August 27. Heimlich Transport will pick them up on Friday morning, August 28. They have reserved the appointment for 8 am. You'll be in control when the truck leaves the terminal."

Ryzhkov picked up his glass of vodka, took a hefty swig, and with his left hand, picked up a cigarette and took a long drag, "Good luck."

"Thank you," said Beltermann.

Chapter Fifty-Two

HANK LUCAS'S RESIDENCE

The Lucas Estate was fronted on Old Dominion Road in McLean, Virginia. They had five acres of land surrounded by an eight-foot-high steel fence connected to a four-inch-thick steel electronic gate. Two security officers monitored the entrance to the gate from their black SUVs. They wore ear mics, and their Glock pistols were lying on the passenger seat. There was a guardhouse inside the entrance, where two heavily armed security officers monitored the premises and opened the gate to guests after they presented a passcode to the officers.

The square footage exceeded ten thousand and comprised seven bedrooms, seven baths, an elegant home entertainment room, family room, game room, living room, dining room, large kitchen, and a study. In the foyer of the two-level mansion, standing off to the door's right to the house stood additional security officers.

Henry Lucas had grown up in Santa Barbara, California. His father built custom homes, and his mother managed the household and raised both he and his two sisters. After graduating from West Point in 1974, he had received a commission as a 2nd Lieutenant in the Army and retired as a major general after twenty-seven years of service.

In 2003, President Ridgeway appointed him to Under Secretary of Defense for Intelligence, overseeing the DIA, NSA, Defense Security Service, and the National Geospatial-Intelligence Agency. He left that agency in 2006 and became an executive vice-president of government affairs for a major defense aviation company. After spending two years there, he was appointed Secretary of Homeland Security by the President.

Sullivan, Geiger, and Lucas were playing poker with three of Lucas's friends. Lucas and his wife, Charlotte, had been married for almost thirty years. When Sullivan arrived with his wife Ann, Charlotte took her into the family room to join three other wives for an evening of bridge.

At nine o'clock, the grandfather clock's chime played Beethoven's Ninth Symphony and struck nine times. Sullivan looked at Lucas, "I didn't realize you were a fan of classical music."

"Beethoven's my favorite composer. When our kids were growing up, they bombarded us with the noise they called music. Thank God we can now enjoy classical music in peace."

At eleven o'clock, the gentlemen finished their game, stood up, and waited to join their wives. Hank and his wife hugged their friends and said their goodbyes. Geiger and Sullivan joined Lucas in his study. Sullivan couldn't help but be impressed with Lucas's large room. There was a strong Japanese influence with pictures of Samurai warriors in battle. He had one photo of being awarded a trophy in a karate tournament. Another photo showed him with Chuck Huntington sparring during a karate event.

On the wall of the study hung a picture of Lucas in his military uniform and three officers standing on the tarmac at Bagram Air Field. The two-star general smiled in the photo.

"What year were you in Afghanistan?" Geiger said.

Lucas immediately answered, his square jaw jutted out like a commander to a subordinate at roll call. "I spent two weeks touring Afghan bases in April 2002."

Sullivan remembered Lucas when he had headed up the Defense Intelligence Agency in the 2001–2002 period. "Did you know Colonel Dawkins?"

He calmly leaned his head toward Sullivan. "Yes. I briefly met him on my tour and in the following year in Iraq when I became the Under Secretary of Defense for Intelligence. He supported the Office for Iraqi Reconstruction and Humanitarian Assistance."

Geiger stepped closer to Lucas and paused. He glanced at the general's picture on the wall.

"Did Dawkins do a good job?"

Lucas's face tensed up with the question. "The DoD appeared satisfied with his work. Personally, I never liked the man. Why do you ask?"

"We're investigating a huge fraud and corruption case that took place between 2002 and 2005. Many military and State Department contractors were involved in billions of dollars of fraud and bribes. The auditors did a piss-poor job. Dawkins, along with a few other names, surfaced, and the government will soon bring him in to help with our investigation," Geiger said.

"I heard he retired and joined Chuck Huntington's private security firm and made a bundle of cash," Sullivan said.

Lucas nodded. "Well, it sounds like the man had good connections. Glad someone else is making money instead of Blackwater."

Chapter Fifty-Three

Abdullah and the Albanian, code name Casino, drove to the Las Vegas airport. After parking their vehicle, they entered the terminal, surveyed the ticket counter area on the first floor, and went up the escalator to the shops.

An hour later, they met two men who were part of the Alpha Team at a coffee shop off Flamingo Blvd.

Two hours later, they drove to the Las Vegas Convention Center and met two men from Bravo Team, and walked around the convention center complex.

HOUSTON, TEXAS

Beltermann met the Chechen, code-name Cowboy. They drove to the George H. Bush International Airport to conduct recon at the airport. They entered the terminal and walked throughout the public areas of the airport. They met two men from the Charlie Team at a coffee shop near the airport.

Two hours later, they met two men in a Houston bar wearing Bauer Transportation uniforms. They came from Delta Team. They talked briefly and then drove out to the Galaxy Oil Company's refinery, checking out razor wire fencing, guard towers, and the facility's general layout.

———

AT SIX AT NIGHT, Abdullah sat down in Starbucks in Henderson, Nevada. He drank tea and read an email from Khalid. Abdullah replied to the email, shut down his laptop, and took out *The New York Times* newspaper to read. Thirty minutes later, he left the coffee shop. In the parking lot, Abdullah saw two vehicles with men dressed in sports casual clothing pull up. He got back into his car and waited. The men entered Starbucks, and five minutes later, they left with their coffee. He noticed all the men had something peculiar bulging beneath their sports shirts, which were draped over their waists. They got into their vehicles and took off. Abdullah thought *They all had concealed guns. Is this a coincidence, or are they following me?*

———

AT EIGHT-THIRTY IN THE EVENING, Beltermann activated the computer through his biometrics log-on while seated at Starbucks at the Galleria Mall in Houston. He sent Abdullah an encrypted email bstallion @ planetearth.com:

Finished the last phase of research and will go over the final plans with the team this weekend. Watchmaker.

Then he sent an email to Khalid at fdancer @ swisstelecom.ch

Per your instructions, all targets have been analyzed and evaluated for efficiencies and capabilities with teams. Watchmaker.

Chapter Fifty-Four

GENEVA, SWITZERLAND

E ricksen arrived at Geneva International Airport on the 28th at 1:30 pm on British Airways flight #726 from London. After retrieving his luggage and cleared customs, he proceeded to the passenger arrival lobby and took a taxi to the Swissôtel's Metropole Hotel.

Jurgen Reiter ushered him into his fifth-floor executive suite office at 3:30 pm. "How are you doing these days, Monsieur Ericksen?"

"Fine, thank you. And you, Mr. Reiter?"

"Life is good." Reiter escorted him to a leather chair across from where he sat. "Would you like some coffee or tea?"

"Coffee please."

He picked up his intercom: "Please bring Mr. Ericksen a cup of coffee." Ericksen took a drink of coffee from a Banque Matthias Reiter mug. "Well, what can I do for you?"

"I would like to check my account."

Reiter attempted to check Ericksen's numbered account on the computer, but it froze. "Shit, something is wrong." He stood up.

"Please wait here. I will check your file and make a copy for you." He left his office.

Ericksen thought *Jacobson told me he would try to penetrate Reiter's computer system. Perhaps he planted a bug in Reiter's computer.*

Five minutes later, Reiter returned with a copy of the most recent activity. "You have two million dollars in your account." He handed the copy to Ericksen.

"Thank you."

An hour later, he entered Caldwell's office. She gave him a hug. "We're working on a sensitive black operation. Besides our primary task, our team gained access to Jurgen Reiter's computer attempting to collect evidence against key Americans involved in fraud, corruption, and tax evasion. One of the targeted individuals is your old JSOC Commander, Shane Dawkins. Unfortunately, we can't link the numbered accounts to any official names of people or companies. More than likely, these Americans have set up holding companies in other private offshore banks."

Ericksen nodded and kept calm.

"When you met with Reiter to open your numbered account, what was his demeanor in his office?"

"Initially, I didn't meet him in his executive office. He escorted me to his conference room and told me to sit toward the front of the table. He excused himself for a few minutes. When he came back, he sat across from me."

"Conference room?"

"Yes."

"Anything unusual about the conference room."

"I can't recall...just a nice conference room."

GSTAAD, SWITZERLAND

Ericksen and Caldwell arrived at the Chateau Rosenberg at seven in the evening. The valet parked his Audi rental while the bellman brought their luggage to the lobby's registration area. The front-desk manager handed Ericksen two room keys, "We hope you find your stay at Chateau Rosenberg most enjoyable. Mr. Al-Bustani reserved an elegant suite, especially for you."

"I'm sure I will."

The bellman escorted them up to their suite. Ericksen noticed two bottles of Carlsberg beer in the ice bucket, a bottle of Pinot Noir from Oregon, and a card.

"Please join me and several of my colleagues for dinner at eight in the main dining room, Khalid."

He heard a knock on the door. He looked through the door viewer and opened the door.

"Hello." A beautiful, tall blonde woman appeared.

"I'm Svetlana, compliments of Mr. Al-Bustani. I'll be your companion during the time you're here," she said in English with a Russian accent.

"I don't think my girlfriend would approve."

"Honey, did you say something?" asked Caldwell.

The Russian woman heard a woman reply and left abruptly.

Sitting around the dinner table were Ericksen, Caldwell, Khalid's call girl, Moritz's girlfriend, and Ziad. Khalid glanced at Caldwell and turned to Ericksen, "I didn't know you were bringing a lovely lady. Elizabeth, what brings you to Switzerland?"

She turned to Khalid, "I work for Prentice and Aubert, an executive search firm in Geneva, and Mark's company has retained us to conduct a search for a european general manager."

"How's the search going?"

Ericksen interrupted, "Elizabeth has scheduled three candidates for me to interview on Monday in Geneva."

"You certainly have good taste in selecting professionals," Khalid said.

Ericksen nodded. "Thank you."

After dinner, both he and Caldwell returned to their suite. She swept the room for bugs and detected two bugs, one located in the light fixture on the ceiling and the other inside the vent on the wall.

Caldwell pointed them out to him. They went into the bathroom, and she turned the faucet on to drown out the sound.

He asked, "Do you think they suspect us?"

"I doubt it."

"Is our cozy arrangement standard operating procedure during clandestine operations?"

"This is the first time," she said. Ericksen nodded and smiled.

She entered the bathroom and changed into a nightgown. He went into the bathroom, closed the door, and took a shower. He opened the door wearing a t-shirt and boxer shorts.

Caldwell pointed to a bug. "I've got a headache. Let's make love tomorrow."

"Good night, honey." Ericksen thought she was the complete package: brains, beauty, and mental toughness. He tried to focus on going to sleep, but sleeping next to Caldwell kept his mind focused on one thing and one thing only: he wanted her right now.

KHALID'S SUITE

Khalid plopped on the couch in his suite. He took a drink of orange juice.

"I believe Ziad knew Omar followed him and called me the moment he lost him," Moritz reported.

Khalid's face tightened, and his eyes narrowed. "You can't be serious. Abdullah and Bin Laden have total trust in Ziad. Furthermore, Ziad has demonstrated countless times his loyalty to me. Omar proved to be a traitor. So don't bother me with your paranoid tendencies."

Moritz and Khalid were control freaks. As head of his protective security detail, Moritz enjoyed being in the loop on Khalid's major security issues, but he also knew Khalid liked to compartmentalize operations. Khalid shared the big picture with only his son Faisal and with Abdullah.

Chapter Fifty-Five

FREDRICKSBURG, VIRGINIA

Randy served as a private contractor for Dawkins at Stealth Dynamics. He had an excellent background: ten years as a SAS British Special Forces operative. He had proved to be a reliable hitman for Dawkins, especially when he needed to terminate individuals. Dawkins had contracted him to warn Ericksen with two well-placed shots on the jogging trail in Hyde Park. Randy only wanted to know who needed to be killed, details on the target, and the job fee. He would do the rest without leaving any speck of evidence linking him to the murder or murders.

Marwan headed south on Highway 95. As he passed the Telegraph Road overpass in Fredericksburg, Virginia, Randy had a clear target. He fired three shots from the brush on the west side of the freeway, and the first shot penetrated the windshield and hit Marwan in the forehead. The second and third shots pierced the left front and rear tires, spinning the Ford Taurus out of control. Marwan's vehicle went off the road and hit several trees in the brushy area.

The FBI undercover officers in the vehicle two hundred yards behind slowed down as they approached the Ford Taurus. They got out of their car and saw Marwan's bloody body trapped between the seat and the steering wheel.

One of the FBI officers put on a pair of latex gloves and checked his pulse. He couldn't feel a pulse. Marwan died at 9:00 pm.

In the meantime, Randy had a good two minutes when the FBI checked Marwan's vital signs. He ran back to his rental SUV, which the trees off the road partially blocked from view. Randy started the ignition, drove the car up Telegraph Road to Russell Road, headed south to Hot Patch Road and Montezuma Avenue before stopping at a shopping center. He got out of his vehicle, walked into Starbucks, purchased a latte, took a seat, and enjoyed his drink.

He took out his secure cellphone and texted Dawkins:

"Yes, happy to report the George project is completed. Randy."

After several minutes he stood up and left the coffee shop, heading north on Highway 95.

Abdullah finished an email to Khalid and noticed a beautiful woman seated two tables from him at Starbucks in Henderson, Nevada. He was married, and his two wives lived in Jeddah along with four children. Being a dedicated terrorist operations leader left little time for romancing a woman. The woman had long black hair and the look of an Egyptian model. She couldn't be more than thirty years of age.

He decided to stay and see if she noticed him. After twenty minutes, he realized she only looked twice in his direction, and he couldn't take a chance of approaching her yet. He left Starbucks, opened the door to his car, and decided to wait for a few minutes. While seated, he saw two vehicles approach the parking lot. Four men in suits got out and entered the coffee shop. *These men look like the last four he saw,* he thought.

A few minutes later, they walked back to their vehicles with their coffee. Again, Abdullah noticed concealed guns under their shirts. He followed one of the cars at a safe distance. A short distance later, both vehicles pulled up at the FBI office on Lake Mead Blvd. in Las Vegas. Abdullah passed the office and drove back to his Las Vegas motel.

After entering his room, he took out his secure cellphone. "We've been compromised. Either Marwan or Ericksen set us up."

"Marwan double-crossed us and paid the ultimate price. He is dead. Go to Plan B," Khalid said.

Abdullah took out his pre-paid cellphone to call. "Watchmaker, this is Black Stallion. The Sheikh ordered us to go to Plan B. Use only the pre-paid cellphones from this moment forward. Please confirm."

"Confirmed."

Chapter Fifty-Six

GSTAAD, SWITZERLAND

Ericksen and Caldwell hiked one thousand meters up a trail to a scenic vista in Les Diablerets in the Bernese Alps. The alpine air smelled fresh and crisp. The flowers were in bloom as they walked along the hiking trail and came upon a wooden log that overlooked the mountains. He liked Caldwell and wished they could develop a personal relationship, but based on their operations' sensitive nature, he had to maintain a professional one.

"The NSA intercepted a call between Abdullah and Khalid. He told him their operation had been compromised," she said.

Khalid might make an attempt on my life, and Elizabeth could be a target as well, he thought.

"Do you think he suspects me?" asked Ericksen.

"I doubt it.

"I hope you're right."

He glanced at her sparkling eyes. "I've never met a woman spook before. Where's home?"

"You might say I'm a country girl from Idaho."

"How did the CIA recruit you?"

She looked at him and thought to herself, *how much should I tell him?* "They recruited me right after I graduated from Stanford. I originally planned to be a high school history teacher. You never know when opportunity will knock on your door."

"This is none of my business, but are you in a relationship?"

She put her head down for a moment and then looked up at him. "Mark, in many ways, I can empathize with you on your loss. I lost a dear person I loved two years ago. He served in the Idaho National Guard. An IED killed him near Ramadi."

"I'm sorry."

She nodded. "That's life."

"That mess in Iraq has to go down as the biggest American foreign policy disaster in history. For the administration to lie to the American people about Saddam's nuclear weapons program and try to link him to Al-Qaeda without proof is criminal."

"You're mistaken. The president had no choice but to invade Iraq. Saddam killed so many of his people without blinking an eye. He had designs on invading other Middle Eastern countries."

"That's bullshit. We invaded Iraq to get rid of Saddam and cut oil deals with their new puppets."

Caldwell tensed up. "We had to maintain the stability of the Middle East flow of oil. Our economic and national security interests were being threatened by this madman…we had no choice but to invade.

"Elizabeth, we've paid too high a price for this pre-emptive invasion. We've lost over four-thousand American soldiers, hundreds of thousands suffered both physical and mental wounds, not to mention the millions of Iraqis who fled their country, nor the thousands of innocent Iraqi lives we wasted. The cost of this war in Iraq alone exceeds one or two trillion dollars. That's money we could have used in our country to rebuild our infrastructure: bridges, roads, schools, our electric grid and most importantly, generate more jobs," said Ericksen.

"I suppose you think we made a mistake in going into Afghanistan too?"

"We had the world behind us when we went into Afghanistan. Our mission was to rout Al-Qaeda and the Taliban from power and leave the region. However, once we had Bin Laden cornered at Tora Bora, the administration didn't want us to capture or kill him because it would have impacted their future agenda, Operation Iraq."

"Didn't the Congress approve the pre-emptive invasion of Iraq?" said Elizabeth.

"Those wimps caved. They probably had their palms greased by the lobbyists and defense contractors. After all, isn't this the way a career politician gets re-elected, exchange promises for campaign contributions?"

"I can't believe it, but I agree with something you just said."

"I hope someday we can elect leaders who have the wisdom, integrity, and backbone to stand up and be counted, like a Harry Truman or a Teddy Roosevelt. But I'm not holding my breath," said Ericksen.

"Right now, our challenge is to prevent another terrorist attack." She stood up, brushed off her shorts, and turned to him. "Let's drop the conversation. It's apparent you're a liberal."

"You're mistaken. I'm a hawk on defense when it truly is in our national interest."

"Really!" She retorted.

"Elizabeth, both parties are sucking the life out of America. I'm an independent and a progressive at heart." He thought she had been brainwashed by all of the right-wing, neo-con propaganda, but he still respected and liked her a lot.

———

AFTER A DELICIOUS AUSTRALIAN lamb dinner accompanied by superb French wine, the party moved into the cocktail lounge, seated around a table Khalid hosted for his guests, Moritz and his lady friend, Ericksen, and Caldwell. Khalid and Moritz drank orange juice while he and Caldwell enjoyed margaritas.

A band played soft rock. Moritz signaled to his lady friend to dance. "Come join us, Mark." They all stood up and moved to the dance floor.

Kupchenko and Ryzhkov stood by the bar when Khalid spotted them and walked toward them. Delgado entered the bar area and took a seat fifteen feet from them.

"I'm ready for a good shot of vodka," Ryzhkov said.

Khalid turned to him and Ryzhkov and said, "You deserve it. We wired the $8 million to your Geneva bank, and in a few weeks, you'll receive the balance."

"The nukes were picked up and are en route to Houston as we speak," Ryzhkov said.

"Good. We're on schedule."

Ericksen and Caldwell danced to the Eagles' hit song *Desperado*. He pulled her closer to his body, and she responded to the warmth of his body. His erection brushed against her body as she put her arms around him and closed her eyes. A few moments later, she opened her eyes, looked into his eyes, and they kissed.

They returned to the table. "Please excuse us, but we're going to call it a night. Ciao!"

They walked toward the lobby, and Ryzhkov looked at her from the bar. He turned to Khalid. "I know her. Her name is Betty Nichols."

"You must be mistaken. Her name is Elizabeth Caldwell, and she is a guest of one of my business partners."

"It's Nichols. She worked at the American embassy in Berlin. They listed her official position as a political attaché, but she took her marching orders from the CIA."

"CIA!" Khalid said as his face flushed with rage. *Shit, Abdullah had been right; it was Ericksen, not Marwan,* he thought.

"Ericksen must be a spy too. We have a safe house about eight kilometers south of Zurich," said Ryzhkov.

"Abduct those CIA pigs and find out what they know. Then kill them!"

"With pleasure."

———

ERICKSEN SHOWERED and entered the bedroom with a towel draped over his muscular body.

Caldwell looked at him, appreciating the view of water droplets cascading down his well-defined abs. Her heart rate sped up. She motioned to him and lifted the covers with her left hand, exposing her well-shaped nude body. "Mark, would you like to join me?"

He smiled from ear to ear, observing and grinning as he strolled over to the bed. "So you're a redhead."

After turning off the light on the nightstand, he slid under the sheets and slid his body over hers. They kissed passionately and made love.

Chapter Fifty-Seven

Beltermann and two members of his Charlie Team pulled their vehicles close to the truck stop off Highway 20 in Brandon, Mississippi. The driver parked the Heimlich Transport truck. When he finished his dinner, he walked back to the truck.

Beltermann walked toward the truck, and as he moved closer to the driver, he pulled out his handgun and slammed the butt of the gun over the driver's head. The driver dropped to the side of the truck unconscious. One of the Charlie Team operatives took his keys, jumped into the truck, turned on the ignition, and drove back on the highway.

Beltermann and the other two operatives followed in two vehicles. As they drew closer to Jackson, they pulled off the road and arrived at the Banger Warehouse Complex. He checked the time. The watch's hands showed 8:30 pm. Two of the Delta Team operatives opened the chained gates and drove the truck to the bay. They opened the container, and another operative drove a forklift to the ramp, where two men assisted in removing twelve ice freezer chests.

Fifty minutes later, they opened the ice freezer chests, removing the nuclear suitcases and C-4 explosives. They put the ice freezer chests back into the container, locked it up, and drove the truck back to

Brandon. Beltermann and his team placed the nuclear suitcases and C-4 in the back of the panel truck.

The Charlie Team parked the truck a few blocks from the truck stop. Blindfolded and hurt, the driver regained consciousness as he lay on the back of the cab. Beltermann climbed to the cab, pulled out his Glock, and fired two bullets into the driver's head. The teams got back on Highway 20 in their panel truck and the SUV, fully loaded with dangerous cargo headed for Houston.

Chapter Fifty-Eight

At seven in the morning on Sunday, August 30, Caldwell left the hotel. She ran to the Saanen Airport and jogged back toward Gstaad via Gstaadstrasse. At 8:30 am, Caldwell entered Heidi's Pastry Shop on Promenade Street. Holding her coffee in one hand and a box of pastry in the other, she walked back toward the hotel.

A gray panel truck on the road drove towards her. Two muscular men in their thirties dressed in casual sportswear walked toward her on the same side of the street. The panel truck pulled up to the curb and stopped while the men grabbed her. They hauled her inside the truck, forcing Caldwell to drop her latte and the box of pastry on the sidewalk, and sped away. Delgado trailed fifty yards behind and charged toward her but couldn't stop the abduction.

Kupchenko bloodied her nose with his fist. She punched him in the groin and thrust the palm of her hand against the bridge of his nose. He slammed his fist against her jaw, knocking her unconscious. A few miles away, they pulled off the road, tied her up, and placed her on the floor of the truck.

Ericksen's cellphone rang. "Gold Eagle."

"Elizabeth has been abducted by some Russians. Get packed and check out. I'll meet you in the lobby in thirty minutes. We'll be able to track her down."

"Track her down?"

"She has an implanted RFID GPS chip located on her upper arm, near the shoulder area."

Ericksen thought *I should have gone with her this morning.*

At nine-ten in the morning, Delgado removed his secure cellphone and called the CIA safe house in Bussigny, near Lausanne. The communications center techie answered the call in French.

"Philippe speaking."

"Tampa here. Venus was abducted! Please activate the satellite tracking system and call me back as soon as you get a reading."

Ten minutes later, his cellphone rang. "Tampa."

"Philippe again. She's traveling on Highway A14, just past the town of Reussbuhl on the road toward Zurich."

"Thanks, keep us updated." A minute later, they checked out of the hotel.

"Late last night, I checked out your car and found a GPS tracking device under the fuel tank. The bastards were planning to kill you. Let's get in my Mercedes."

"Elizabeth's life is hanging by a thread. Fico, we must find her." At one in the afternoon, they arrived at the CIA safe house in Zug.

They went upstairs and picked up three duffel bags filled with weapons, ammo, black stealth clothing, thermo-imaging cameras, night vision goggles, and Kevlar body armor, then turned to an Agency IT guy.

"Where is Venus now?"

"We've tracked her to a large house in Kusnacht, about eight kilometers south of Zurich. It's on the lake."

"What's the address?"

"The first number is three on Hornweg. It has a Swiss flag and a boat ramp with a 20-foot boat."

"Take a closer satellite look," said Delgado.

"The Estate sits on an acre or two. There are two cars and a panel truck in the driveway."

"We're on our way."

———

MORITZ JOGGED OVER TO KHALID, who rested on a lounge chair at poolside. "Ericksen checked out. He must have support; the Audi is still here."

"Shit!" Khalid said in Arabic.

———

SULLIVAN AND CAMPBELL finished their racquetball game and walked past the karate class, catching sight of Hank Lucas practicing karate with the instructor. Lucas had achieved a third-degree black belt in karate. The men were members of the Neptune Athletic Club of Washington.

Sullivan and Campbell showered and went into the sauna room. A few minutes later, Lucas joined them. "What is this about, Bill?" asked Lucas.

"Two things. Al-Bustani is in negotiations with a Pakistani nuclear scientist and is in the process of purchasing an eight-kiloton nuclear warhead which at some point will be on a container ship heading for the Port of Los Angeles."

"Shit! Have you touched base with the Pakistani Intelligence?"

"I have alerted their director, and they're investigating the principals right now."

"Let me know ASAP," said Campbell.

"Number two: the Swiss Federal Police notified me this morning Banque Matthias Reiter in Geneva will be raided Friday, September 4. We're hopeful the records confiscated will provide us with names of individuals involved in financial terrorism as well as Americans who profited illegally from the Afghan and Iraqi wars."

"We need to indict these corrupt bastards and put them away for life without parole," Lucas responded.

"Who is taking the lead role in concert with the Swiss authorities?" Campbell asked.

"The FBI, Justice, and Treasury are conducting a joint investigation. Their efforts are in sync with the Swiss government."

―――――

AT TWO IN THE AFTERNOON, Campbell picked up his secure cellphone.

"Hello," Reiter said, from his home near Geneva.

"Spotlight here." He leaned against his bookcase in his study. "Please transfer all of my Palm Financial Holdings' accounts first thing Monday morning to my Trilogy Palm Group Holdings at the Waldmann and Tessier Bank, Grand Caymans. Only my personal account shall remain at your bank."

"Why the rush?

"The Swiss Federal Police are planning to raid your bank on Friday. Is that urgent enough for you?"

"What! Are you sure?"

"What do you think?" Campbell's face tensed, and he shook his head. "I have reliable intel from the highest sources."

"I'm departing at 21:55 for Singapore this evening. I'm a guest speaker at a function Tuesday afternoon."

"Is there anyone at your bank who can accomplish this without any problems?"

"I'm the only one who can do these sensitive transactions. No one in the bank is aware of our secrets."

"When is the earliest you can get back to Geneva?"

"I can take the 1:00 am. flight back on Wednesday and be in my office by one in the afternoon."

"Fine. Please don't disappoint us."

―――――

LUCAS LIFTED up his Louis XIII Remy Martin cognac decanter and poured his cognac into a brandy snifter. He walked over to the CD player in his study and placed Beethoven's Ninth Symphony CD into the tray. After he had taken a swig of his cognac, he hunkered in his leather recliner and made a call on his secure cellphone.

"Iron Fist here," Dawkins said, as he recognized Shogun's Swiss cellphone number.

"The fortress is going to be raided next Friday. I talked with Spotlight a few minutes ago and he has been in contact with our man in Geneva. All of our funds must be transferred by Wednesday afternoon. Please wish him well for me and put his mind at rest. Do you copy?"

"Yes, sir," Dawkins said.

WHITE HOUSE SITUATION ROOM

Campbell, Sullivan, Lucas, Geiger, the National Security Advisor, the Secretary of Defense, the Secretary of State, and their key staff were seated around the conference table in the White House Situation Room with President Porterfield at seven in the evening.

The president came into office in January, and now the honeymoon period was starting to come to an end. Porterfield faced an enormous financial crisis inherited from the previous administration: the meltdown of Wall Street, high unemployment, the housing crisis, out-of-control defense spending, increased deficits, and being locked into two unpopular wars in Afghanistan and Iraq.

Besides those issues, Porterfield faced many geopolitical risks around the world: China's emerging military threats, North Korea's erratic, unpredictable dictator and their nuclear arms proliferation threats, the Russian prime minister's long-term strategic vision for the Russian Federation, containing Iranian nuclear arms ambitions, global terrorism, and a gridlocked Congress.

"We intercepted a call placed to Khalid's Swiss cellphone. Voice analysis confirmed it came from Abdullah. He discovered our operation. They've shut down their communications," Campbell said.

President Porterfield looked around at his senior intelligence directors and key cabinet heads. "Shit. We don't have much time.

According to the DOE, three kilograms of fissionable plutonium material would kill everyone within a half-mile to a mile radius. What are our options?"

"Mr. President, we have a call into Saudi Intelligence right now," Sullivan said.

The president stood up and slammed his hand down on the conference table. "God damn it, we don't have the luxury of time. We don't even know what their targets are in Vegas and Houston. Find those terrorists before they hit us again."

"We'll find them, sir!" *I need to send the Special Operations Group to Jeddah immediately.*

ZURICH

Ericksen and Delgado left their car near the Marina in Zurich, where two CIA officers met them. One of them gave Ericksen the keys to a 25' Bayliner. They loaded their equipment and weapons onboard and left at ten in the evening. They slowed down and cruised to a boat ramp two hundred yards from the Russian safe house at eleven. Tall hedges were separating one mansion from the targeted Estate.

In the living room of the Russian safe house mansion in Kusnacht, Ryzhkov and Kupchenko looked at Caldwell, her hands tied behind her back, her face bloodied and swollen. "Tell me what you know!"

"Go to hell."

"Take her downstairs," Ryzhkov said in Russian.

The Russian guard #1 opened the basement door and took her downstairs. Ryzhkov turned to Kupchenko, "I'm going to the airport motel right now and will depart for Moscow tomorrow morning. Call me immediately after you extract the information...then kill her!"

"I'm looking forward to it. Give my best to Sasha." Ryzhkov nodded and left the house with his suitcase. Kupchenko kicked Caldwell in the back and punched her in the face, bruising her left cheek. Blood flowed down from her mouth. He removed her clothes and shoved her down on the chair. "You better start talking."

"You're going to kill me anyway."

He slapped her across her face. The Russian guard #1 lifted Caldwell up. Kupchenko grabbed her by the hair and held her head under the bathtub water for thirty seconds. After dunking her two more times, he lifted her head up from the water. She gasped for air.

"You're a fucking CIA pig!"

Two men guarded the front of the mansion, and three men guarded the rear, near the boat ramp along the lake. Both Delgado and Ericksen were in full combat attire: dark green camo clothes, night vision goggles, headsets, assault rifles with scopes and suppressors, sharp Special Operations Forces' knives and handguns.

From one hundred yards out, Ericksen spotted Russian guard #2 in the front and fired: zap, zap, hitting the Russian in the head. From seventy-five yards out, he aimed his M4 rifle at Russian guard #3 and fired: zap, zap, another killed. Russian guard #4 heard something near the water and from fifteen yards out, a burst of bullets from Delgado's handgun killed the Russian. Ericksen spotted Russian guard #5 and cut him down with three shots to the head.

Delgado made a move toward the house, with Ericksen trailing behind.

They reached the back door of the Russian safe house and heard some sounds coming from the basement. Their handguns at the ready, they opened the door, and a Russian started firing at both of them. They returned fire, and the Russian somehow managed to get to the side door, opened it, and ran toward the boat ramp. Ericksen charged in hot pursuit after him. He stopped, took aim, and fired two shots, killing the Russian guard #1.

A woman's screams could be heard, yelling, "Bastard!"

"Shut up, bitch," Kupchenko said in Russian. He heard the racket, put his pants back on, and climbed the steps with his gun in his right hand. As he opened the door to the main floor, Delgado shot his gun out of his hand. He punched and kicked Kupchenko, and both men exchanged blows. After Delgado grabbed his handgun, he struck Kupchenko's jaw, knocking him out. Then, he dragged him to the wall and tied his hands behind his back with flex cuffs.

Entering the basement, Ericksen spotted Caldwell stripped naked on the bed with her hands tied to the bedposts. He rushed over and worked as fast as he could to untie her hands.

"My clothes are on the chair in the corner."

He picked up her clothes and handed them to her.

"Give me your gun," Caldwell said, her face tensed and red, and filled with anger. Ericksen gave her his handgun, and with a firm grip on the weapon, she moved towards Kupchenko, who regained consciousness.

"Don't do it! He might have important information," Delgado yelled.

She walked up to Kupchenko, who rested against the wall with his hands tied behind his back. "You scumbag. I hope you rot in hell!" Caldwell squeezed the trigger and shot four bullets into Kupchenko's head and chest.

Tears flowed down her cheeks. Ericksen extended his hand out to her, and she hugged him. He held her in his arms for several seconds.

She turned to Ericksen. "Thanks."

"The nightmare is all over," Delgado said.

MONDAY, AUGUST 31, 2009

They arrived at the Auerbach Emergency Clinic in Zurich at 0100. Over the next two hours, the doctor and nurses treated and patched her up. By 5:30 am, they were on the road heading toward the Agency's safe house in Bussingny.

"I received a text from Jacobson's cellphone. He and Scharz checked his office thoroughly and couldn't find anything of substance to prosecute them on," Caldwell said.

Ericksen shook his head. Caldwell sat in the front passenger seat, her face black and blue with bandages over her right eye, forehead, and neck, and sporting a split lip.

———

MORITZ APPROACHED Khalid in the cafe. "I've got bad news." He tensed up and whispered in Khalid's ear, "Oleg and several of the Russians are dead. Their Russian maid found their bodies this morning. They were all shot to death. Ericksen apparently rescued Caldwell."

Khalid shook his head in disgust. "Shit!"

———

AN HOUR LATER, Dawkins picked up his secure cellphone.

"Iron Fist."

"I'll be leaving today for Jeddah. Can you meet me at one in the afternoon at the café Richemont in Nyon?"

"See you there."

The Mercedes sedan with Swiss plates pulled up to Café Richemont in Nyon. Khalid got out and walked into the café. He spotted Dawkins, who pulled up a chair and joined him on the terrace overlooking the lake. "I have a job for you. It's worth three hundred thousand dollars. I want you to find Mark Ericksen and his girlfriend and kill them."

"Consider it done."

He took out an envelope. "This is a down payment."

Dawkins handed a piece of paper to Khalid. "This is my new bank in the Cayman Islands."

"Call me when you have completed the job, and I'll wire the balance of the money to your new bank account." Khalid stood up, shook hands, and left the restaurant.

Chapter Fifty-Nine

SEPTEMBER 1, 2009

Z iad knocked on the door to Khalid's office in Jeddah.

"Come in," Khalid said, motioning with his hands. "In ten days, the American Satan will feel Allah's revenge."

He got up from his chair and walked toward the photograph of Falcon Dancer. He slid the picture to the left, revealing the wall safe. He placed his right index finger on the optical scanner and pressed it. The safe opened up, and Khalid put a USB drive into it.

He looked at Ziad. "You've earned my trust. The red-marked one has our American operations, and the blue-marked one has a list of our Red Sea Brotherhood members. The one I'm holding is the third USB flash drive. Its contents detail the nuclear warhead Faisal purchased from leaders of a Pakistani Al-Qaeda and Taliban group. We're going to load a tactical nuclear warhead on a container ship in Karachi the first of January bound for Jakarta and reload it to another container ship with a final destination of the Port of Los Angeles." He closed the safe and slid the photograph of Falcon Dancer back.

"Khalid, that is great news. The Great Satan will feel our thunder."

"This land belongs to the Caliphate, not Royal Bluebloods." He looked at the report Ziad had in his hands.

He handed the report to Khalid. "Here are the latest financial statements from Herr Steiner. Our balance is one hundred ten million Swiss francs left in our Zurich bank."

He took a minute to browse over the statements. "Good. On Thursday, the tenth of September, I'll be transferring about $40 million to my personal account in Dubai. I'll need you to fly to Dubai on the 10th to complete a joint venture deal for me with Moosa Al-Dhaheri's company."

"I'll put it on my schedule," Ziad said.

Two hours later, Ziad entered a Jeddah bookstore. He went to the history section, and the dentist made eye contact with him, twenty feet away. He picked up a book, looked around, and placed a piece of paper in the middle of the book. He laid the book flat over several books in the section. When he turned the corner of the history section, his face froze in shock as his eyes met by the sudden presence of Faisal.

"What a coincidence seeing you," Faisal said with a smirked expression.

"Yes, I was thinking the same thing. What brings you to the bookstore?" asked Ziad.

"I'm looking for a spy book," Faisal said in a serious tone.

"Most of the good ones are in English," Ziad said, smiled, and exited the bookstore.

The dentist approached the section, picked up the book, and proceeded to the cashier. Moritz signaled two men in the car outside the bookstore to take photos of the stranger who just left the bookstore.

FBI HEADQUARTERS

Lucas walked into FBI Director Geiger's office at eight-thirty in the morning. The Undersecretary of the Treasury for Financial Intelligence and Terrorism handed Lucas a photo of Campbell and Dawkins and the Swiss banker Jurgen Reiter in Dubai around February 2005.

"The DOJ is getting ready to arrest both of them for graft, fraud, and corruption," she said.

"Nothing would surprise me about Dawkins, but Campbell, I can't believe it," Lucas said as he tensed up and tossed around in the chair.

"A sniper shot and killed Marwan Haidar on Highway 95 traveling south in Virginia."

"One less spy to worry about. How's Elizabeth Caldwell?"

"She's recovering from her ordeal."

"Thank God. Where's Caldwell and Ericksen now?" asked Lucas.

"They're safe for the moment. Caldwell is awaiting information from Jacobson on certain Swiss numbered bank accounts Campbell and Dawkins maintained at Banque Matthias Reiter in Geneva."

Lucas tensed up, and sweat formed on his forehead.

CIA HEADQUARTERS

Sullivan was holding the president's daily briefing in his hands when he heard a beep. He glanced at his laptop computer monitor and checked his encrypted email messages.

"What's this," he said under his breath. *An urgent email from General Al-Jabr, requesting me to call him immediately.* He picked up the secure landline phone and made the call.

"Al-Jabr."

"Phantom, what's new?"

"Our operative informed me today that Khalid has the complete nuke attack plans hidden in a wall safe in his office and protected by a fingerprint scanner. They reside on a USB flash drive. He also added another plan, a container ship set to sail with a tactical nuclear warhead, destination Port of Los Angeles. We believe it is going to carry an eight-kiloton explosive yield. The targeted date of the shipment from Jakarta is sometime in January."

"That's right."

"General, I can arrange to have a black ops team up with your special operations forces and Ziad by Friday to make a surprise attack on the headquarters."

"First of all, we don't know the names of the traitors within our armed forces' ranks, and I suspect they would tip off Khalid, and he would hide the flash drives or destroy them."

"This is his last mission. He will only work with Ericksen, whom he trusts with his life."

"All right, we'll get Ericksen. I'll need to get back to you on the details."

———

SULLIVAN RETURNED to his Great Falls home early after a meeting with the President, Lucas, and Geiger. His cellphone rang. Sullivan glanced at his watch, which read two o'clock.

"Hello."

"Hi, Bill. Given the urgency of the mission, I could assemble a four-man Delta team immediately. They could join up with the Saudi spy in Jeddah," Lucas offered.

"Thanks, but the Saudi spy will only work with Ericksen. Anyway, we'll have a backup plan while the mission is in progress." He walked toward the dining room. "The Swiss intel officer and Jacobson have a flash drive with the information on the numbered bank accounts at Banque Matthias Reiter. He'll email the data in a word document soon, once he gets confirmation on a wire transfer to a Cayman Islands Bank."

"Great job," Lucas said.

Sullivan picked up his secure landline phone and called Ericksen at nine-thirty in the evening. "Hello, Gold Eagle, this is Phantom. Sorry to wake you."

"It's three-thirty in the morning. What's up, sir?" asked Ericksen.

"Khalid has a hidden fingerprint biometrics wall safe which holds his operational plans on two USB flash drives – one drive has the nuke attack plans for Las Vegas and Houston, and the other has a plan to ship an eight-kiloton nuclear warhead on a container ship bound for the Port of Los Angeles."

"Holy shit!"

"Wolverine will pick you up in two hours from the safe house and drive you to the Geneva International Airport. He'll give you Khalid's copied fingerprints on a latex glove. Place your right hand in the glove and use your index finger to gain access to the safe. Our Gulfstream jet will be ready for take-off to Jeddah to meet Ziad at 0730 hours. Our medical team will insert a GPS-implanted microchip into your shoulder before take-off America is counting on you for this mission."

"Hooyah, sir!"

"Glad you got that SEAL spirit. We're having a special reunion of old spooks in December at the Bellagio in Las Vegas. You'll be my personal guest."

"Thank you, sir."

Chapter Sixty

At nine in the morning, Ericksen heard the Gulfstream pilot's voice on the jet's intercom, "Mark, pick up our satphone."

"Where are you?" asked Ziad.

"I'll be landing in four and a half hours. Where are Moritz and Khalid?"

"Khalid is in Riyadh. Not sure about Moritz. I received your bank information. Call me when you arrive at the Sheraton."

"I can't thank you enough," Ericksen said.

"It's a small measure of the damage I've done."

Sullivan mentioned Bellagio. The painting. Yes, yes. Ericksen jumped up and approached a staffer. "I need to make use of this satphone again. It's urgent!"

"Go for it!" the staffer said.

He called Caldwell. "This is Gold Eagle."

"Venus here. What's up?'

"I recalled something odd about the bank's conference room. Maybe it's nothing. There is a beautiful stained glass painting of Bellagio, Italy, on the wall to the right of where I was seated and to the left of where Reiter sat down. I glanced at the artwork several times. Something about it didn't seem right. The painting captured Bellagio on the right side, the center, Lake Como, and on the top, the Swiss Alps. The rays of the Sun depicted in the scene appeared bright and surreal. But in the middle of those rays, in a small rectangle, they appeared dull."

"What's the size of the painting?" asked Caldwell.

"Probably ten-feet in height by seven-feet in width."

"What is the size of the rectangle?"

"About two-inches by four-inches."

"Mark, I think this could be the break we need. I'll call Dave right now. Be safe."

JEDDAH, SAUDI ARABIA

Ziad placed his tape recorder next to the speakerphone and made a call. At Monch and Schneider Private Bank, Zurich, Hans Christian Scharz's phone rang. "Herr Scharz speaking."

Ziad activated the recorder. "Khalid Al-Bustani, Account number MSPB8880076/OS," said Ziad, impersonating Khalid's voice.

"Mr. Al-Bustani, please type in your code."

He keyed in Red Sea on the computer. "What is your employee I.D. number Herr Scharz?" asked Ziad.

"477, sir."

Ziad took a drink of water. "I would like to make a wire transfer to VikingMercerIslandDK, account number #BMR0534986JR/1 – Banque Matthias Reiter, Geneva, for thirty million Swiss francs."

"Is this correct, Mr. Al-Bustani?" asked Herr Scharz.

"Yes."

"The total comes to thirty million Swiss francs. We'll put the wire transfer through within the hour. That leaves you with a balance of eighty million Swiss francs, sir."

"Thank you, Herr Scharz."

GENERAL INTELLIGENCE DEPARTMENT, RIYADH

Colonel Mustapha looked at the facial recognition database terminal. After inputting a photo of the dentist into the computer, he pressed Enter. Scrolling through thousands of pictures yielded no match. He inputted Ziad Al-Kabbani's photo, and nothing showed up either. He shook his head in frustration, walked over to the classified archives section, and approached two GID (General Intelligence Department) guards.

After producing his smartcard, he placed one of his fingers on the scanner for positive I.D. recognition. A few seconds later, the system granted him access. The GID guard approached.

"Do you have the authorization, colonel?" the guard asked.

"Yes." Colonel Mustapha produced the necessary paperwork, and the guard left him alone. He entered the room and glanced at another facial recognition database terminal. He began scrolling through hundreds of pictures. Finally, a match appeared of the dentist.

Profile: Fouad Al-Kharusi, born February 10, 1953, Al-Khobar, Saudi Arabia. Dental degree: King Saud University, Riyadh, 1980; Saudi National Guard, 1980–2002; and retired with the rank of colonel. In private practice, Jeddah, 2002–present.

The colonel tried Ziad Kabbani's photo. After ten minutes of scrolling the database, his face appeared with the name Zamil Al-Rasheed. An asterisk seemed to be next to the name – contact General Al-Jabr if there are any questions. The colonel left the Saudi GID and immediately made a call from his secure cellphone.

"Hello," Khalid answered.

"The dentist operates in the shadows, and I believe he assists deep-cover intel officers."

"What about Ziad?"

"He's a spy who reports directly to General Al-Jabr."

"Shit! I'll personally kill that traitor!" Khalid yelled.

AL-BUSTANI GROUP OF COMPANIES

Ericksen and Ziad approached the main entrance to the headquarters building. Ericksen looked like a Saudi, dressed in a typical Saudi robe. Beneath his dishdasha, he wore combat boots.

The security guards recognized Ziad but still asked for his I.D.

Ericksen showed them his phony passport and a badge from Al-Bustani's companies, verifying his employee status. The wall clock read 5:30 pm.

They were waved through the lobby and continued to walk by a row of elevators before they reached the security department's facility door. They knocked on the door with a security camera overhead and heard a voice coming from the security officer behind the door. "One moment, Ziad."

The security officer pressed a button, the door opened, and a bank of video camera security was in full view. He and Ziad walked in and, within two seconds, zapped two of the security guards with tasers. While they were immobilized and on the floor in shock, Ericksen injected the officers with a sedative. They proceeded to cut off the power on the video security cameras focused on Khalid's office.

After entering Al-Bustani's office, Ericksen slid the photograph of Falcon Dancer to the left, exposing the wall safe.

"We only have twenty minutes to get in and out," Ziad said. He put on the latex glove, placed it over the biometric optical scanner, gently lining up his right index finger to the scanner. He pressed Enter, and the safe opened up. He removed three USB flash drives.

Faisal walked from his dining room to his study. He placed some reports on his desk and sat down by his computer, and started his logon. His phone rang. He picked up his secure landline phone.

"The colonel just confirmed Ziad is a traitor! It's a long story. His real name is Zamil Al-Rasheed, from the Ha'il area," Khalid said. "Find him and bring him to *The Dolphin Prince*. I'll meet you at the marina in four hours."

"Yes, Father."

Faisal's face tensed up as his eyes fixed on empty chairs in the security department facility. He glanced around the room and noticed two security officers unconscious on the floor.

The drive from his condo to the headquarters took no more than ten minutes. He lifted the phone and made a call.

Ericksen and Ziad went over to Khalid's computer and powered it up.

"Let me send the Red Sea Brotherhood members' flash drive first," Ziad said.

"Okay." He placed his USB drive into the USB port, and a prompt symbol asked for a passcode. Ziad keyed in Khalid and pressed Enter. Nothing happened.

"This isn't any ordinary USB flash drive. It's a Fortress Keyguard. You get four attempts at the passcode," Ericksen said.

Ziad tried two more: redseabrotherhood and dolphinprince.

Again and again, nothing happened.

"We have one last attempt. What does Khalid value the most?"

"Jihad, Islam, power, wealth." Ericksen looked up at the photograph of the horse, turned around the office, to the windows, and back to the horse. "The ring. Try falcondancer."

Ziad keyed in falcondancer and pressed Enter. "Amazing!" He placed the E06 CD into the laptop computer's drive and pressed Enter.

The CD enabled Ziad and Ericksen to send their emails in an encrypted format without being compromised. The encrypted software sent the emails to an overseas server and then changed I.P. addresses every second. After the messages had been sent, the software deleted the emails, making them virtually impossible to recover. On Khalid's computer monitor, the flash drive's files began appearing in Arabic and listed The Red Sea Brotherhood members. He scrolled down the extensive list of a few thousand names. He immediately removed the original flash drive, placed his USB flash drive into the port, and made a copy, and downloaded the entire file. He then keyed in: swordsman88 @ swisstelecom.ch, and his email address: ZAR39 @ arab.net.sa.

"Swordsman, here's the info in the attachment. ZAR." Ziad then removed the flash drive from the USB port.

Three security officers arrived in the security room, and they re-activated the video cameras. They spotted Ziad and an Arab talking in Khalid's office. They called Faisal, and when he received the news, he gave an order: "Get someone up on the balcony of Khalid's office. Now!"

Ziad recognized the cameras were re-activated. He aimed and shot out the three cameras.

Ericksen placed his flash drive labeled USA plan in Arabic into the USB port. A minute later, the entire USA attack plans for Las Vegas and Houston popped up in Arabic. He scrolled down as Ziad interpreted the critical elements of the file to him.

"It lists the names of sleeper cell operatives in each city, storage areas, safe house locations, targets, plan, and the date of the attacks. Khalid must have moved up the date. It's now Monday, September 7," Ziad said.

"Damn it!"

Three security men jumped onto the balcony with their guns drawn. "Did you hear that?"

Ziad opened the shutters covering the bullet-proof windows and saw three men on the balcony. He closed them. "Mark, hurry, we don't have time."

Ericksen placed his flash drive into the USB port and began downloading the files. He put the last flash drive into the USB port. This one detailed the nuclear warhead plans to be loaded in Karachi on a container ship destined for the Port of Los Angeles. After Ericksen had made copies, they walked back to the wall safe, placed all three flash drives back, closed the safe, and slid back the photograph of Falcon Dancer.

Ericksen inserted both USB flash drives into the hidden compartments of his combat boots. Ziad ran over to an indoor plant, hid his copy under the plant, ran back to the computer, removed the E06 CD, broke it into many pieces, and dumped them under the rug. Faisal and four security guards were outside Khalid's office with their guns and AK-47s drawn.

"It's no use," Ericksen said. They placed their guns on Khalid's desk and opened the door.

"Put your hands behind your back," Faisal yelled. At that moment, his security guards placed plastic flex cuffs on both of them.

They were shoved into a Honda van, followed by two SUVs filled with armed guards. Faisal's armored Hummer led the way. Two Agency men followed them at a safe distance. Twenty minutes later, Faisal and his team arrived at the Jeddah Marina with Ziad and Ericksen, and they were pushed by the guards up the ramp of *The Dolphin Prince*.

One of the CIA officers made a call.

THREE HOURS LATER, Sullivan led a teleconference meeting in the Situation Room. Seated around the table were President Porterfield, his national security advisor, the Secretary of Defense, and staff. On the screen, in General Al-Jabr's office, were the Saudi Minister of Defense, a Saudi Naval Admiral, and staff. Listening in via satellite communications: the USSOCOM commander, an American Naval Sub Commander, Centcom Commander, and a SEAL Team Six commander, based on an aircraft carrier in the Arabian Sea.

"We have an American sub in the Red Sea. It's about five hours from Jeddah. We need to rescue Ziad and Ericksen. We don't have much time. Can you launch an air assault on *The Dolphin Prince*?"

"Director Sullivan, we'll plan every contingency and coordinate with you and your naval assets in the area."

"Director Sullivan, General Al-Jabr, let me and the Saudi Minister of Defense develop a plan for both an air and surface assault to board the vessel as soon as you conclude the conference," said the Commander of the United States Special Operations Command.

Sullivan looked around the conference table and nodded his head to all principals seated. "Thanks, Admiral, and thanks to you, your highness and General Al-Jabr, for arranging this meeting."

BANQUE MATTHIAS REITER

Scharz and Jacobson went down the hall on Wednesday evening to the conference room. They looked at the stained glass painting of Bellagio, then left, and went next door to a small utility room marked Bank Research Group *Salle de securité.*

The door had a cipher lock on it. Jacobson took out his drill and broke the cipher lock. They opened the security room and observed two large metal file cabinets, a bookcase, and against what appeared to be a tiny two-way mirror separating the utility room from the conference room. A 35 SLR digital camera is mounted on a tripod and focused on a 2" X 4" area within the stained glass painting. This confirmed their suspicions; the camera setup took pictures of new clients.

Jacobson picked the lock of the first metal file cabinet and opened it. He found one flash drive with a label on it with the word CH/BMR/Accounts.

He uploaded the flash drive into his laptop computer, and the prompt asked for the password for www.BMR.CH. He took out a piece of paper for the passcode: Grindelwald1890 and pressed Enter.

Once they arrived at the site, they searched for management personnel. Scharz clicked on Jurgen Reiter's name, and a password prompt appeared. They entered Matterhorn55JR. A list of 250 private numbered accounts came up. He scrolled down until he came to BMR0534986JR/1 and entered Ericksen's passcode: VikingMercerIslandDK. In fifteen seconds, his bank records appeared. It showed dates of deposit and amounts in Swiss francs. A letter symbol seemed to be next to each entry: I.P. (in person), T (by phone), and W.T. (wire transfer). To the right, an entry of Mark Ericksen/F#244. Scharz clicked, and up came a picture of Mark Ericksen, his private numbered account, passcode, and monthly activity. Apparently, the software had built-in redundancy.

They clicked on another folder under Jurgen Reiter's personal file: My Pictures and scrolled through several account holders' photos. Each file showed the private numbered account, passcode, monthly activity, and the name of the individual or company name.

Scharz thought the other cabinet in the room stored identical records to the flash drive. The tech specialist picked the steel cabinet lock. After five minutes, they located the client file folders in the second drawer. The file listed all 250 of Reiter's clients, names, photos, and activities. The flash drive had all of the same information on it. Reiter's cautious management style required an extra layer of security, which the backup delivered.

They couldn't take a chance of security, making another round on the floor. The tech specialist installed another cipher lock with the exact code on the utility room door.

On the road back to Bern, Jacobson took a deep breath in. He thought they had sufficient evidence to prosecute the bastards.

Chapter Sixty-One

K halid entered his office at 2100 hours. He slid the photograph of Falcon Dancer to the side, opened the wall safe, removed four passports, three USB flash drives, $500,000 in wrapped hundred dollar bills, and credit cards. His secure landline phone rang.

"Hello."

"This is Steiner. Herr Scharz told me you transferred thirty million Swiss francs from your numbered account this afternoon to a numbered account at Banque Matthias Reiter. Is this correct?"

"What!"

"Herr Scharz said he received the call from you, and you requested a wire transfer to account number BMR 0534986JR/1."

Khalid picked up a paperweight and threw it against the wall. "I never called Scharz!"

"Someone must have recorded your voice and knew your account number."

"It's Ziad. He's a Saudi spy." Khalid wiped his brow and clenched his teeth. "Immediately transfer to the following private numbered accounts in US currency: $20 million into Faisal's account, $8 million into Ignacio Martinez's account, and $2 million into Vance Bullock's account at Waldmann and Tessier Bank, Grand Cayman Islands; $30 million into Faisal's account at Waldmann and Tessier Bank, The Bahamas; and $10 million into Abdullah's account at Waldmann and Tessier Banque, Luxembourg."

"Yes, Khalid. It will be done immediately."

The captain greeted Khalid, who boarded *The Dolphin Prince* along with Moritz. Khalid wore the traditional Saudi robe, and around his waist, he carried an ivory-handled Jambiya knife resting in its sheath.

"Set sail for Yanbu," directed Khalid.

"Yes, Sheikh." Khalid's men disengaged the ramp at 2200 hours, and *The Dolphin Prince* departed from the marina with a crew of twenty and ten terrorist operatives from the Red Sea Brotherhood.

The ship traveled twenty-three miles northwest of Jeddah. Khalid and Moritz entered one of the guest staterooms, where three bodyguards held Ericksen and Ziad. Their faces, bruised and bloody, showed the effects of a severe beating. They were stripped naked, seated on two chairs with their hands tied behind them.

"Stand them up!" shouted Khalid. He stared into Ziad's eyes. "You were one of my most trusted men. You betrayed me," said Khalid in Arabic.

"No, Khalid, you betrayed your country and Islam. Hell awaits you."

With the speed of a magician's hands in motion, Khalid pulled his sharp, steel, curved Jambiya knife from its sheath and plunged it into Ziad's chest. He groaned in agony, blood spurting out, losing consciousness as he hit the floor. He gasped for air. Khalid bent over Ziad's body, twisted the knife for good measure, and pulled it out. "Throw this piece of shit overboard," he said. He shifted his glance toward Ericksen. "You almost ruined my plans, but it is too late. America will feel real pain soon."

"Go-to-hell!"

Before Khalid could respond, Ericksen kicked him hard in the knee. Khalid grimaced in pain. Two guards tightened their grip on Ericksen. Khalid landed a hard right hand to his jaw, followed by a left hook to his mouth, dropping him to the floor of the cabin.

The captain entered the cabin. "Colonel Mustapha has been arrested."

Khalid appeared startled. "Tie him to the chair." He looked at Ericksen. "I'll be back for you shortly."

"Go to hell!" Ericksen thought *This is it. Hopefully, they'll make it swift.*

The US Navy Sub, USS *Cunningham,* followed two miles behind *The Dolphin Prince.* An American drone buzzed over the mega-yacht at an altitude of 10,000 feet, twenty-five miles northwest of Jeddah. Complete blackness covered the night sky except for the stars.

The Agency received specs from the builder of *The Dolphin Prince*, a German company, and recommended a maximum of fourteen passengers and a crew of twenty. The ship had seven staterooms, including the owner's suite, located on the main deck toward the bow, and five staterooms and the captain's quarters resided on the upper deck. A helicopter landing took up a portion of the sun deck. The 280-foot vessel could reach speeds up to twenty-three knots per hour but was designed for cruising at eighteen knots per hour. A security firm had outfitted the ship with modern warfare weaponry.

The Navy captain of the sub looked at the satellite video link shown on the command center monitor and noticed that the thermal imaging cameras from the drone above captured heat patterns from various stateroom locations. "I hope he's still alive. Can you see any pulsing activity being transmitted from Ericksen's enhanced RFID implanted microchip?" asked the captain. A Navy lieutenant commander observed signals pulsing on one of the monitors.

"Yes."

The USS *Cunningham* captain lifted his satellite radio phone. "Hello, this is the Commander of the Saudi Naval Special Forces. We're set to depart from our base in thirty minutes with four Apache gunships, each with a sniper and a CH-46 Sea Knight helicopter carrying joint Saudi navy commandos and your SEAL Team-Six operators."

"Commander, we'll be launching our two SEAL boat teams in

twenty minutes. We should complete the control of the lower and main decks by the arrival of your helicopter-borne assault team. Good luck."

One torpedo-shaped SEAL Delivery Vehicle (SDV) powered by lithium polymer battery entered the water with two SEAL Team Eight operators seated and four SEALs armed with assault silenced rifles and knives.

Ten minutes later, one rubberized, inflatable Zodiac manned by a coxswain, who controlled the tiller arm of the outboard engine, cruised toward *The Dolphin Prince* with a total of six armed SEALs.

Khalid turned to the chef, who brought a lamb dish and a glass of orange juice to him. "Rafiq, bring me a machete and the German butcher knife right now. Hurry!"

Moritz nodded as he faced Khalid, "Sheik, I can't wait to see you butcher Ericksen into bits of meat and bones."

Khalid's face was filled with anger as he yelled to his personal bodyguard, "Oskar, I'm going to cut this CIA pig to pieces and take great pleasure of throwing his remains overboard to the sharks!"

"I'll bring the vinyl tarp to Ericksen's stateroom," said Moritz. Minutes later, the SDV Team pulled up to the port side, and once positioned beside the ship, threw a hook with an attached ladder to the deck and climbed onboard. They each fanned out with their M4 carbines with suppressors in two-man assault teams. The first two-man team found an armed guard by the vessel's stern and fired and killed him. The next two-man team killed an armed guard toward the bow of the boat. They combed the lower and main decks and killed two more armed guards before one guard on the main deck discovered the team.

A few minutes later, the SEAL Team in the inflatable combat boat approached from the starboard side.

The chef came back to the Bridge with the tools and handed them to Al-Bustani when they heard several shots. Pop-pop-pop sounds were fired from the guard, alarming the crew and terrorists.

The captain, the first mate, and Khalid stopped talking when they heard shots. Inside the Bridge, they turned and saw Moritz run inside.

"I spotted helicopters. They're coming towards us."

Khalid switched the intercom on. "We've been boarded. Kill the infidel dogs." The SEALs were now in a firefight as bullets riddled the ship.

Once the USS *Cunningham* emerged, a terrorist sighted it from the bow. He rushed onto the Bridge. "Sheikh, a submarine has surfaced and is one kilometer in front of the bow."

Khalid yelled, "Oskar, take the waiter with you to the helicopter. Hurry, the pilot is waiting. Tell the pilot to take you to Mecca."

A Saudi Navy Al-Riyadh Class frigate moved toward *The Dolphin Prince*. Khalid glanced at the sub moving closer, and in the distance, he spotted a large vessel coming toward his location. He grabbed his duffel bag and his handgun. He made his way down to the lower deck without being spotted by the SEAL teams. The ship's first officer joined him as they passed a couple of crew members and opened the engine room door. They went into a utility room and went to a bookcase. There he went to the third shelf from the top and moved four books. He pushed a switch up, and the bookcase slid to the side. He placed the books back where they belonged. The two men were now inside.

Khalid pressed a button from the inside, and it closed the sliding bookcase. The hidden compartment had piped-in air conditioning, bottled water, and a box of cereal. His two-man submarine rested on the lower deck in a garage-type hold.

From the Saudi frigate, a Saudi naval officer with the aid of night vision binoculars spotted a man dressed in a dishdasha carrying a duffel bag along with another man who fit Moritz's description boarding the helicopter. He picked up his satphone.

"Sir, I think it's Khalid and his bodyguard, Moritz."

"Take down that helicopter," General Al-Jabr said. Two minutes later, a Saudi Special Forces operator took out a Stinger missile launcher, placed it on his shoulder, and with the assistance of a satellite comms spotter, targeted the helicopter as it reached one-thousand-feet, squeezed the handguard, and fired the missile. Within a few seconds, the missile hit the aircraft, which exploded into a gigantic fireball with a loud boom. Pieces fell from the sky and into the Red Sea.

Two Apache gunships flew over the ship, snipers on the ready.

Both the pilots and the snipers wore night vision sensors. The forward-looking infrared detected the amount of light released by heated objects. The SEAL teams forced the engine crew to climb upstairs to the main deck's lounge area, where they were in flex cuffs.

The main deck was now secured. Two more Apache gunships arrived, and snipers aimed their rifles at anything that moved. The CH-46 Sea Knight helicopter arrived on the scene, and the SEAL Team-Six and Saudi naval commandos fast-roped onto the main deck. They burst into the Bridge, secured it, and tied up the captain. The naval commandos escorted three engine crew members from other mega-yachts down to the engine room. These three now operated the engine room.

On the upper deck, SEAL Team-Six searched the stateroom cabin by cabin.

"I'm in here," shouted Ericksen. Two SEALs heard him, spotted the guard positioned outside the cabin door, and shot two bullets into his head. They shot the lock off and entered the room. Ericksen smiled. "You're just in time." They cut his flex cuffs with a wire cutter.

"Sir, follow us," a SEAL said.

Ericksen motioned with his hands, "We need to find my combat boots. Follow me." After reaching the upper deck master stateroom, they entered and checked the room thoroughly for his clothes and boots. "No luck here."

They exited the cabin and bolted to the next room, a utility room. Ericksen looked into a laundry bin against the wall and found his clothes and boots under dirty clothes. After getting dressed, he followed the SEALs to one of the inflatable rubber Zodiac boats and jumped in.

They arrived back on the USS *Cunningham*. Ericksen entered the command, control, and intelligence center and gave the USB flash drives to the Commander.

"Director Sullivan is expecting these babies," he said.

"Thank you, Mr. Ericksen." The Commander inserted the flash drive into the USB port of his computer and pressed Enter. He put his hand on Ericksen's shoulder. "The Lieutenant will take you to your quarters, get you clean clothes and some rest. You have an Agency Gulf Jet scheduled for departure from Jeddah to Geneva, at 1400 hours."

The Saudi frigate arrived, and their Special Forces teams boarded *The Dolphin Prince*, putting the mega-yacht under the control of the joint Saudi and American Special Operations Forces. When the mega-yacht came within one mile of the terminal, the frigate turned and cruised toward a naval base.

Khalid opened the hidden compartment and reached the garage hold alongside where the mini-sub was located. He opened the hatch to the two-man submarine while the first officer activated the lower deck garage, pressing the hydraulic system button. The first officer then turned a switch that gently guided the mini-sub into the water. He heard one man from the engine room move closer to them and shot him with the suppressor on. He got into the sub's other seat. Khalid guided the submarine under the water's surface to an initial depth of 40 meters. Once they were 100 meters from *The Dolphin Prince*, they submerged to a depth of 60 meters and moved at a 4 knots per hour clip. Their destination: the Fakieh Aquarium area.

When they reached the seawall near Al-Kurnaysh Road, Khalid maneuvered the mini-sub to the seawall, opened the hatch, reached the top of the seawall, and grabbed his duffel bag, and lifted himself onto the surface, followed by the first officer. They walked toward the Pizza Hut, just north of Suri Road. He took out another satphone and called one of his aides.

"We'll drop you off at a shopping center. Make arrangements to meet Faisal and tell him I'll be meeting Ignacio. He'll understand."

An hour later, a Land Rover pulled up, and they both jumped into the SUV and drove off.

The Dolphin Prince arrived at the Red Sea Gateway Terminal at 0100 hours, Thursday, September 3. The Saudi National Police and intelligence services waited for orders to board.

———

At 8:00 AM, the Saudi National Police and Saudi Intelligence Services placed a gangway alongside the ship. They boarded the vessel, relieving the Saudi commandos and SEAL Team-Six of their duty. After inspecting the entire mega-yacht, they discovered a crew member killed and the mini-submarine missing.

Chapter Sixty-Two

GENEVA, SWITZERLAND

Dawkins' cellphone rang at three in the morning and woke him up. He reached over the woman sleeping next to him and grabbed the phone. "Hello."

"Shogun here. Timberwolf will meet you at ten in the morning. He'll give you several passports, cash, a makeup kit, and a ticket for your one-way commercial flight to Rio de Janeiro, scheduled for Friday morning. The Feds have issued an arrest warrant for you and Spotlight."

Dawkins' face turned ashen-white, and he scowled in disbelief. "Will someone be meeting me when I arrive?"

"A man will be waiting for you when you clear customs. He'll have a sign up there saying 'Diego Iron.' Good luck."

"Thanks."

———

Jurgen Reiter closed the door to his mansion located on Chemin de Ruth in Cologny, an expensive Geneva suburb. He walked toward the circular driveway to his Maserati sedan. When he started the ignition, the car exploded, engulfing Reiter and his car in flames.

At nine in the morning, Sheridan lifted his cup of coffee in his hotel room in Geneva. His secure cellphone rang. "Hello."

"Shogun here. Is everything okay?"

"Yep."

"Caldwell, Delgado, and Jacobson should all be at the safe house this evening. Jacobson will have the evidence with him."

"What about the Swiss Federal Police?" asked Sheridan.

"The Swiss aren't going to divulge any private bank numbered accounts held by foreigners unless our government provides evidence the account holder committed serious illegal activities. If our government doesn't have the contents of our numbered accounts, I believe we have a good chance of not being caught."

In the background, Beethoven's Ninth Symphony played.

"Terminate them; otherwise, we're toast!" Lucas directed.

"Randy and I will take care of everything."

———

SCHARZ AND JACOBSON arrived at the Swiss Federal Police headquarters building on Nussbaum Strasse 29 in Bern at four in the afternoon. At 5:00 pm, they placed the thirty-two-gigabyte memory card filled with images into a photo printing computer hookup. A few minutes later, many photos of men and women appeared on the monitor, along with a reference number affixed to each picture. The reference number tied to each private account number should confirm Reiter's system.

To check their theory, they inputted Ericksen's private numbered bank account: BMR0534986JR/1, the passcode prompt appeared, and he entered: VikingMercerIslandDK. Mark Ericksen's name appeared, and File #244 and his photo. Swiss Federal Police Director Muller ordered Scharz to wait until he returned at six this evening before releasing Jacobson's information.

They scanned the files and the photos and matched them up:

BMR7073385JR/1; passcode: IronFist = The Conestoga Fund. F#202: Photo of Shane Dawkins – listed eight million Swiss francs in the account.

BMR7073642JR/1; passcode: Bermuda60 = Palm Financial Holdings. F#225: Photo of Steve Campbell – listed four million Swiss francs in the account.

BMR7073388JR/1; passcode: Timberwolf = Saber Recon Fund F#205: Photo of Nate Sheridan – listed five million Swiss francs.

BMR7073380JR/1, passcode: Shogun = Opal Stream Foundation. F#190: Photo of Rupert Henry Lucas – listed twenty-five million Swiss francs.

BMR0534986JR/1; passcode: VikingMercerIslandDK. F#244: Photo of Mark Ericksen – listed thirty-three million Swiss francs.

Muller arrived and spent the next twenty minutes going over the files.

"The note you found in his top drawer could be used to indict Campbell, Dawkins, Sheridan, and Lucas. The fact that Lucas requested Reiter to transfer all his funds to Waldmann and Tessier Private Bank in The Cayman Islands on Monday, August 31, made me suspicious. Lucas must have calculated if we audited the bank after liquidating all of his Swiss account holdings, there would be no record to indict him. The same holds true with the other conspirators: Campbell, Sheridan, and Dawkins," said Muller.

"Perhaps they assumed once the funds were transferred Reiter could pose a problem for them. They didn't waste any time. He was blown to bits," Jacobson said.

"Sir, we discovered a file referenced to Dawkins, which mentioned Pulaski and Huntington at various times. I wouldn't be surprised if their funds were merged amongst these four conspirators' accounts," Scharz said.

Jacobson nodded. "Dawkins murdered Pulaski, and Huntington died last year in a small plane accident."

Muller looked at Jacobson and leaned toward him, "Okay, Herr Jacobson, take whatever intel you need. I hope your government prosecutes and convicts these criminals."

Jacobson downloaded the information to a USB flash drive. He sat down by a desk and opened his laptop computer, did the log-on, and placed his USB flash drive into the port. A few minutes later, he emailed Director Sullivan with the information, with a copy to the under secretary for financial intelligence and counterterrorism, and Caldwell.

He called Sullivan's direct number, and it routed him to voicemail:

"Emergency, please check your email. Wolverine."

He stopped for a quick dinner on the road to Lausanne. *I can't wait to celebrate tonight with Caldwell and Delgado.*

Chapter Sixty-Three

BUSSIGNY, SWITZERLAND

The CIA safe house was on a one-acre plot of land with views of the mountains and Lake Geneva. The two-story Tudor home on the Rue des Alpes blended in with other charming homes.

Caldwell and Delgado were in the living room watching a movie on television from the comfort of a couch. One Agency security man guarded the front of the home. He hunkered down in a lounge chair on the front porch and could see and hear anyone approaching the house from the front.

Randy had conducted a brief recon and surveillance on the property using a small UAV earlier in the day. At 9:30 pm, he had spotted the security guard. When Randy came within twenty feet of the security man, Randy approached from the property's side and fired two shots into the man's head with his Glock. The suppressor he used significantly reduced any noticeable noise.

Sheridan wore a camouflaged outfit and moved closer to the safe house. He managed to enter a neighbor's property that backed up to the safe house, climbed the six-foot fence, and jumped down on the lawn.

He approached the property, cut the landlines, and employed communication jammers.

Sheridan looked into the window and observed Caldwell and Delgado watching television. He cut the window glass by the kitchen door near the back patio, placed his hand on the deadbolt lock, and opened the door. Then Sheridan bolted into the living room from the dining room and aimed his Makarov 9mm handgun at them.

Delgado and Caldwell saw a flash of a man burst out of nowhere.

Their eyes were glued to him in shock.

"Get your hands up," yelled Sheridan as he threw a pair of flex cuffs on the floor. He looked directly at Caldwell. "Cuff Delgado."

"What's this all about?" Delgado asked.

"Where's Jacobson?"

"He is in Bern."

"Then we'll just wait for him. Now get down on the floor and lay on your stomach with your hands behind your back."

Caldwell followed his orders. After he had cuffed her hands, he lifted her up and placed her next to Delgado. He opened the door and looked at Randy. "Drag the guard's body to the back of the house. Jacobson should be coming within the hour." Sheridan stepped out of the safe house for a minute.

CIA COUNTERTERRORISM CENTER

"The secure cellphone number we intercepted belonged to Jurgen Reiter. He also had six other cellphones listed on his phone bill," said the CTC Director.

"What's the number?"

"The number is 41-22-919-8816. The last two intercepted calls were placed on the hour, and we heard chimes from a grandfather clock in the background."

"Have the scientists do a voice analysis. Also, have the NSA pinpoint the GPS origination of the calls." Sullivan picked up a phone in the CTC and made a call.

"Wolverine," said Jacobson.

"Phantom speaking. I tried calling Venus and Tampa's cellphones as well as the landline a few minutes ago. No one answered. I just got off the phone with the Bern station chief, and they're going to dispatch a team in a few minutes...Be careful."

Sullivan called another number.

"Gold Eagle," Ericksen said.

"Phantom here. Where are you?"

"I just cleared customs."

"Did you catch the breaking news this morning?"

"No."

"The Saudis made it official and released a statement on Al-Bustani's death. *Al-Jazeera* reported 'Saudi mastermind terrorist killed by Saudi commandos last night.'"

"Apparently, his body vaporized upon impact. Couldn't happen to a nicer guy."

"Just got off the phone with Wolverine. He is near the safe house. Be prepared for trouble."

CIA SAFE HOUSE

Sheridan came back into the house. "Where's your laptop?"

"In my trunk," Caldwell said.

He opened the front door and saw Randy. He threw the car keys to him. "Open Caldwell's car trunk and bring me the fucking laptop computer."

Randy retrieved the computer and handed it to Sheridan. Sheridan plopped down on a dining room chair and placed the laptop computer on the table. He powered it up, and the prompt asked for a passcode.

"What's your passcode?" asked Sheridan.

"I'm using EyeD4 Comm's palm vein biometrics."

"Damn it!" Sheridan's face got red with anger.

He looked at both of them. He hurried back to the patio and opened a duffel bag. He pulled a pair of wire cutters out and came back to the living room.

After he had cut Caldwell's flex cuffs, he held his gun aimed at the back of her head. "Get your ass up here and log-on."

She sat down. *Stall.*

Two minutes later, Sheridan glanced over Caldwell's shoulder and read the most recent emails. "Shit!" *Jacobson's email has all the fucking private account numbers.*

He placed another pair of flex cuffs on her and lifted her up. "Sit down on the couch."

He took out his cellphone and called. Lucas answered it at his office. "Hello."

"Timberwolf speaking. We're toast! Jacobson emailed Caldwell, Sullivan, and Treasury all the private account numbers."

"Damn it!" said Lucas. Then silence.

"Now that you have the information, when do you expect to release us?" asked Caldwell.

"Who said anything about releasing you. Randy, get back outside and secure the place."

Silence prevailed. Sheridan aimed the gun at Delgado's head. "Fico, it must have been you who told Ericksen about our Spin Bolak operation. I'm sorry, but your history!" Then he fired a bullet into Delgado's head. The blast pushed Delgado backward as brain matter and blood splattered in different directions, some splashing on Caldwell. Sweat ran down her tense and somber face.

"You rotten bastard!" She screamed and shook her head, numb to the cold-blooded, brutal execution of Delgado.

Jacobson rambled along until he came within seventy-five yards from the property. The Agency informed him that the family who owned the property next to the safe house had left a few days ago on vacation. He jumped their fence and crawled one hundred feet to the fence, separating the two properties. He put on his night-vision goggles.

Then he heard a noise, something like a person moving slowly on the lawn. He saw a tall, slim man holding a handgun in his right hand, partially hidden by bushes along the side of the safe house. He crawled closer, aimed his Sig-Sauer gun with the suppressor, and shot off a burst of bullets into the man's head. Randy toppled over into the bushes and died.

I've got to get in there. Jacobson went around the back and spotted a dead body on the patio, slumped over and leaning against the brick. He removed his night vision goggles. Moving with stealth through the unlocked kitchen door and toward the dining room with his handgun drawn, he leaned toward the living room and spotted Sheridan.

Jacobson had him in his sights as he bolted from the dining room into the living room. Sheridan heard a sound, turned around, glanced at a man, and in less than a split-second, Jacobson fired two shots at him: one in the shoulder and one in the knee, dropping him onto the Persian rug. Jacobson kicked his gun away and stood over him.

"Dave, you son-of-a-bitch," he said, groaning in pain.

"Turn over and place your hands behind your back." Jacobson placed flex cuffs on Sheridan's wrists and left him on the ground. He grabbed a wire cutter and cut the flex cuffs off Caldwell. Then he embraced her. For a few moments, she didn't say a word. Finally, she looked into Jacobson's eyes.

"Thank God."

Caldwell cut Delgado's flex cuffs and picked up her cellphone. "Hello, Venus speaking. Get some people over to the safe house immediately. It's an emergency. Fico Delgado is dead."

"The team should be there in a few minutes," an Agency case officer said.

Jacobson searched Sheridan. He took his cellphone from his jacket pocket and removed his sim card.

"I would have enjoyed killing you, but a life sentence in prison will give you more time to reflect on your sordid, sick life."

He inserted the sim card into a sim card extractor reader, connected it to the USB port of Caldwell's laptop, and sent the information to the CIA Counterterrorism Center.

HENDERSON, NEVADA

Beltermann finished loading the nuclear suitcases and C-4 explosives into a van on Thursday, September 3, and left the Jackson Storage facility off East Sunset Road in Henderson. The safe house's address was in the five hundred block of Hickory Street, not far from its intersection with Constitution Avenue in Henderson. He met up with Abdullah and several of his team.

Abdullah, Beltermann, and Ryzhkov arrived at the Henderson safe house. They entered through the garage, where he began programming the clock timers for the two suitcase nukes. He locked in the date: Monday, September 7, at twelve o'clock noon.

Two cell operatives pulled up in their SUVs; Beltermann got into one and Ryzhkov the other vehicle. After a thirty-minute drive, they arrived at Las Vegas International Airport. Both men took their carry-on luggage and fake passports and received their boarding passes for flight to Houston.

———

THE CTC DIRECTOR handed Sullivan a number. "The last number sent to Dawkins' cellphone came from 8649 Old Dominion Drive in McLean. The number is 703-555-0148. The other calls to Reiter also came from the same number."

"Old Dominion Drive," Sullivan said, and returned to his office. His chief of staff entered the office, handed him the email and attachments from Caldwell. "Wow! Swiss, Dubai, and Cayman Islands private numbered accounts." *We finally have the evidence to indict all of them. Lucas and Sheridan, you sons-of-bitches, you fooled us.*

Chapter Sixty-Four

FRIDAY, SEPTEMBER 4

Ryzhkov and Beltermann arrived at the safe house on the 2100 block of Old Legend Drive in Sugarland, Texas. Ryzhkov completed the clock timers' programming on the two nuclear suitcases set to go off at 2:00 pm, September 7, 2009. They closed the garage door to the entrance of the laundry room. Cowboy and his two team leaders went over the plans again with Beltermann. Ryzhkov got into the back seat of a Mercedes SUV for his ride to the airport to catch his flight back to Europe.

———

Sullivan, Geiger, FBI agents, and Virginia State Police staked out the area that abutted Lucas's estate. At six in the morning, he opened his garage, drove his Porsche SUV from the driveway, and passed the security guards before being surrounded by law enforcement teams.

"Rupert Henry Lucas, we've retrieved your Opal Stream Foundation private numbered account transactions. Unfortunately, the twenty-five million Swiss francs in your bank won't help you where you're going," Sullivan said.

Geiger butted in, "You're under arrest for fraud, tax evasion, corruption, money laundering, and being a co-conspirator for the murder of several US Army soldiers."

Lucas sat in silence.

"I'm sure we can prove your culpability in the murder of Jurgen Reiter too," said Geiger, as he adjusted his tie.

Sullivan shook his head in disgust. "We have all of your numbered bank account records and your calls to Dawkins and Reiter. We discovered you ran Alpha Group from 2002 to 2005 while you were the director of DIA and continued as Undersecretary of Defense for Intelligence."

"Do we have that right, Hank?" said Geiger. "By the way, we just received word that last night your buddy Campbell killed himself."

Lucas looked stunned. His jaw dropped a bit, and he shook his head a few times.

"Handcuff him, read him his rights, and take him away."

The FBI agents led Lucas away.

SATURDAY, SEPTEMBER 5, 2009

At 6:00 pm, Geiger, Sullivan, senior FBI, Department of Energy, and Homeland Security staff were seated in the FBI Headquarters conference room.

The Deputy Director of the FBI stood up. "Three days earlier, we received actionable intelligence from the Agency identifying the two safe houses; one in Henderson, Nevada, and the other in Sugarland, Texas, where the nuclear suitcase bombs and C-4 are stored. Those sites have been under surveillance for the past 48 hours. Director Geiger will now fill you in on your task."

Geiger walked up to the podium. "Experts from the Department of Energy are set to disarm the nuclear suitcases once the FBI's HRT (the Hostage Rescue Team is the counterterrorism unit of the FBI) takes control. The operation will commence at 3:00 am. Monday morning

Pacific Time, and 5:00 pm. Central Time, respectively. He looked around the room, and continued, you know the drill: neutralize the nukes, kill the terrorists, and take no prisoners. We only have a 5-second window once we burst through. Please synchronize your watches; we have 36 hours to launch time. Your aircraft departs in 2 hours. Good Luck."

SUNDAY, SEPTEMBER 6

General Al-Jabr arrived early in the morning and conducted a search and recovery operation to gather any bits of the helicopter and burnt bodies. The Saudi Navy recovered body parts and one of the officers turned to the General. "It will be difficult to make any ID, sir."

Ziad's body had been recovered on Saturday by a Saudi Coast Guard vessel twenty miles due west of Jeddah. General Al-Jabr was saddened by the death of his best spy who played a massive role in helping eliminate a significant threat to the Royal Family and the United States of America.

MONDAY, SEPTEMBER 7, SWITZERLAND

Scharz and two Swiss Federal police officers entered Steiner's office in Zurich.

"Herr Steiner, I'm with the Swiss Federal Police. You're under arrest for conspiracy to commit murder, nuclear weapons procurement, terrorist arms financing, and money laundering," said Hans Christian Scharz.

"You…"

MONDAY, SEPTEMBER 7, UNITED STATES

The FBI's HRT unit conducted surveillance on the houses in Henderson and Sugarland using thermal imaging cameras. At 3:00 am sharp, PDT, they raided the home killing all the terrorists. DOE people rushed into the garage and disarmed the nukes. At 5:00 am sharp, CDT, the HRT unit, raided the house in Sugarland, killing ten terrorists, and the DOE experts swiftly neutralized the nukes there too.

———

CNN REPORTED on a breaking news event. FBI Director Geiger addressed the public in front of the cameras and made an announcement: "Earlier today, the FBI's Hostage Rescue Teams killed several terrorists in both Henderson, Nevada, and Sugarland, Texas, who were planning attacks on the United States. The terrorists were members of the Red Sea Brotherhood. We are looking for the following individuals [their pictures appeared on the television screen]: Wolfgang Beltermann, Abdullah Al-Suhaimy, and Sergei Ryzhkov. These people are dangerous and armed. Please notify law enforcement immediately if you know their whereabouts. There is a reward of $5 million on each one of them."

Chapter Sixty-Five

DIRECTOR OF NATIONAL INTELLIGENCE

The President entered Sullivan's office on November 10, followed by his Chief of Staff and his National Security Advisor. CIA Director Norstad, FBI Director Geiger, Caldwell, Jacobson, and Ericksen stood next to him and greeted President Porterfield. After the greetings, the president looked at everyone present and spoke.

"The CIA's Hummingbird Operation delivered critical intelligence, and your efforts stopped the terrorists from executing a nuclear attack on our homeland, as well as working with Pakistani intelligence in stopping the shipment of a nuclear warhead on a container ship en route to the Port of Long Beach. I thanked the Pakistani President for ISI's efforts in retrieving the nuclear warhead and arresting members of the Pakistan Taliban and Dr. Gull. Saadi Al-Fulani escaped, and there is an ongoing manhunt for him. I want to personally thank all of you for your heroic task in stopping the planned attack by the Red Sea Brotherhood. Our nation owes you all a great debt of gratitude."

Everyone nodded their heads and smiled. President Porterfield smiled and continued, Unfortunately, none of you will have that honor publicly, but it's fair to say your dedication to your country and its citizens have served our nation honorably."

Then the president gave each of them a presidential pen and portfolio. He shook everyone's hand and left Sullivan's office, followed by other staffers and FBI Director Geiger.

"I received my reward. Khalid is dead," said Ericksen.

"Let's hope it's true," Sullivan said. He thought *General Al-Jabr said a two-man submarine was on the ship when SEAL Team-Eight assaulted the vessel. When the ship arrived at the terminal, it had disappeared. Did Khalid make an escape from The Dolphin Prince?*

He sighed, looked at Ericksen, and smiled. He thought *his son Ryan was a lot like Ericksen, with sterling character, integrity, discipline, and country love. In a way, Mark was like a son to him.*

"We'll soon be talking with the Treasury and Justice Departments and the Swiss government in seizing all the assets from the Swiss private numbered accounts belonging to Dawkins, Campbell, Sheridan, Lucas, and your account," said Sullivan.

"Hopefully, with your help, our government can donate some of the Swiss bank proceeds to several veterans charity organizations like The Wounded Warrior Project, The Special Operations Warrior Foundation, and The Navy SEAL Foundation," said Ericksen.

"Mark, we'll do our best to make that happen."

"Thanks, sir. When are you planning on getting back to work?" Sullivan asked.

"Dave and I are taking a week off and going deep sea fishing on Maui."

"Sounds great."

CIA Director Norstad walked up to Caldwell and smiled. "We finally have you back at headquarters. Effective today, you've been promoted to director of the clandestine service's European Division, and it comes with a big salary raise."

"Thank you, director."

Sullivan turned to Jacobson. "I am appointing you to become the director of the national clandestine service, effective December 1."

"Thanks, sir."

The next day Ericksen drove out to Charlottesville, Virginia. He went to the cemetery and visited his wife's grave. Ericksen placed a bouquet of flowers and knelt down. He glanced at his wife's headstone and thought, *Karen, I will always remember the love we had for each other. I'm finally ready to move on with my life.*

That evening, he enjoyed the company of Elizabeth Caldwell. After a nice seafood dinner at the Market Street Grill and Bar, inside the Hyatt Regency in Reston, the waiter brought over a dessert menu. The waiter smiled. "Have you decided on dessert?"

Caldwell looked at Ericksen and smiled. "No, thank you. But I would like a Drambuie."

He glanced over the menu again and looked up at the waiter. "I'll have your carrot cake and the Galliano Ristretto liqueur."

She shook her head and chuckled, "Better watch it, or you're going to lose that hot bod of yours."

He extended his hands to her, and she placed her hands on his. "Elizabeth, I'm going to miss working with you."

"Me too."

"If you ever have business on the West Coast, please call me in advance so we can plan an exciting get-together. We've shared a lot of history together. I think you know what I mean."

She smiled again. "Yes, I do."

Chapter Sixty-Six

At five in the morning, an Air Force pilot focused on his computer console/monitor and his sensor operator at Creech Air Force Base in Nevada. He received a live feed through a video link via the satellite from a Reaper Drone flying high over Yemen. The time in Yemen was 3:00 pm, and their targeted house was located ten miles west of Tarim's city, in the Hadramaut Mountains of Yemen. Ryzhkov got out of the SUV and met Abdullah, Faisal, Beltermann, and Al-Fulani. Six security guards armed with AK-47s left their SUVs and stood to watch outside.

In the Communications Auditorium of the National Intelligence Building in Virginia, Bill Sullivan, the Director of National Intelligence, CIA Director Susan Norstad, and the Director of National Clandestine Service, Dave Jacobson, looked in front of a series of large television monitors viewing the live satellite video footage over Yemen. The camera on the drone zoomed in as everyone entered the house. Both Sullivan and the drone operators at Creech Air Force Base were in communications.

"Officer, fire the missile now!" ordered Sullivan.

"Yes, sir." A few seconds later, a white flash occurred on the screen when the Hellfire missile hit the house and exploded. The screen dissolved into a cloudy picture.

Sullivan made a call at noon to Ericksen from his office in McLean, Virginia.

"Hello."

"Phantom here. I have good news for you. 4 hours ago, a Hellfire missile took out Abdullah, Ryzhkov, Faisal Al-Bustani, Beltermann, and Al-Fulani."

"Fantastic! That's the best news I heard in a long time. Perhaps you can help me with another subject. I wanted to call Langley to reach Elizabeth but realized that wasn't her real name. I think about her a lot."

"She resigned in November. She's helping her brother and sister-in-law with their Alpaca business."

"Can you give me her forwarding address and telephone number?"

"I'm sorry, Mark, I can't. She's in treatment for PTSD and doesn't want anyone to contact her."

"I understand. Please give her my best."

"I will. Are you still in therapy?"

"No. My meditation and daily exercises have reduced those memories substantially. Thanks for asking."

"That's good to hear. Last month we brought Jannan, his wife, their children, and Bashir's daughter, Laila, to Fremont, California. They're living rent-free for one year in a condo rental provided by an Agency's old Afghan friend. Jannan asked about you, and we told him you would call him soon. I'll email his phone number and address to you."

Ericksen choked up. "Thank you, sir."

Chapter Sixty-Seven

APRIL 15, 2010

The palm tree-lined beaches of Copacabana in Rio de Janeiro, Brazil, had more than sun-tanned, beautiful, bikini-clad women parading in the soft sandy beaches and luxury hotels and resorts. They also had plastic surgeons who earned substantial money reshaping their bodies and faces, making them look younger and more beautiful or handsome. They also altered people's appearance to the point where no one could recognize them again.

In a medical office building on the Copacabana, a plastic surgeon in his late forties with thinning dark brown hair smiled confidently at his patient, Mr. Ignacio Martinez, a clean-shaven Argentine man, formerly known as Khalid Al-Bustani. After two months of recovery time, he appeared for his final visit.

The surgeon activated the large, 50" flat-screen hi-def TV monitor that showed the before and after results from the surgery. His nose from the rhinoplasty surgery was now shorter and slimmer, more like the actor George Clooney's nose. The surgeon showed Khalid the original photo of his facial features before and after. The darkened circles and bags under his eyes were resolved with double eyelid surgery, accompanied by a cheek lift that restored his cheeks' fullness. The surgery made him look younger and more vibrant. His cosmetic facial transformation enabled his mouth to spread wide when he smiled now, showcasing his new veneers.

The medical technician, a woman in her early thirties, smiled. "Señor Martinez, you look fabulous."

He smiled back and gave her a small present. She opened it, and her eyes lit up at an emerald necklace. "Thank you very much." She held it out, looked at it, and gave it to him. 'Would you please put it around my neck?" They both smiled.

His new appearance made it virtually impossible for any law enforcement or intelligence agency to identify him. With his new passport and prescription designer eyeglasses on, he strolled down the streets of Rio de Janeiro with the confidence of a successful South American businessman, followed by two tough-looking bodyguards.

For the past seven days, he was staying at the luxurious Miramar Hotel on the beach. He had to address one problem. His two Chechen bodyguards had flown into Rio five days earlier on a contract arranged through layers of anonymous communications techniques. Khalid made an appointment with the surgeon to meet him at his office. He promised him a bonus of an additional fifty thousand dollars.

The surgeon arrived at the medical office building at nine in the evening and admitted Khalid into his office. No one else appeared to be working at that time. Khalid gave him an envelope with fifty thousand dollars in counterfeit money. The surgeon's eyes widened with excitement, and his smile lengthened. "You're too kind, Señor Martinez."

"The cash is a gesture of my appreciation of your fine cosmetic surgery services." The surgeon turned away for a moment. Khalid took his Makarov handgun from his pants pocket and fired one shot from a distance of eight feet into the back of the surgeon's head. Blood splattered on the floor and the wall. Khalid changed clothes and placed his clothes in a small duffel bag. He opened the door for the two arsonists. An hour later, fire engulfed the entire six-story medical building.

MAY 10, 2010

Khalid entered the Waldmann and Tessier Bank in Georgetown, Grand Cayman. He wore a business casual outfit. The last time Khalid visited the bank as Ignacio Martinez had been nine or ten years earlier. He approached an executive officer of the bank and produced his private numbered account, and the officer escorted him to a private and secure room.

Within minutes he completed his transactions and walked out of the bank with two million dollars in cash in two briefcases, giving one to Dawkins, who now went by the name of Diego Ramirez. They walked back to the marina and up the gangway to board a 150-foot yacht called *Sweet Juanita.*

Dawkins sat across from Khalid in the yacht's salon lounge, drinking cognac from a crystal snifter. "Just think, four months ago, the US government seized all your assets from your Swiss, Bahamas, and Grand Cayman accounts, and today you're sitting with $1 million in that briefcase. He raised his glass of orange juice in a toast to Dawkins and said, "Cheers."

Looking at the briefcase by his sandals, Dawkins said with a smile, "Today, my spirits are lifted. What now?"

"We're first going to drop you off in Panama so you can open up a private numbered bank account with the million dollars. Then we'll pick you up in Veracruz at the end of June to begin our mission. I've sent two operatives to Portland to obtain Ericksen's home security alarm codes. Once we kill that son-of-a-bitch I'll wire two million dollars into your new Panamanian bank account."

"Sounds like a plan." The heavily bearded, dyed-jet-black-haired Dawkins took another swig of cognac and stared at Khalid. "I'll be frank. I don't respect your fucking Islamic Jihadist shit. After we kill him, I'm going my fucking way."

"Shane, we're all the same. We're cold-blooded killers. You murder for money; I kill to eliminate the infidels from exploiting our resources and occupying our lands. I need your help. This mission will make you a few million dollars, which will go a long way in Brazil."

Several days later, Dawkins was dropped off in Panama.

JUNE 28, 2010

Dawkins waited at the Veracruz, Mexico marina for Khalid to arrive. A few minutes later, his yacht docked. "Any news on Ericksen's codes?" Dawkins asked.

He turned to Dawkins as they walked to the Mercedes limo at the port. "One of our men works in dispatch at the security alarm company, and the other one drives for a limo company."

The taxi driver opened the door for the men and drove them to the Veracruz airport, where Vance Bullock greeted them.

He and his pilot flew them on his private corporate jet, a Cessna Citation, directly to Santa Barbara, California. They landed in the late afternoon at the Santa Barbara Municipal Airport. Bullock provided them with new American passports, California driver's licenses, and a condo address listed in Santa Monica.

"I don't know what you're planning, but leave me out of it. I'm taking a huge risk of helping you. Here are the keys to my condominium in Sausalito. You can stay for up to two weeks, but afterward, I need you to leave," said Bullock.

"Who are you kidding, Vance? You greedy bastard!" He shook his head and stared into Bullock's eyes, his eyebrows almost touching the bridge of his nose. "The only reason you're helping me is you need Al-Bustani Construction to continue doing business in the Kingdom. I'll be back here soon, and you're going to fly us where I tell you!"

Chapter Sixty-Eight

JULY 9, 2010

Ericksen stood with two bouquets of roses and waited for Jannan, his fifteen-year-old daughter Farah, and Laila, his brother Bashir's twelve-year-old daughter he had adopted a few years earlier. Their flight on Alaska Air Lines left San Jose and landed at 3:15 pm at Portland International Airport.

Fifteen minutes later, Ericksen spotted Jannan Sadozai with a carry-on and duffel bag. Each of the girls walking alongside Jannan carried their small duffel bags and slowly made their way past security. Standing off to the side near an airport store, Ericksen maintained his composure and approached Jannan. It was the first time he had seen him since their meeting in Kandahar five years earlier.

Jannan wore a blue short-sleeved dress shirt, khaki slacks, and brown casual shoes. They looked at each other, and Ericksen gave him a big hug. Jannan cried as he received the hug. "I'm so happy to see you and want to personally thank you for helping get our family out of Afghanistan. My wife and I, and all the children, finally feel safe here in the States."

Tears continued to flow down Jannan's cheeks. He lost his

composure and took a handkerchief out of his back pocket and wiped some of the tears away.

"Welcome to Oregon. I'm overjoyed, finally seeing you here in America."

"Thank you. My wife and son couldn't make this trip, but my wife wanted you to know whenever you're in the Bay Area, she would like to make you a typical Afghan dinner."

Jannan stepped aside for a moment and introduced the girls. He motioned with his outstretched arm. "This is my daughter Farah and my youngest daughter Laila."

Ericksen presented each girl with a beautiful bouquet of red roses. The girls were wearing dresses and the hijab, the head covering.

"Thank you, Mr. Ericksen," both girls replied and smiled.

He looked intently into Laila's sparkling large coffee-colored eyes. He saw a young girl who had witnessed so much war, trauma, the loss of her parents and sister. Her olive complexion and sweet smile made him feel happy. "I've planned a weekend of activities for all of you. First, we'll go down to the baggage area and gather your checked luggage." Everyone nodded.

Both girls spoke some English and were registered to attend school in the fall in Fremont, California. For now, they would be his guests over the weekend. He planned to take them on a sightseeing trip down the Columbia Gorge to visit Multnomah Falls and make the loop from Hood River to Mt. Hood to enjoy a dinner at the Timberline Lodge.

On Sunday, he invited Jeb Templeton, his wife, and their children for a salmon barbecue.

This was the moment he had been waiting for over eight years, some way to redeem himself for taking an innocent life. He couldn't bring back Bashir, but he finally felt a sense of happiness in knowing his efforts had saved a good Afghan family from the threat of death and a miserable life for their children. He owed a lot to Bill Sullivan for making his dream a reality. While driving back to his home in West Linn, they talked and laughed about being together as good friends.

Chapter Sixty-Nine

WILSONVILLE, OREGON

A caterer brought in all kinds of sandwiches, salads, and a birthday cake into EyeD4 Systems' lunchroom. Today was July 13. The employees enjoyed their lunch and then gathered around the table where Ericksen blew out the candles. The occasion was his fortieth birthday. The company had grown to fifty employees and anticipated exponential growth over the next five years with their biometrics access control systems' initial success and their biometrics communications encryption systems' roll-out.

After the birthday luncheon party, he went back into his office. He sat down with his executives: Jeb Templeton, recently hired as senior VP of marketing and sales, and Sofia Kastrup, the Chief Financial Officer.

"Jot down August 17 on your calendar. Poul Kastrup is having a corporate meeting at Cyberburst Communications with its board of directors. He asked me to present a conservative three-year business plan. Let's get together the first week of August and prepare the plan to anticipate the questions they'll more than likely raise."

At four in the afternoon, Ericksen's executive assistant passed his office and glanced inside. "Here's a FedEx package addressed to you." She placed it on his desk.

"Thank you."

He noticed it was shipped from Sandpoint, Idaho. Curiosity got the best of him. He opened the package and discovered an oil painting, 12 inches by 18 inches of a Swiss mountain landscape, a box of Lindt Swiss Chocolate Hazelnut candy bars, and a birthday card. He opened the card:

Dear Mark,

Happy birthday! I'm sorry for ignoring you. I recently received two job offers for an executive recruiter position in the banking industry. One is in San Francisco, and the other is in Lake Oswego, on Meadows Road. Both jobs start around the first week of September. My real name is Kate McDonald. I don't blame you if you decide never to call or write to me. However, I hope you do. You can reach me at 208-555-0029. My current mailing address is 7550 Schweitzer Mountain Drive, Sandpoint, Idaho. You're in my thoughts, Kate.

Ericksen's parents entered his office with Thor, their four-year-old Belgium Malinois. When his parents' dog Bjorn died, they were devastated. After searching for a rescue dog, an old SEAL buddy of his located Thor in a California rescue shelter. He hugged his mom and dad and patted Thor on the head. They were leaving for Denmark to visit family, and he agreed to take care of Thor for two weeks. "Mark, please don't be too strict with him. Please give him some hamburgers once in a while. He likes human food better than dog food," his mother said in Danish.

"Mom, don't worry, he'll be my jogging partner every morning."

Thor looked up at Ericksen and barked.

His cellphone rang. "Ericksen speaking."

"Phantom here. You and Templeton make a great team."

"Thanks for giving us a strong endorsement to the board of directors of Cyberburst Communications."

"I heard from Kate, and I'm glad she finally contacted you. She told me a company in Portland offered her a position. I wouldn't get surprised if there's a future for both of you. As they say, the ball might be in your court. If you ever get bored in the private sector, there will always be a future for you in the CIA."

They both chuckled.

"On a serious note, we believe Khalid Al-Bustani is alive and somewhere in the United States. Several months ago, a plastic surgeon performed surgery on a man claiming to be a citizen of Argentina, using the alias of Ignacio Martinez. The surgeon was shot to death, and their medical office building burned to the ground. An eyewitness who worked as a nurse for the surgeon claims to have seen this man wearing a gold ring with an image of a horse's head and the inscription Falcon Dancer on it."

"Don't tell me that butcher is alive!"

"The intelligence community went into high gear and verified this same individual, Ignacio Martinez, visited the Waldmann and Tessier Bank in The Grand Caymans and withdrew two million dollars. The bank executive who processed his private numbers account also noticed the gold ring and gave us a good description of this man. We're not sure where he went from there. But here's what we do know. That same day two men walked away from the bank with two briefcases and boarded a large yacht. The man accompanying him had a bushy black beard and a striking resemblance to Shane Dawkins. The name of the yacht is *Sweet Juanita*. It is registered in the Bahamas and was hired to pick up two men in Rio de Janeiro matching those descriptions."

"Sounds ominous."

"It could be our worst nightmare. The captain of the boat said he dropped off Dawkins in Panama and Khalid in Veracruz. In checking all modes of transportation, the only plausible one had to be flying out of Veracruz. So far, we checked all commercial airline carriers which departed on the 28th, and nothing showed up. I have several agencies looking into all private jets. Both Homeland Security and the FBI are also checking out all leads. I'll get back to you if something pops up."

"Thanks, sir."

———

Dawkins and Khalid boarded the Cessna Citation late morning at the Santa Barbara Municipal Airport and arrived at the Aurora Municipal Airport, Aurora, Oregon, on July 14, at 2:30 pm. They were met by a man who carried their bags and placed them into a van, then drove them to the Lakeshore Inn in downtown Lake Oswego, where they checked in. Over the next several days, they drove past Ericksen's home, his office, ClubSport, and otherwise, stayed mostly in their rooms. They ate in fast-food restaurants and walked to Peet's Coffee a few blocks away for their morning espresso.

CENTURY CITY, LOS ANGELES

Three men in suits approached the main office lobby of The Bullock Group. One man was the special agent-in-charge of the FBI office in Los Angeles, another with the Department of Justice. The other was an executive assistant director for national security. They showed their credentials and, escorted into the private office of Vance Bullock.

"What is the occasion for your visit, gentlemen?"

The FBI man looked directly at Bullock. "Mr. Bullock, you have a serious problem. We talked with your corporate pilot, and he told us that you and he picked up two men at the Veracruz Airport in Mexico on June 28 and flew them to Santa Barbara, California. We have eyewitnesses who will testify to your Cessna Citation's flights from Mexico. Your pilot told us he flew them to Aurora, Oregon, two days ago."

Beads of sweat formed around Bullock's head.

"Gentlemen, please be seated. Is there anything wrong with picking up some American friends in Mexico and flying them back to the States?"

The Justice Department official sat across Bullock and placed his hand on the expensive executive desk. "Not if you didn't violate any federal laws. Mr. Bullock, your pilot, identified one of the men who went by the name of Javier Cortez of Santa Monica, California, and whose previous alias was Ignacio Martinez. The man recently had plastic surgery and wore a large gold ring with a horse's head and an inscription. The man was reported killed in Saudi Arabia last year. Khalid Al-Bustani is his real name, and he is a wanted fugitive and terrorist mastermind. You're in hot water! We could charge you with harboring a known fugitive terrorist, providing false American IDs, and allowing your pilot to fly both Al-Bustani and Shane Dawkins to the Portland area."

"What do you want from me?" Bullock asked.

"If you cooperate, we could perhaps recommend to the Justice Department to reduce some of the charges, but you better act now because if either of these men kills anyone, you'll be an accessory to murder."

"I don't know what they're doing in Portland. They told me they're planning on departing from Oregon, but I don't know when or where in Oregon."

"How do they get in touch with you?"

"They contact me via my secure cellphone."

"Good. You'll be coming with us. We're placing you in a safe house in Santa Monica and waiting for Al-Bustani's call."

Chapter Seventy

ERICKSEN'S HOME

At 5:30 pm, Khalid and Dawkins, wearing Hakkinen NW Doors and Repairs uniforms, opened the van bearing the same name.

They took their tool chests and walked along the side of the home on Rawhide Drive. One of Khalid's sleeper cell operatives parked the van along the curb between Ericksen's home and his neighbor's house. Most of the homeowners parked their cars in their garage or in their driveway. Vehicles parked along the curb belonged to individuals or companies hired to perform service.

Khalid followed Dawkins to the garage entry door on the side, and in a matter of seconds, opened the lock to the garage. They entered and used the same burglar tools to open the door to the laundry room. On the wall next to the door, sat the home security alarm module. Their inside man at the alarm company had provided them with the access code to neutralize the alarm–6498. They checked the lower level of the house and eventually made their way up the stairs. Khalid entered Ericksen's master bedroom and opened some of the drawers.

"We'll stay up here until he comes home." His cellphone rang.

"He just left the office. He has a Belgian Malinois dog with him," said one of his men.

"Follow him and tell me when he is close to the house."

"Yes, Sheikh."

———

ERICKSEN DROVE a few miles north on Southwest Parkway and pulled into the Costco Warehouse parking lot.

At 6:20 pm, the Hakkinen NW Doors van took off from Rawhide Drive.

Khalid's cellphone rang. "Yes. Where is he?"

"He spent fifteen minutes at Costco in Wilsonville. Just turned off the West Linn 10th Street exit. He'll probably be there in ten minutes."

"You and your buddy get here at 7:00 pm. Get room reservations for us tonight in Eugene."

"Yes, Sheikh."

Dawkins took out his handgun. "I'm going to enjoy seeing Ericksen's face when he sees us." Khalid turned to him, took out his pre-paid cellphone, and made a call.

Bullock's cellphone rang. "Hello."

"This is Falcon Dancer. I want you to have your jet available for take-off from the Medford Airport tomorrow afternoon at three sharp. Make sure the jet is fueled-up."

"Okay."

———

ERICKSEN DROVE the Porsche into the garage, opened the door for Thor to get out, put his house key into the lock to the laundry room, and opened it. He deactivated the alarm, went back to his car, and brought in the groceries. When Ericksen re-entered the house, he heard Thor growling. He walked into the kitchen and put the groceries away. Thor continued barking, and Ericksen bent down, patted him, and gave him a dog bone.

"Calm down, Thor." He went to the cabinet and took down Thor's favorite dog food. After placing the dog food in the bowl and filling another bowl with water, he removed a Carlsberg beer from his fridge.

Ericksen picked up his landline phone and placed a delivery order for Chinese food from the Pine Garden Restaurant in Cascade Summit. He picked up a book, *Up Country* by Nelson De Mille. He slumped down in his recliner in the family room, and Thor joined him, lying alongside the recliner.

Ericksen's cellphone rang. "Hello."

"Phantom speaking. A private jet owned by a wealthy architect, Vance Bullock, flew Dawkins and Khalid Al-Bustani to the Aurora Airport several days ago."

"What the fuck!" Ericksen blurted out.

"We established Bullock's architectural firm does a lot of business with Al-Bustani Construction in Saudi Arabia and Dubai. Just got off the phone with Geiger. The Portland FBI's Hostage Rescue Team should be there any minute."

Thor started barking again. Ericksen heard a noise, looked up, and saw two men entering the kitchen from the dining room with weapons drawn.

Ericksen dropped the cellphone on the hardwood floor, got out of his recliner, stood, and held his book. They both stared at him. In heavily accented English, Khalid said, "I've been watching you."

"Khalid!" He thought, *Fight to the death.* "What a surprise, or should I call you Ignacio Martinez?"

Khalid held an Israeli Desert Eagle handgun in his right hand, and Dawkins had a Glock with the suppressor on, both aimed at Ericksen's head.

"I don't give a fuck what you call me. Your friend Ziad transferred thirty million Swiss francs of mine into your bank account. All of my money in your account has been seized by your government. You and the CIA pigs destroyed my operations, killed my colleagues, and my son Faisal. You were rescued from certain death on my ship, but today Mr. Ericksen, you are going to die!"

"Shane, you were always a fucking, unethical asshole, but to align yourself with an Islamic Jihadist terrorist is outright insane."

Dawkins' face turned red with anger. "Fuck you, Ericksen."

Thor barked and growled. His menacing large canine teeth were in full view of both men.

"If he doesn't stop, I'll kill him."

A loud horn startled Khalid as he turned to look at Dawkins. The sound of bullets broke the silence outside.

"Angribe!" Ericksen yelled in Danish.

Thor charged Khalid and jumped onto him. He grunted and yelled as the dog knocked him down. The gun dropped near the fireplace. Dawkins took aim at Thor, but the hardbound book hurled by Ericksen hit his hand. He bolted toward Dawkins, delivered a karate chop to his wrist, and the gun dropped on the floor. He threw a left-hand punch smashing Dawkins' right ear, then followed up with a closed-fist punch to the solar plexus, sending Dawkins into the kitchen cabinet. Ericksen kicked the gun away. Dawkins momentarily recovered, got into a martial arts stance, and caught Ericksen with a blow to the chin, forcing him back to the kitchen granite countertop island.

Dawkins threw a menacing right-hand shot to Ericksen's left eyebrow, cutting him with a deep gash. Blood spurted out and down his cheek. He kicked Ericksen in the knee and drove him into the kitchen table. When Dawkins attempted a roundhouse kick to the head and missed, Ericksen threw a hard right to Dawkins' temple. He followed up with a palm thrust against his nose, knocking him back into the family room. Dawkins collapsed to the floor. Ericksen dove on top of him, pummeling him with shots to the face and head. Blood covered Dawkins' entire face.

Loud sounds were heard from the firefight outside Ericksen's house between the terrorists and the FBI's HRT counterterrorism unit. Thor kept biting and clawing at Khalid's face and shoulder. Suddenly he pulled out a knife and slashed the dog's shoulder. The dog began whimpering, blood pouring out of Thor's wound.

Ericksen heard Thor's cries of pain, got off Dawkins, moved into a martial arts stance facing Khalid, who charged him holding a sharp ten-inch knife in his right hand. Ericksen quickly grabbed his wrist with his left hand and exerted pressure on his forearm with his right hand, pushing Khalid off balance. In a split-second, his right hand reached for the back of Khalid's head while holding the knife at bay with his left hand. Ericksen pushed his head down, kneed his head, and kicked him in the groin. Khalid dropped the knife, got hammered with a right hook, and fell backward onto the desk. He slammed Khalid's head against the desk, threw him on the floor, landing elbows to his head and face. Ericksen turned him over, placed his forearm around his neck, and clamped down with all his strength. Within seconds the chokehold rendered Khalid unconscious, and ten seconds later, he was dead.

Dawkins regained enough strength to stand. He spotted the gun twenty feet away, raced over, and picked it up. Ericksen heard him and pushed Khalid off him to his left, reached into the bottom drawer of his desk, grabbed his Heckler & Koch 45, and rolled to his right. Dawkins fired three shots that missed Ericksen, who hid behind the desk. Ericksen spotted him, took aim, and fired two shots, hitting Dawkins in the head and heart. He dropped dead onto the hardwood floor. Blood splattered out on the wall, cabinets, island, and floor.

Ericksen checked Thor. The dog continued to bleed from his shoulder injury. Two minutes later, several HRT men ran around to the back of the house and spotted Ericksen. He saw the team and opened the kitchen door. They entered and viewed the bodies. "The ambulance should be here momentarily," one HRT man said.

Ericksen placed a towel over Thor's shoulder wound and applied pressure to stop the bleeding until the EMT arrived. He sat on the hardwood floor next to Thor and waited.

Chapter Seventy-One

F ive days later, Ericksen opened the door, and the heavily bandaged Thor jumped into the back seat of his Chevy Silverado pickup. The veterinarian who performed the surgery told him the recovery period could take up to several months. Thor had saved Ericksen's life, and he wanted him along for the trip.

He was driving along the Columbia Gorge when his cellphone rang. His SUV had Bluetooth, and he checked the caller ID.

"Sullivan here. The dental records have confirmed Khalid's ID. What are you going to do with the $15 million reward money?"

"Several things come to mind, a vacation home on Maui for my family, $1 million to Jannan's family, $1 million to Fico Delgado's family, $1 million to Jeb, and $1 million to Lars."

"Sounds good. One last thing, Dave Jacobson handed his resignation this morning to Norstad. It's not every day someone decides to no longer head up the National Clandestine Service. I talked with him, and he told me you hired him to be your company's new Executive Vice-President and COO. I hate to see the CIA lose a good one, but I'm sure he'll be happy in Portland working with people he loves and respects. He'll be overjoyed to be called by his real name."

"I informed Cyberburst Communications that Lars Wahlberg would be joining us as of September 7. I'll have to get used to calling him by his real name."

"Good luck and say hello to Kate for me."

After a day of driving along the Columbia Gorge, up through Tri-Cities to Spokane, they stopped at a dog-friendly motel in Coeur d'Alene, Idaho. After breakfast, he gassed up and left at eight in the morning. An hour later, he reached a house at 7550 Schweitzer Mountain Drive. He rang the front doorbell, and a moment later, a pleasant-looking woman in her mid-sixties opened the door. Ericksen identified himself as a personal friend of her daughter, and she gave him directions to her son's ranch where he would find her.

Ericksen drove toward Hope, Idaho, climbed some hills, and finally reached a dirt road. He turned at the entrance to McDonald's Alpaca Ranch and drove up the gravel road to the top of the hill over-looking Lake Pend Oreille and the Cabinet Mountain Range. He looked up at the sky and spotted a bald eagle flying over the lake, perhaps searching for a Kokanee salmon.

Ericksen spotted McDonald 200 yards away. Her brother's little daughter, probably five or six-years-old, stood next to her. McDonald's horse and the little girl's pony were tied up by the fence, while a yellow Lab strolled nearby.

McDonald recognized Ericksen as he drove within 100 yards of her. He opened the door of his pickup, and he and Thor got out. The little girl looked up at her aunt as Thor walked briskly alongside him. McDonald and Ericksen stared into each other's eyes for several seconds and embraced each other in a long hug. He gently moved back, holding her hands. She looked at him with tears in her eyes and said, "I love you."

They both smiled as he pulled her closer to him. "Kate, I love you too."

And then they sealed their lips with a kiss.

Afterword

Dear Reader,
I hope you enjoyed reading my novel, "The Ericksen Connection." If
you would like to review and rate my book on Amazon.com, please go
to the Amazon.com website.
Key-in "The Ericksen Connection."
When you reach the page, please scroll down to the section [write a
customer review]. Letting me know what you think of my book is very
much appreciated.
Thank you,
Barry L. Becker

Acknowledgments

Many thanks go to my good friends Jack Rieber and Dennis Porter, for providing me with their feedback.

In the fall of 2020, I used Grammarly editing software to correct grammarical errors and make my story more readable. Finally, special thanks to my wife, who provided me additional editing, constructive criticism, unwavering love, and support.

About the Author

Barry L. Becker retired in 2013 after spending twenty years as a sole-proprietor for an independent manufacturers' representative company in Oregon. Also, he has provided marketing consulting services for corporations in the biometrics technology industry.

Mr. Becker previously served as vice-president of international sales and marketing for Eyedentify, an Oregon company specializing in eye-retinal scanning technology for positive ID in sensitive facilities. In 1987, he wrote an article entitled "Eyedentify Counters Security Threat," which appeared in the Journal of Defense and Diplomacy.

The Ericksen Connection is his first novel.